ANN APTAKER
MURDER AND
GOLD

Bywater
BOOKS

Ann Arbor
2021

This book is dedicated to everyone who won't let jerks push them around.

ANN APTAKER
MURDER AND GOLD

Chapter One

Cantor Gold's apartment, New York City
Late September 1954
A few minutes before dawn

There are lots of women in my life, and I like it that way. I don't want to fall in love, not again. I was in love once, and she was perfect. But she's gone. Gone in a storm of gunfire on a tropical street. My heart's as good as dead. I can't even say her name. If you know my story, you know her name. And if you don't know my story, her name doesn't matter.

And besides, domestic bliss would interfere with my criminal life. Domestic bliss would distract me from keeping my senses sharp, senses that protect me against danger: from cops, from gangsters, from rival thieves and smugglers. So no thank you, lady, you can share my bed but not my heart. It's out of business.

I didn't say any of this to last night's red-haired, blue-eyed amusement, only that she was swell but this was it, there'd be no more. She slapped my face—not the first woman to so honor me— and told me I give butches a bad name, that we were supposed to be chivalrous. I told her I'm chivalrous to a fault, one woman at a time, one night at a time. I guess she didn't like that explanation because she slapped my face again, got out of my bed, put her dress on—a nice little form-fitting black satin number with a flaring

1

skirt—grabbed her coat and scrammed fast, hollering, "They should arrest creeps like you!" as she slammed the door of my apartment on her way out.

She doesn't know the half of it. She doesn't know how many times the boys with badges have tried to arrest me, flatten me, run me out of town. She doesn't know because I didn't tell her about my life, how I make my dough. I didn't tell her I steal high-priced art and other treasures from faraway places, smuggle it into New York for clients who pay me fistfuls of cash but don't give a damn that I risk my life to satisfy their acquisitive lusts. I didn't tell her any of these things. I don't talk about my outlaw life with any of the women who share my bed. Except one.

The exception is Rosie Bliss, one of the most skilled cabbies rolling on New York's streets, and that's saying something. What Rosie does behind the wheel of her big yellow Checker is a performance worthy of a top-ticket Broadway show. She can make the cab dance, she can make it glide or make it kick, and best of all she can use those skills to ferry me out of sight and out of reach of cops and other nosy parties when I'm carrying hot goods. Rosie Bliss is the best wheel spinner a thief could hope for.

Rosie used to be in love with me, but she gave it up a couple of years ago after my heart went cold for good. But Rosie and I have operated on the taboo side of the Law for several years now, and we're loyal to each other in our way. We take care of each other's needs, if you catch my drift.

We also protect each other, make sure the cops have no idea what we're up to. Protecting my business is what's on the menu this morning. I need to move a small clay statue, a forty-five-hundred-year-old wide-eyed Sumerian votive figure I brought into New York a week ago—smuggled it out of Baghdad right under the noses of the British military and Hashemite princelings currently running the place. From there, the eight-inch fellow standing in perpetual prayer with big staring eyes and long wavy beard sailed with me wrapped in canvas and oilcloth in a damp cabin of a tramp steamer, then slipped into the Port of New York aboard Red Drogan's tugboat, and finally rode with me in the backseat of Rosie's cab in the dark of night. The little Sumerian has been residing peacefully ever since on a shelf in the basement vault beneath my dockside office, cooling off while the Baghdad authorities scour the ancient smuggling routes of the Near East, searching everywhere but New York and my underground vault.

But at nine o'clock this morning my praying Sumerian will have his prayers answered and find a home with a woman who has big money, big political connections, and a Gramercy Park townhouse. I don't want to drive my Buick down there, not with the goods in tow. The cops make it their business to know my car, even the new one I buy almost every year, and they pull me over sometimes just for the fun of it. But they can't pick out Rosie's cab, one of countless Checkers working the streets of New York. So I'll meet Rosie at my office, a well-hidden spot in an unnoticeable little corner building shadowed by the elevated West Side Highway and across from the Hudson River docks. She'll slip the cab through the alleys behind the building, then drive me downtown to Gramercy Park.

A hot shower is followed by a cup of coffee. I turn on the radio, snap my fingers a few times to a current hit number, "Shake, Rattle and Roll," before this new music—rock and roll, they call it—gets on my morning nerves. I turn the dial to something smoother but with just enough pep to get me going: Ella Fitzgerald crooning a Gershwin tune, "Nice Work if You Can Get It." Yeah, my work's damn nice, and I get enough of it to keep me in new cars, custom-tailored silk suits, and good scotch. But the nicest thing about my work is that I get to poke my finger in the eye of the Law that wants to jail me—or worse—just for my love of women and taking them to my bed. So I figure if the Law has no respect for the most beautiful part of my life, I have no reason to respect the Law.

While the velvet-voiced Miss Fitzgerald sways me in the tune, I more or less comb my always disobedient crop of short brown hair. Women have called my hair a mop, or an old broom, or a pile of sticks. I work in a little hair tonic, not too much. I don't like the oily look. It's the best I can do to keep it all down.

3

Groomed, I rub a warm cloth over my face, soothe the scars I've collected over the years: the curved scar above my right eye, the jagged one on my left cheek, the straight line cut into my chin, and Rosie's favorite, the one she likes to tickle with her tongue, the small knife-shaped number above my lip. I think of my scars as the artistry of my outlaw life and brazen freedom.

I slip into the trousers of my pale gray silk suit, button up a crisp white shirt, adorn it with a gray and pale green striped tie, and strap into the shoulder rig holding my .38 Smith & Wesson revolver, the chambers full. My suit jacket, which I finish off with a pale green pocket square, is tailored to hide the bulge of my gun. I put my wallet, keys, and extra rounds of .38 slugs into my trouser pocket, grab my black wool overcoat and my gray tweed cap, and I'm ready to start another day in my underworld Shangri-La.

My street, like the others in my Theater District neighborhood, is ordinarily pretty quiet at this early hour. Windows in the old brick or brownstone five-story walk-ups, or in more recent apartment buildings like mine, are still dark, the blinds closed or the shades pulled. My night owl neighbors, those troupers who sing and dance on Broadway's stages or croon in the nightspots, don't put a toe on the pavement until noon at the earliest, and that's only if they have a two o'clock matinee. But this morning there's a drama in front of my building, right outside the door. Uniformed cops keep a handful of rubberneckers back while a plainclothes cop makes notes as he stands over the dead body of a woman. I know the body's dead, not just some sweetie passed out from too much booze or fainting from hunger. I know it by the way her legs and feet are splayed at odd angles and by the blood that's spreading from her midsection onto the sidewalk.

And I know the body. She slammed my apartment door about an hour ago.

Chapter Two

Lieutenant Norm Huber of Homicide, tall and skinny with a dry, stubbly, hollow-cheeked face, bears an uncanny resemblance to a dead tree. His brown tweed coat is cop-drab and shapeless. Smoke from the stubby ten cent cigar between his teeth clouds under the brim of his beat-up brown fedora. Seeing me through the cigar smoke as I walk through the lobby, he pushes his hat back on his head and lets the smoke drift away, the better to show me the hate in his hooded eyes.

He doesn't really see me, at least not all of me, and it's not because of the cigar smoke. He sees my face and form all right, but he doesn't see the shock and misery behind my eyes at the sight of the woman lying dead on the pavement with a bloody wound in her chest, her face contorted in terror, the woman who'd lain beneath me in my bed. He doesn't see that part of me because I don't let him. And even if I did, he wouldn't see it anyway. His soul went blind years ago, if he even has one, which I doubt.

Maybe homicide cops' souls always go blind, a survival tactic protecting them from being crushed by all the savagery they see. But hate like Huber's isn't from a blind soul; it's from a tight, empty space too small for a soul.

If you ask Huber why he hates me, he might say it's because I got in his way on a murder case a few years ago and I've been a thorn in his side ever since. Or he might say he hates criminals

5

generally, and people of my romantic persuasion especially. But if you ask me, I'd say hate is just Huber's nature, the only emotion with enough heat to warm his cold heart.

Taking the cigar from his mouth, he gives me a toothy, tobacco-yellowed grin a month too early for Halloween, but its effect is just as spooky. "When the call came into the precinct," he says, his phlegmy voice gurgling through his teeth, which makes that grin even creepier, "I told the captain this one's mine. And you know why, Gold?"

"Lemme guess. You recognized my address."

His grin spreads wider, nastier, his eyes narrow with sour joy. "And here you are, all spiffed up on a sunny morning, a stiff at your doorstep. I suppose you're gonna tell me you've got nothing to do with this and you've never laid eyes on this woman?"

"Listen," I say, keeping it light and easy, burying my acquaintance with the deceased behind an *I've got nothing to hide* performance my showbiz neighbors would appreciate. "I can't be two places at once, can I, lieutenant? I just came off the elevator, and the woman is already lying here dead."

Huber sticks his cigar between his teeth again, keeps it clamped while he stares at me as if I'm a sewer rat he'd love to drown. After a second or two of his laughably silent bullying, he pulls the cigar from his mouth. "How do I know you didn't knife her and then—"

"Oh, is that how she was killed?"

His hard look warns me not to give him any more back talk. "Yeah, that's how she was killed," he says. "My gut says you did it, Gold; then you went back upstairs to wash the blood off and change your bloody clothes for another of your snappy suits." He says this like he wants to arrest me just for dressing better than he does. "And when you heard the sirens you came back down and ambled through your lobby innocent as Sunday."

"Except today is Tuesday," I say, "and your story assumes I'm stupid enough to kill someone on my own doorstep and leave her here. You hate my guts, Huber. You've called me everything from sewer filth to perverted scum, but you've never called me stupid."

He's been grinding his teeth all the time I've been talking, and now that I've stopped, he spits out his other accusation. "And I suppose you don't know who the dame is?"

"And I suppose you do?" It's easier on my guilty soul to throw his question back at him than admit I'm a cad who never even asked her name.

"Her name's Lorraine Quinn, age thirty, according to the driver's license we found in her handbag. With an address on the bleaker end of Bleecker Street."

I know more about her now than I did when I'd buried my face in her lush chestnut hair and held her body against mine while we danced at the Green Door Club. I still didn't know any of it while I luxuriated in her breasts when she was in my bed. I feel pretty crummy that she had to die for me to find all that out. But feeling crummy could show up in my eyes, come across as the wrong kind of guilt, give Huber the wrong idea. So I squelch it.

With a tip of my cap, I say, "I'll be on my way now, lieutenant. You have a murder to solve, and far be it from me to stand in the way of the police." I start to walk away, but Huber grabs my arm.

"You're not off the hook yet, Gold."

I give him my best Broadway smile, full of razzamatazz charm. "Am I the worm or the fish?"

He puts the cigar back in his mouth with a sharp jerk of his arm, making it clear he's not impressed with my little joke. "Get out of my sight," he says, turning away from me and back to the business of the dead Lorraine Quinn.

After the hell of finding cops at my doorstep and the ache of seeing the woman who shared my bed dead at their feet, I take a little comfort from the sight of the familiar busted pink neon sign that reads PE E'S LUNCHEONETTE instead of PETE'S. The wacky sign sets my world back on its regular axis.

The joint is down the block from my place. Its broken sign

helps dissuade tourists from venturing inside, which is why Pete never had the sign fixed. Mom and Pop Tourist linger too long and tip too little, making the counter help cranky.

It's not quite seven-thirty when I walk in. The scattering of early morning patrons eating breakfast at the counter or at the few small tables are agreeably quiet, except for the clink of spoons stirring coffee, the rustle of newspaper pages being turned, and the occasional shuffle of feet or scrape of chairs on the scuffed green-and-black checkerboard linoleum floor. The room has the welcoming aromas of strong coffee and tobacco. Cigarette smoke curling through the air makes the place look almost pretty.

Behind the counter, Doris, the pink-uniformed, gray-haired, thin-faced waitress who's been here since the linoleum was new, is pouring a cuppa for a guy in a dark blue coat and gray fedora, a neighborhood guy I nod to. He nods and taps a finger against the brim of his hat, and that's all the acknowledgment needed or given. Nosiness is not a feature of my neighborhood. Not this early in the morning anyway.

On my way to the phone booth in the back, I hang my coat and cap on the rack and give Doris my order for black coffee and two eggs sunny-side-up on a warm bialy. Her smile of acknowledgment, with her cherry red lipstick as usual smudged between her teeth, provides additional assurance that my world is steadying itself.

After the clink and rattle of my dime dropping down into Ma Bell's lap, I dial Judson Zane. Judson's my right hand, a young guy of twenty-five with the clicking brain of an Einstein and a talent for secrecy that makes the government's spy boys look like a bunch of blabbermouths. He loves obscure details, loves digging for information, and he's put together a network of sources that police departments from here to Shanghai would lust after. Working a phone, Judson can generally find out just about anything about anyone. Oh, and he's popular with girls. Behind his wire-rim glasses, they think his alert brown eyes and chiseled cheeks are adorable.

I dial his apartment.

He answers on the third ring.

I say, "Judson, it's me. Listen, I'll meet you at the office around eight-thirty. Rosie will get there around the same time to ferry me and the goods down to Gramercy Park."

"Yeah, I know," he says. "So why the call?" The guy doesn't miss a trick.

"I want you to get started on something right away. Start working your contacts and dig into the life of one Lorraine Quinn, age thirty, lived somewhere on Bleecker Street."

"Lived?"

"Yeah. Lived. She was knifed to death just outside my apartment building. Huber caught the case. Or rather, he laid claim to it."

Judson takes a moment to absorb this news and calculate its ramifications, then says, "So he wants to pin you for the killing?"

"That's the gist. But I want to get ahead of him. That's why I need you to find out anything you can about Miss Quinn. Where she was from. Where she worked and what she did. Who loved her. Who didn't. Who might've wanted her dead." I tell him I'll see him at the office and hang up.

My breakfast is waiting for me when I slide onto a stool at the counter. Doris is pouring me a cup of coffee.

"Just brewed a fresh pot," she says through her cigarette-ragged voice. She puts down the coffeepot, looks me over through a smile loaded with street savvy. "You look like you could use a good cry."

I stop my forkful of egg-soaked bialy halfway to my mouth. "C'mon, Doris. When have you known me to cry?"

"Never seen it, but I bet you do."

"Haven't in a long time, a couple of years." I take my bite of breakfast.

Doris says, "Maybe you should. Not healthy not to cry. Anyways, you look lousy, like someone or something caught you in a hard grip." Leaning across the counter, she puts her hand under my chin, says as tenderly as her savvy smarts allow, "It wouldn't have anything to do with all that excitement—cops

9

and everything—going on down the block? That's your place, ain't it?"

Doris doesn't know how I make my dough, but after years of sharing coffee together, she's wise to the general contours of my love life. She doesn't judge, and she's even provided wise counsel and a sympathetic ear now and then when some cutie has cut me off at the knees. So the best thank you I can give her for her generous spirit and bottomless cups of the best coffee in town is to keep her uninformed of my criminal activities. That way, if the cops ever question her, she can tell them with a straight face and clean heart that she has no idea what they're talking about. Works out great for both of us.

But Doris is no fool. No doubt she already has some of that part of me figured. She was smart enough to ask about the cops at my door.

I slide her hand from my chin, give her a smile. "Cops don't like me, that's all. They want to arrest me just for doing this," I say, and kiss her on the knuckles.

That earns me a sassy laugh and another cup of coffee, "On the house! Enjoy your breakfast, Cantor. And try not to get arrested. You're the best tipper I've got."

The ancient Sumerians knew a thing or two about hedging their bets. In their rocky desert world where the nights were very dark, the silence pierced only by the distant roar of lions or the nearby hiss of snakes, praying to the gods seemed like a good idea if you hoped to wake up alive in the morning. But a body's got to sleep and eat and work and can't be praying all the time, which is where my little votive statue earned his place in the affections of his human tribe. His eyes wide in eternal wakefulness, the little fella and his similarly carved sisters and brothers stood in constant prayer on your behalf while you and your family were otherwise engaged in the business of living.

I wrap him in batting and cloth for his trip downtown, but linger for a while in the vault in the basement of my office, enjoy some of the treasures temporarily in my care. I'm rather fond of the little gold-trimmed alabaster box Howard Carter brought up among the goodies he discovered in Tutankhamen's tomb in 1922. The Cairo Museum is still looking for it. The curators at the Louvre in Paris are still scratching their heads about the strange disappearance of a pair of silver Rococo candlesticks that once belonged to a handsome courtier in service to King Louis XVI. The overly fussy candlesticks, full of flowery vines and animal head gewgaws, aren't to my taste, but I have to admit the silverwork is first rate.

The priciest thing on my shelves right now is a spectacular little French Gothic illuminated manuscript, a prayer book with illustrations possibly attributed to Master Honoré. To my eye, the illustrations are certainly skillful enough to be Honoré's, with their zesty use of color, confident handling of line, and bold rule-breaking of space and frame. It's a book of hours, inscribed with prayers to be recited by the Christian faithful at appointed hours of the day and evening. The client who hired me to lift it from the collection of an aristocratic family in France and smuggle it to New York made a bad bet on Wall Street and couldn't come up with the rest of the dough to deliver the book to his Fifth Avenue apartment. He swears he's good for the money. I told him, "Sure, just let me know when you're ready to fork over." I'm not holding my breath. I've already made arrangements to offer it to another interested party when she returns from her country place in time for the holidays.

Look, I run a business, not a cultural charity. I even make museums pay.

It's nearly eight-thirty. Time to take my little Sumerian upstairs.

Judson's on the phone at his desk when I walk into the office, the receiver tucked under his chin as he writes notes on a slip of paper in his neat handwriting. His pack of Lucky Strikes is folded into the sleeve of his white T-shirt. Seeing me, he raises a finger to indicate he'll be off the phone any second and I should hang around for information.

He hangs up after a "Toodle-oo" to whoever's at the other end of the line, then says to me, "I've got something on Lorraine Quinn," and hands me the slip of paper. "It's not much, but it's a start. I'll keep digging."

Judson's right. It's not much, just a start, but it's a damn good start.

It seems Lorraine came to New York nine years ago from a beach town on the South Jersey shore, and after the usual succession of waitressing jobs while pursuing a career as an actress she gave up on her Broadway dreams two years ago. She took a course to be a legal secretary, which landed her a job at a shady law firm near City Hall, the office of Otis Hollander, Attorney at Law. Hollander specializes in divorce cases involving cheating spouses, what's known on the street as a Tail-and-Snap outfit: tail the spouse to a hideaway love nest, kick down the door or peer through the window, and snap their picture in the arms of someone other than their wife or husband. Big alimony for the spurned wife of the can't-keep-it-in-his-pants husband, or save the cuckolded husband from paying his no-good cheatin' wife a dime in the divorce.

And Lorraine called *me* a creep.

"Good work, Judson," I say.

Never one for showy emotion, he just shrugs, pulls a ledger from his desk drawer, and starts to work on our business records. They're written in a dense code only Judson and I can untangle.

I'm on my way into my private office when I hear, "Good morning, Cantor," in Rosie's soft, lilting voice.

She's in her cabbie's duds: gray-brown chinos, blue work shirt, unzipped brown leather jacket, and a dark green eight-point cabbie's cap, the shiny black brim pulled low, barely revealing her sweet blue eyes. Her misty blond hair spills out from under her cap, accenting a complexion creamy as a rich dessert. Rosie's just as tasty from the neck down, filling her cabbie's duds with plenty of curves. I'm always happy when I roam those curves. And as far as I know, Rosie is happy when I'm roaming, though I know there's a part of her that wouldn't mind if I dropped dead. That's the hurt part, the part that once loved me but didn't get my love back. But she didn't abandon me. She just changed the game to one we both could live with. We play with others, but now and then share a night of first-aid sex that soothes life's wounds.

"I'll just get my coat," I say, put the wrapped little Sumerian on Judson's desk and walk into my private office.

This room is my haven, sometimes my home-away-from-home when I need to spend a few nights here, lie low for a while until a situation cools down. I've furnished the place with first-rate stuff because I like good design and my racket brings in the cash to afford it. My oxblood leather couch is comfortable enough to sleep on. The leather of my pale green club chair is so supple that sitting in it is like sitting in a woman's embrace.

But the furnishings are also practical. The wall safe behind my big walnut desk is stashed with plenty of cash, spare guns, and ammo. I've got a stall shower, a wardrobe with fresh clothes, a small refrigerator and hot plate so I don't go hungry. There's a radio and good supply of Chivas scotch so I don't go nuts.

The cops have no idea about this place. Besides me, only Judson, Rosie, Red Drogan, and my lawyer know who this joint belongs to. And my lawyer buried the ownership information so deep in a mountain of paperwork, even a pickaxe wouldn't uncover my name because it isn't there.

I grab my coat and cap, go back to the outer office, pick up the little Sumerian, and leave with Rosie.

Her cab's parked in the back alley. She gets into the driver's seat. I get into the backseat, just another passenger chauffeured around by a New York cabbie, of no interest to anyone, not even cops.

Chapter Three

Rosie threads us through the tangle of traffic in the Garment District a few blocks east of my office. Shouting guys pushing wheeled racks of dresses or handcarts piled with bolts of fabric compete for space with delivery trucks double-parked on both sides of the street. Mixed in with the muscle of truckers and rag trade labor are delicate beauties in elegant clothes, models on their way to and from the lofts and showrooms of the clothing manufacturers and fashion photographers in the skyscrapers towering over the streets. As Rosie finagles the cab through the throng, I light up a smoke to accompany my satisfying eyeful of pretty faces, shapely legs, and bodies swaying inside the current style of swing-y coats that ripple with every movement of hip and torso. These beautiful sights take a little off the edge of how crummy I feel about the murder of Lorraine Quinn and the lousy way I treated her.

"One of these days," Rosie says, breaking into my sightseeing reverie, "the city is gonna do something about all this double-parking around here. It's hell on the cab business."

"Not until the Mob lets go of the rag trade and the truckers," I say.

"Yeah, and that's never. Driving through here knots up my muscles."

I feel a carnal smile spread across my lips. "You know I'm always good for a massage, Rosie," I say.

"And I'm happy to take you up on it."

I park my cigarette at the corner of my mouth, lean forward in the cab, press my fingers against her shoulders, and start to gently rub. "How about tonight?"

"I'll let you know," she says. "I might have plans." She rolls my fingers off her shoulders.

There it is, the occasional slap in my face from the part of Rosie that still hurts because I couldn't return her affections. It's not a big part, just a little bit of chilled blood deep in her veins.

I rest again into the backseat, my carnal smile reduced to a defeated pucker. I keep quiet with my smoke while Rosie drives us through the city.

Below Thirty-Fourth Street, Park Avenue becomes Fourth Avenue, and fancy apartment buildings and hotels give way to slightly less fancy residences and eventually to office buildings. Rosie makes a left turn at East Twentieth Street, which here, along the small, verdant, private enclave that gives the neighborhood its name, is called Gramercy Park South.

At the far end of the park, she lets a woman walking a poodle, a guy in a lumber jacket and beat-up cap, a bored-looking guy in a tweed coat and gray fedora, and a kid on a bicycle cross the street before she makes another left turn onto Gramercy Park East. I tell her to pull up in front of the place on the corner, an ornate brownstone townhouse with lots of tall, well-tended shrubbery around the front and side. The house is two stories chockablock with neoclassical exterior. Never mind that Ionic columns and classical scrollwork look peculiar in New York brown. Enough money can buy you any century you want to drape on your shoulders. If you want your front door to greet you as if you're a Greek hero or a Roman emperor, all you have to do is tell your architect to throw in some columns and statuary.

This particular imperial residence is the home of my client, Eve Garraway, the thirty-two-year-old only child of the late John Garraway, known as Boss Garraway, at one time the most powerful politician in the state of New York. As the Speaker of the State Assembly, he handed out committee assignments and chairmanships, which meant if a politician wanted any influence they had to go through Garraway. He could get your neighborhood streets paved or neglected, could get a railroad station for your new suburban town, or have your upstate village bypassed. He could raise up your political career or make sure you were never elected to anything more than dogcatcher. And of course, he made sure you, your town, your village, or your city paid for it. The guy made a fortune in graft.

His daughter is the beneficiary of all that cash slipped into daddy's pockets. The old man invested it wisely, turned thousands into millions, and gave his wife and daughter the imperial life befitting his extravagant house, which he stole from the bankrupt robber baron who'd had it built for his own imperial dreams.

Eve Garraway lives here alone now, except for a butler. Eve's mother, the famous beauty Mary O'Neill Garraway, outlived her husband but passed on three years ago after a losing battle with pneumonia. Eve, no slouch in the looks department herself, is the last of the Garraway line. She's determined to maintain the family name and influence as long as she's alive and beyond, which is where my smuggling job to bring her the little Sumerian comes in. Since her mother's death, Eve's been aggressively assembling a collection of the world's art treasures, everything from ancient artifacts to medieval icons to paintings by Renaissance, Baroque and Rococo masters, dangling them in front of curators and directors of major museums across the country. Every art bigwig from New York to California wants the Garraway hoard. All it will take is obeisance to Eve and building a museum wing for her collection. The Garraway Wing.

I get out of Rosie's cab, walk up the half dozen steps to the portico of the house and with a smile on my face ring the bell at the side of the brass-handled door. Thirty thousand dollars is waiting for me on the other side of that door, which puts me in a very sociable mood.

The door's opened by Desmond, the longtime Garraway butler, a gray-haired, gray-faced stick of a guy who looks like he'd turn to dust any minute. He smiles at me. He likes me. And why shouldn't he? Before his respectable spot as a butler, Desmond Mallory pulled off some of the smoothest bank heists in the annals of old New York crime. But illness after a rough stint in Sing Sing prison dulled his senses and slowed his hands. His crime spree was over. Boss John Garraway, a fan of Desmond's thieving career, took him on as the household butler, trusting him not to lift the family silver. Desmond's been loyal to the Garraways ever since. I bet he'd die, or maybe even kill, for Eve.

I greet him with an extended hand. "How's everything, Desmond?"

"I cannot complain," he says, his thin, breathy voice melodious as reeds in a breeze. He returns my handshake, takes my coat and cap and leads me through the vestibule and into the main hall.

I hold the wrapped Sumerian close as we walk through the hallway, a baronial stretch paneled in dark walnut. The stained-glass window over the entry door throws colored light onto the walls, the carved Victorian side tables, and me. A thick Persian carpet silences my footsteps. The whole place could pass as a dream.

"Eve must've had a swell time growing up in this make-believe castle," I joke.

Desmond gets a kick out of the memory, gives it a smile. "Oh yes," he says. "She especially liked playing hide-and-seek. Lots of places for a little girl to hide in this house."

"And for Boss Garraway to hide his cash," I say.

"Actually, it was Mr. Aloysius Sloan, the original owner, who hid things here. They did that in those days." We've reached the broad stairway. "Miss Garraway is waiting for you upstairs in her office, Cantor."

Eve's office is along the second floor's open mezzanine at the top of the stairway. After a knock on the door, I hear, "Come in," in Eve's deep but easygoing voice, a voice comfortable in its owner's power over people.

She smiles when I walk in as she gets up from behind her desk, a sleek oak piece of furniture in an equally sleek room of warm pale gray walls lined with contemporary and classic paintings. A few of the classic pieces were supplied by me. But it's not me Eve's smiling at. She's smiling at the bundle in my hands. Her shoulder-length honey blond hair shines, softly framing a porcelain-delicate face whose blue eyes twinkle with acquisitive pleasure. "Ah," she sighs as she walks around to the front of the desk, her white silk blouse and beige pencil-thin skirt hugging her body the way a body should be hugged. "Show me."

I push the desk clock aside to make room for the bundle. The clock's luminous dial throws a green tinge on the wrapping. "Eve, how about if you do the honors?" I say. "You're certainly paying for it."

"Yes." The word passes through her lips in a whisper.

I watch in fascination as each perfectly manicured finger carefully unwraps the cloth and peels back the batting. Luminous green from the clock tints Eve's fingers while light from a window glints off the sapphire-and-gold ring on her right hand and the ruby-and-gold ring on her left. The jewels sparkle their colors as her fingers move. As the statue is revealed, Eve's breathing slows. "He's magnificent," she says so softly I barely hear it as she takes the statue in hand, runs her fingers along the grooves of his beard and rippling hair, then down the smooth sides of his simple garments. Finally turning to me, she says, "How did you ever get it out of Baghdad?"

"You're paying me to do it, Eve," I say with a smile, "not to tell you how."

She gives that a shrewd laugh and a "Touché." The look on her face is just as canny, but curious, as if seeing me for the first time. "You know, Cantor, when you smile, those scars on your face almost seem to dance."

"Thirty thousand dollars can make anything dance."

"Indeed," she says, shrugging with the amusement of someone for whom thirty thousand dollars is nothing but palm grease. "Follow me. It's time I showed you something."

Frankly, all I want to see is her thirty grand greasing *my* palm. But Eve's the client, and it's not my policy to argue with clients, especially rich ones who make regular use of my services.

And besides, Eve Garraway has never stiffed me before. I trust she won't now, so I just follow her across the office to another door.

She opens the door. We walk through into a small vestibule. There's a door on my right to what I assume is a closet. In front of us is a vault door nearly as big as the door to the vault in the basement of my office.

Eve looks back over her shoulder at me, her hair sliding smoothly along her cheek. "Stand back from me," she says with a cunning smile.

Sure, she's afraid I'll see her dial the combination and memorize it.

I do as I'm told, take a few steps back, adding a short, playful bow.

"Well, you *are* a thief, Cantor. Why should I make it easy for you?"

"Afraid I'll steal your money?" I say with a laugh.

"In a way."

She dials the combination, turns the wheel to unlock the safe. When Eve opens the door it's not cash that confronts us. It's treasure. Shelf after shelf of paintings, jewelry, statuettes, religious artifacts, decorative objects in precious metals encrusted with jewels. It's the history of art from all the cultures of the world. It's the famed Garraway Collection.

"People ask me why I haven't married," she says, apropos of a question I didn't ask but have often wondered about. "I haven't married because it wouldn't matter if I did. The Garraway name ends with me. A husband's name would supersede it. I won't allow that. I don't want the Garraway name buried by another. All of this," she says, sweeping her arm around the vault, "ensures that the Garraway name lives on. Go ahead, Cantor. Go inside and look around. You've certainly contributed your share to this enterprise."

I step inside the vault, marvel at the treasures there. I spot some of the pieces I've added to this hoard: a Caravaggio portrait of a prince from 1605; a sketch by Leonardo in preparation for his circa 1508 painting of Saint John the Baptist; a Fragonard portrait from 1767 of a voluptuous young girl; a preclassical Greek amphora from the Geometric period, around 750 BC; a Roman portrait bust of an aristocratic woman, circa 50 AD; a Neolithic clay pot from China, dated to around 3000 BC; and a filigreed gold and ruby-encrusted cross from medieval Tuscany that the Vatican still won't admit is missing. In addition to what I've brought in, there's more, much more. The abundance of color and the gleam of jewels, the shine of silver and gold, all of it threatens to overload my senses.

There's no unifying theme to all this, no narrative idea to tie it all together. It's all just acquisition for acquisition's sake, and now I know why every museum in the country wants it. There's enough here to enrich every curatorial department in the building: ancient art, medieval art, Renaissance and Rococo paintings, art from Asia, carvings from Africa, pottery from the pre-Columbian Americas.

"So you see, Cantor, this will be the Garraway legacy. No husband will ever get his hands on it."

There was something cold in her eyes, a chill I'd never noticed before. She didn't love these treasures. She only loved the power and prestige they bring. I'm suddenly sorry I've provided any part of it.

"An impressive collection," is all I say as I walk out of the vault. I'm not about to insult someone who owes me thirty thousand dollars.

"Thank you. It's in honor of my father, so I wouldn't want it to be anything less than impressive."

"Yeah, well, you've certainly succeeded. Who else has seen it?"

"A few museum people here in New York, and a few from Chicago. My representative has shown photographs to important curators elsewhere. As a matter of fact, I'm expecting someone shortly."

"No doubt you'll place it in a major institution."

"When the time comes."

"Speaking of time," I slip in with a nod to my wristwatch, "I have to—"

"Oh yes, of course. I don't mean to keep you. Let's go back into my office and complete our business."

Yes let's.

An envelope stuffed with thirty thousand dollars creates quite a bulk in the inside pocket of my overcoat, so I'm anxious to get back to my office and lock the cash away in the wall safe behind my desk. Judson will record the transaction in code in the ledger books and figure in his cut and Rosie's and Red Drogan's. Another Cantor Gold operation will come to a satisfying end.

Too bad it comes on a less than satisfying day. Sure, I'm happy that I'm thirty grand richer than I was this morning, but the morning brought murder and cops to my doorstep. No amount of money is going to fix that. It sure as hell can't ease the kick to my guts over Lorraine Quinn ending up dead and bloody an hour after she left my bed. The woman never did me any harm. On the contrary, she gave me plenty of pleasure and a few hours relief from the pain of that wound that won't heal. And the thirty g's can't get rid of the irritating problem of having a homicide cop bent on hanging the murder on me.

I figure I have to do two things to make that situation better. One is to find out all I can about Lorraine Quinn in order to set Huber up with another suspect, and the other is to drown my guilt-ridden mood over Miss Quinn's death. I hope to do the former with whatever information Judson digs up, and then maybe a night at the Green Door Club, tossing back tumblers of Chivas scotch and dancing with a pretty woman, can take care of the latter. Maybe the crowd at the Green Door can even fill in what I don't know about Lorraine Quinn.

These thoughts accompany me down the front stairs to the street, where my luck seems to be returning as a cab comes around the corner. I quickly hail it, but I needn't have bothered. The cab stops in front of the Garraway place. I guess it brought the next salivating museum representative Eve mentioned she's expecting. I hope the guy's prepared for equal amounts of the big chill and the big thrill.

But stepping out of the cab is no guy. It's one of the few women curators in New York, or anywhere else in the world for that matter. Standing in the street in a softly swinging red wool coat trimmed in black chinchilla is a spectacular woman who's reached the pinnacle of the museum world by the twin blessings of family lineage and hard work. The family name, Parkhurst Trent, got her through the door. Her brilliant mind and dedicated work resulted in becoming a respected expert in European Renaissance paintings, hired by the top museum here in New York. And the fact that she's a stunner probably didn't hurt. Such is the way of the world.

As I come down the steps, the woman seems surprised to see me, then not surprised at all. Her softly coiffed waves of shoulder-length brunette hair shimmer below a red hat edged in chinchilla. Her big green eyes—probing, confident, haughty, like those of a pampered cat—regard me with the slightly derisive humor that's the privilege of the privileged. Her half smile, the lipstick on her frankly voluptuous lips the exact shade of her coat and hat, of course, prefaces her simple greeting, "Cantor." Her voice, even though just two little syllables, flows smooth as soft silk.

"Vivienne," I say, with a tip of my cap.

"Adding to the Garraway collection?" she asks.

"In my modest way," I answer.

"There's nothing modest about you, Cantor."

"Except when I'm around you, Vivienne."

She likes my answer, at least I think so. It's hard to tell with Vivienne. She has the breeding that allows her smile to remain cool and aloof, but there's a spicier element, too, a bloodline that runs from her up-from-the-gutter great-grandfather, Malachi Trent, a brute who founded the family dynasty by brawling, bullying, and bribing his way to creating a maritime shipping fortune in old New York. Vivienne's aristocratic Parkhurst breeding and the bawdier Trent bloodline are both evident in her eyes and in the way she moves her body, even the way she's standing here in the street: chin up in high society arrogance, one hand on a thrust hip in a manner better suited to a streetwalker.

"Oh my god," she says, which I think is a rather harsh response to my feelings about being in her presence. But I realize she's not looking at me. She's looking up at the door to the Garraway house.

I turn and look up, too. Desmond's in the doorway, his eyes wide, his face tight, his butler's getup askew. I can't tell if the poor guy is relieved or surprised to see me still in front of the house. He finally raises his arm, stiff as a stick, awkwardly waves me to come inside, but casts a leery eye on Vivienne.

"It's okay," I tell Desmond when Vivienne and I are up the stairs and at the door. "I can vouch for Miss Parkhurst Trent. Eve was expecting her." I leave out that I've worked with Vivienne before, supplied her museum with some of Europe's finest Renaissance and Baroque artwork.

Nodding his acceptance of my assessment, the old thief leads us inside and upstairs, back to Eve's office. His hand shakes when he opens the office door.

My life of crime has hardened me to many things. I'm no stranger to violence, no Nervous Nellie in the face of death. But seeing Eve Garraway face down in a pool of blood on her office floor, a fancy knife with a carved ivory handle plunged deep in her back, shakes me to my core.

The Sumerian votive statue is smashed to pieces beside her.

Chapter Four

A day that started off with two slaps to my face has rolled into the horror of two women dead at my feet. My whole world is tilted at a dizzying angle with nothing to grab onto to right it. And the breath that usually moves freely in and out of my lungs now stings, as if tainted with deadly poison. Wherever I breathe, someone dies. I'm afraid that my next exhale might poison Vivienne.

Until I realize that she's not beside me. Only Desmond and I and the corpse of Eve Garraway are in the room. I might figure that the murder scene is too gruesome for Vivienne to bear, except I know that she's a first-rate huntswoman, a crack shot who's been known to bring down game, skin it, gut it, and have it served at her table with a savory sauce and fine wine. I know it because Vivienne's skill with a rifle saved my life one night a few years ago after an art deal gone bad. She put a bullet into the forehead of a guy whose gun was aimed at me, and she did it from across the room, calm and calculating as a jungle cat. Vivienne Parkhurst Trent may have a society belle's poise but she has Malachi Trent's spine.

My assessment's right on the mark when she walks back into the room, cool as a Park Avenue cocktail. "I've telephoned the police," she says, her voice steady.

My annoyance is matched by Desmond's alarm. Though he doesn't know about the murder of Lorraine Quinn at my doorstep, he knows all about me. He knows about my criminal life. He knows that the cops would be only too happy to put me away for whatever they can make stick. With all that knowledge in his own outlaw mind, he grasps the situation fast. "Cantor," he says, his bony frame tense under his butler's duds, his thin voice edgy, "you must leave here immediately, before those blue-coated rascals arrive."

"Sure," I say, "but before I go, Desmond: tell me, did you hear anyone come into the house? The place has a back garden, yes? Did you see or hear anyone roaming around back there?"

"No, no one," he says, his voice cracking as if he might break down and cry.

"What about any strange sounds around the house? Like someone hiding inside, waiting for Eve to be alone?"

"No, I didn't hear anything after you left. As far as I know I was alone in the house. Except for Miss Garraway, that is."

If I didn't know any better, I might raise an eyebrow about Desmond being the only other person in the house besides Eve. But an old pro like Desmond, an ex-con who knows the ropes, wouldn't set up a murder that fingers him as the killer. And besides, the guy's so loyal to the Garraways he'd probably walk in front of a truck to save Eve's life.

He says, "Listen, Cantor, after you left, I went to the kitchen to organize the lunch order from the Plaza. Miss Garraway has a standing order for them to supply lunch and dinner each day if she's not dining out. After that, I went upstairs to talk to Miss Garraway about other household business. Like I said, I . . . I heard no one else, saw nobody, just Miss—" The poor guy can't even look at Eve on the floor. Fixing a watery, worried eye on me instead, he says, "Leave here, Cantor. You must leave here now. The young lady and I will handle the blue devils."

I start to walk out, but Vivienne grabs my arm. "Just a minute, Cantor. Why are you worried about the police? You were outside with me when—oh," she stops short. "Yes, of course. The police might think you killed Eve before you left the house. But what motive would you have?"

First Desmond and then Vivienne look at me as if horns are slowly sprouting from my head. I can guess what's on their minds, so I take my cap off to give them a better look. I even smile, a wiseacre smile that lets them know I'm on to them.

There's something especially snide in Desmond's eyes. He knows to forget all that honor among thieves baloney. In the crime world, it's grab what you can, kill if you must, and don't trust anyone.

I keep my smile, but back it up with a steely stare at Desmond and Vivienne. "I don't have any motive. None. But I had thirty thousand reasons to be very happy with Eve Garraway," I say, and pat the bulk where the thirty grand resides in my inside pocket, "and high hopes for an equally fruitful future. So you two can just ditch your crummy suspicions. And you, Desmond, you should know better. People like us never kill the golden goose. Well, almost never." I put my cap back on.

He snickers at my reference to the suspicion widely held in the underworld that he'd knocked off a guy who'd paid him to knock over a telegraph office back in the old days, before his career as a bank thief.

Vivienne says, "Desmond, you're sure you heard no one else in the house?"

A gravelly answer arrives. "Yeah, what about it, Desmond?" The familiar croak of Lieutenant Huber twists deep in my gut.

Desmond was right. I should've scrammed when I had the chance.

That chance is gone. I'm trapped in this room between a dead woman on the floor and the narrowing stare of Lieutenant Huber throwing equal amounts of surprise and cold triumph at me. "Well, look who's here. How many women are you gonna kill today, Gold?"

"You tell me, Huber. You're the one keeping a tally."

There's so much accusation all over Huber's bony face that I half expect his brown eyes to turn red. Instead, his stare grows even colder, as brittle as dead leaves in winter. He says, "All I know is this is the second time today some dame has wound up dead and bloodied, and whaddya know, you're inches from the body. And I bet your fingerprints are all over that knife in her back."

"You'd lose the bet."

"So you wiped 'em. You're a pro, Gold."

"And maybe so is whoever killed Eve. My bet is you won't find any prints at all."

Vivienne grabs my arm, looks at me with confusion, and for the first time in all the years I've known her, fear. "Cantor? What is he talking about? What does he mean this is the second dead woman today?"

Before I can even open my mouth to answer, Huber slaps Vivienne's questions aside. "And who would you be, missy?"

Vivienne's newly minted fear of me dissolves into the haughty annoyance she was bred to feel for those lesser beings on the public payroll whom her crowd merely considers the help. "My name is Vivienne Parkhurst Trent, lieutenant. And if you don't explain yourself and your reference to dead women in connection with Cantor, I'm sure the police commissioner will be more than happy to provide the information. He owes me a drink. Perhaps I'll take him up on it this evening. I'll be sure to mention your name."

I enjoyed that, and so did Desmond, who's trying to hide the tiny smile his outlaw soul is savoring down to his marrow. Getting the better of cops is always entertaining.

The expression on Huber's face goes from cold and hard to pasty. He looks like he's been force-fed a pill he can't quite push down his gullet. He not only recognizes Vivienne's family name, he's aware of its influence.

But a cop is a cop, and that badge, especially a lieutenant's gold shield, gives him plenty of power too. Only a moment ago, Huber looked like he might gag. Now he looks like he could spit right in Vivienne's face. "I don't care what you say to the commissioner, Miss *Parkhurst Trent*." His smug exaggeration of her name has enough acid behind it to eat through the walls. "Just make sure you get my name right—Huber, Lieutenant Norm Huber—when you tell him about one dead woman at the door of Gold's apartment building this morning and the other dead woman here on the floor. Oh, and remember to mention that the woman on the floor is the daughter of old Boss Garraway. If I recall, Miss Parkhurst

27

Trent, John Garraway was what you might call a mentor to the commissioner."

"And my family financed them both," Vivienne counters with a smile that could peel the flesh from Huber's bones. "And now, good afternoon, lieutenant." Vivienne takes my arm as if we're on our way to high tea at the Plaza.

Huber steps in front of us, blocks us from leaving. "You're not going anywhere yet, not until you answer a few questions. And if I don't like the answers, the only place you and Gold are going is the lockup."

Vivienne says, "I don't like your tone, lieutenant."

"You don't have to like it, lady. What you have to do is tell me what you and Gold are doing here."

The look on Vivienne's face is a study in umbrage. Umbrage at being challenged by someone so beneath her. Umbrage that such a person would have the nerve. I usually disapprove of snobbishness, but Vivienne's wielding it like an elegant weapon, and there's no one I'd rather see her use it on than Huber. "What do you think I'm doing here, lieutenant?" she says. "I'm a curator, and Miss Garraway is a collector. We had an appointment to discuss acquiring her collection for my museum. Now, if you don't mind, Cantor and I will be on our way."

Huber blocks us again. "I mind plenty," he says. He shifts his focus to me, pushes his hat back on his head, gives me the full weight of his cop stare. "And what about you, Gold? What was your business here? That broken bric-a-brac on the floor next to Miss Garraway's corpse have anything to do with it?"

"I don't break things, lieutenant. I have too much respect for—"

"The money those fancy knickknacks deliver to your handbag?" he says. "Oh, my mistake, you don't carry a handbag, do you." His smile is so slimy it wouldn't surprise me to see snakes slither through his teeth.

I've had it with this guy. "If you have any more questions, lieutenant, call my lawyer." Vivienne's hand is still on my arm. I clutch it tight while I maneuver us past Huber.

He says, "Don't leave town, Gold."

ᔓ ᔓ ᔓ

I hail a cab, intending to take Vivienne to a cozy spot I know nearby where we can chat over coffee, which I'll tell the waiter to spike with a shot of booze to loosen the knots in my gut. The murder of two women in one morning is tough for anyone to take. Add my guilty feelings about my rotten treatment of Lorraine Quinn, plus the relentless Lieutenant Huber determined to see me fry for the murders of Lorraine and Eve, and it's fair to say I'm not in the best of moods. It doesn't help that as soon as we're in the cab, before I can give the cabbie the address of the spot where a boozed-up coffee is waiting to greet me, Vivienne directs the driver to her museum, that big joint on Fifth Avenue at the eastern edge of Central Park. All I can do is lick my lips, disappointed there's no scotch whiskey to lap up.

Vivienne is silent as the cabbie drives his hack uptown, weaving through traffic in that terrifying way only a New York cabbie can do. Kids on roller skates, shoppers with Fifth Avenue hatboxes, and office types out to grab some lunch skitter out of this guy's path. He's not as smooth as Rosie.

I can't figure Vivienne's silence. It's not exactly cold, but the set of her face, her beautiful aristocratic face, looking out the window as if surveying the golden city that her great-grandfather Malachi bent to his will, makes it clear that conversation is not invited.

Just as well. Vivienne's silence gives me room to think about my lousy morning and try to figure out why the hell murder is following me all over town.

As a senior curator of European paintings, Vivienne's office is a cushy spot with elegant gray-green walls covered in ornately framed masterpieces: from the late medieval Italian religious dramas of Giotto to the succulent French Rococo amusements of François Boucher. The furniture is just as elegantly eclectic. Two nineteenth-century French walnut armchairs upholstered

29

in needlepoint face Vivienne's English eighteenth-century George III mahogany desk. Its green leather top hosts an early twentieth-century abalone and brass desk set and cigarette box. A sparkling cut-crystal ashtray with plenty of heft and enough sharp edges to brain someone is next to the cigarette box. A similar ashtray hoards most of the space on the spindly Rococo table between the two needlepoint chairs. The whole place, an assemblage of delicate things and weighty things, is a subtle expression of a connoisseur's taste and a not-so-subtle expression of the Parkhurst Trent influence. It's that influence which was able to slide me out of Huber's grip.

Vivienne removes her coat, hangs it on a rack in the corner, removes her hat, and hangs that on the rack, too. With the nonchalance of a woman who assumes beauty is hers by right, she runs her fingers through her dark hair, restoring its style and bounce from the grasp of her hat. Moving to the window, she angles the Venetian blinds, simultaneously cutting the glare of the late morning sun on Fifth Avenue and canceling the view of any nosy neighbors from their windows in the fancy apartment buildings and remaining Gilded Age mansions across the street. With the sashay that's natural to her and that never fails to grab my attention, she moves to the front of her desk and leans against the edge, her slender charcoal wool skirt hugging her smooth curves while her ivory silk V-neck blouse catches light where light should be caught, to my unabashed pleasure. I've always had a taste for Vivienne, a taste she let me indulge one night four years ago. She was delicious, but one taste is all she gave me. I think our night of passion scared her. Maybe I scared her. Maybe she scared herself. Whatever it was, she's retreated into the safety of male companions at the town's better restaurants.

She's all cool and patrician now. With a wave of her hand, Vivienne directs me to one of the needlepoint chairs. When I'm seated, my cap in my lap, she folds her arms across her chest in a quick, annoyed fashion, the gesture a strategy to hold onto her fraying patience. From her perch against her desk, she looks down at me. I think she wants me to squirm. She should know better.

Her green eyes on me as if considering whether to behead me or merely scold, she turns away briefly to take a cigarette from the box on her desk, tilting her head back to offer one to me.

"I have my own," I say, and take out my pack of Chesterfields from my inside coat pocket.

Vivienne lights her smoke with the lighter on her desk, then bends down to light mine. If she's aware that I'm enjoying the view, she doesn't acknowledge it, doesn't smile, doesn't even tease. She just closes the lighter and leans against the desk again. Saying nothing, she continues to look down at me, cigarette smoke curling along her face, drifting around her pampered courtesan's eyes, creating a lacy veil that can't quite hide her displeasure with me.

I have better things to do—like digging for more of Lorraine Quinn's story to find out who'd want her dead—than be kept hostage in Vivienne's office, pleasant as the company, the view, and these surroundings may be. "Why did you bring me here, Vivienne?"

One of her hands remains clamped against the edge of her desk while the other slowly lowers the cigarette from her mouth, her lipstick leaving a smear of red. She's still looking at me, but her eyes are less scolding now. Something else is creeping into those eyes, or rather creeping back: fear, that unfamiliar fear I saw in Vivienne's eyes back at Eve Garraway's place. It takes Vivienne a minute to be able to speak past it. "What did Lieutenant Huber mean about two dead women, Cantor? What the hell have you dragged me into?" There's an edge to her usually silky voice, an edge of frustration, an edge of anger. "I can't afford scandal. I could lose everything I worked so damn hard for here at the museum. I'm the only female senior curator in this institution, and I could lose it all in a minute. Why are you doing this to me, Cantor?"

"Why am I—?"

"Yes, you. I thought I knew you. I mean, I know about the things—the things you do. The museum world is highly competitive, every curator lusting after the best works, and I'm no different. So while

I'm grateful for your help in securing superior acquisitions for me at the museum, if you committed murder—"

"Do you really think I'm a murderer, Vivienne?" It's my turn to look hard at her.

She returns it, stare for stare, her eyes probing me, but the expression on her face is someone looking for safe haven. I guess she didn't find it because she looks away, stamps out her smoke, slowly circling the cigarette at the bottom of the crystal ashtray. She finally shakes her head, then looks at me again. "I believe you can kill."

"And I know you can, Vivienne. But that doesn't make you a murderer."

She can't escape what I just said, can't escape our shared night of violence and the crack shot that saved my life. With a tight-lipped swallow followed by a slow breath, she says, "No, no I don't believe you're a murderer, Cantor. But your world is, well, criminal. I can't be seen by the police to be associated with it."

"Then get your masterpieces legitimately if you want to skirt around scandal, and don't do business with the likes of me."

I know that stung her. I see it in the slight but quickly controlled tightness around her eyes and mouth.

How many times today am I going to be a cad? I gave Lorraine the brush-off this morning, and I barked at Vivienne just now. Less than an hour ago Vivienne was at my side, and together we faced down the Law. She deserves a better Cantor Gold than the lout sitting in the fancy needlepoint chair.

I'd better smooth out my attitude. "Listen, Vivienne, you were simply at the wrong place at the wrong time, just like me. Only it's happened to me twice today, and now Huber is out for my hide. If I don't figure things out fast, he just might skin me. And by the way, thanks for helping me get past Huber's handcuffs at the Garraway place. I mean it. I'm grateful."

"You're welcome, but you owe me, Cantor Gold. You can start by explaining the deaths of two women and why the lieutenant thinks they're connected to you."

"Maybe you're better off not knowing, Vivienne. You're better off not getting dragged into something ugly and dangerous."

"It's too late for that. I was in a room with a corpse with a knife in her back when the police arrived. I'm already dragged into it. And I need to be prepared in case that lieutenant decides to drag me in deeper."

"I wouldn't worry about it. Being in the room isn't enough for Huber to arrest you, Vivienne."

"I'm not worried about getting arrested," she says, waving away the ridiculous idea of someone of her social standing seeing the inside of a jail cell. "But I bet he resents me after I rubbed his nose in the police commissioner's name today, so I have no doubt Huber would enjoy burying me in mud. There are some gentlemen here at the museum who might even help him. They think the only job for a woman at the museum is a secretary, or better yet, one of the after-hours cleaning ladies. Those gentlemen would be only too happy to use a scandal to ruin my professional reputation, which would give them the excuse to show me the door. If I hope to survive this, I need to know what's going on. So let's hear it, Cantor."

The fear's creeping back in her eyes, but there's determination, too, and the determination is winning. The iron-willed bloodline of Malachi Trent is making itself felt in Vivienne's veins. She's no longer grasping the edge of the desk for support. She's leaning against it as if it's a perch from which to command the obedience of the mere hireling seated before her.

It looks good on her. I get a charge from strong women. So okay, I'll play along. She's earned an explanation, anyway.

I kill my smoke in the crystal brain basher on the spindly table next to me. "I don't know what's going on," I say, "but I'll fill you in on what little I do know."

I lay it out, tell her about Lorraine Quinn, one minute in my bed, the next minute dead on my doorstep. I tell her about bringing the little Sumerian to Eve Garraway, and Eve's plans for her family's legacy.

Through a cool smile with plenty of disdain behind it, Vivienne says, "Yes, she'd hoped a museum wing with the Garraway name on it would be her ticket into—"

"Your crowd?"

Her smile's still cool, but the disdain's gone. There's a bit of amusement in it, accompanied by a shrug acknowledging her own snobbishness.

An idea occurs to me. "How bad did she want in, Vivienne?"

"Well, let's just say she pressed a little harder than was seemly. She never married, but she did all she could to chummy up to the more important families in New York, especially the wives. Eve knew it's the wives who hold the social power."

"And you know these wives?"

"Many of them. What are you getting at, Cantor?"

"I bet those wives know a thing or two about Eve Garraway. Things I'd like to know, things that might send Huber looking in a direction other than mine." If I could send Huber chasing in one direction about the Garraway killing, and another direction for the Quinn murder, with any luck he'll trip over his own feet, fall flat on his face, and get out of my way. "Would you do something for me, Vivienne?"

Chapter Five

Judson's still busy with the ledger books when I get back to my office. "We're in good shape, Cantor. If you've got the Garraway money, I'll figure it in."

I pull the envelope of cash from my coat pocket. "Thirty grand," I say. Blood money, I can't help thinking as I take out four thousand—Red Drogan's cut and walking-around money for my pocket—and hand the rest to Judson. "Take your cut and set Rosie's aside, too. I'll settle up with Drogan. Put the rest in the safe."

My young genius eyes me, reads me. "What's wrong, Cantor? Since when does handling a bundle of cash make you look like you've just buried your mother?"

I pull my cap off and sit at the edge of his desk. My bones feel heavy. My mind and spirit aren't feeling any too frisky either, not with the corpses of two murdered women at my feet. My connection to either woman wasn't particularly deep, but they were part of my life, and for better or worse I was part of theirs, even though one of them ended our night of passion by hating me and the other considered me merely for hire. "Eve Garraway's dead, Judson. Murdered as soon as I left the house, maybe even while I was still inside, on my way to the door. Knifed, just like Lorraine Quinn. And Huber's reaching for my neck again."

Judson's not one for syrupy sentiment. The gears of his brain keep all of that in check while those gears turn through all the permutations of a problem. Behind his wire-rim glasses, his eyes stay steady on me but he's not really looking at me. His view is inward, no doubt watching all the possible scenarios go by. I hope an escape scene is one of them.

I can't wait around for the verdict. "Anything new on Quinn?" I say, pulling Judson out of his mental gymnastics.

"Uh, oh, yeah," he says, back with me now. "Something odd. It seems part of Quinn's job at Hollander's law office was to keep tabs on their clients' wayward spouses and arrange the photo surveillance of their trysts. She even did a lot of the photo tails herself."

That raises my eyebrows. I didn't know much about Lorraine when we tumbled into my bed, figured maybe she was an office girl or shop girl, but I wouldn't have pegged her as a snoop. "She must've seen plenty," I say, "which made a lot of those cheating spouses pretty mad. Any one of them look angry enough to kill?"

"More than one, I'd guess. But here's that odd thing. One of the wayward spouses was Tap Tenzi."

My eyebrows inch up even higher. Johnny Tenzi, nicknamed Tap, shortened from Tapioca because of the bumpy tapioca-like skin on his face. The guy's a smart aleck. A boozer. A sometime soldier for the Mob. Married to the former Alice Lamarr, if that's her real name, which I doubt. Always did, even when we had our little fling.

But my connection to Tap Tenzi and Alice Lamarr isn't the only thing grabbing my attention. Something in the whole setup feels off. Otis Hollander is a sharp shyster who knows better than to cross the Mob, even its lowest players. Keeping tabs on Johnny Tenzi is risky business. He wouldn't do it without a damn good reason or a client with enough cash to make it worth the risk.

Where would Alice get that kind of money?

"Judson, see what you can dig up on Alice Lamarr."

"The showgirl you used to run around with?"

"That's the one. She married Tenzi a couple of years ago. Looks like she wants out. And dig around for goods on Tenzi, too, but be careful."

He assures me with a nod, then says, "And what about the Garraway situation? Want me to work on that?"

"Sure. Vivienne Parkhurst Trent agreed to chat up her high society sisters and pass me any gossip about Eve's attempts to crash into their circle. Together with whatever you dig up, it could lead to something to make Huber look in another direction and away from me."

Judson pulls his pack of Lucky Strikes from the folded sleeve of his white T-shirt. He leans back in his chair as he pulls a smoke from the pack. "Parkhurst Trent, huh," he says before he puts a cigarette between his lips and lights it, the match flame reflected in his glasses. "Been a while since we've seen any business from her. She involved with Garraway?"

"Vivienne showed up as I was leaving. She had an appointment with Eve about acquiring stuff from the Garraway collection. Every museum in the country wants it, and Vivienne was going to make her pitch."

But Judson's left the conversation. His eyes crinkle behind his wire rims, the result of a wiseacre smile. "Just don't let her walk all over you this time."

A phone call to Sig Loreale's office lets me know that he's out at his place on the ritzy North Shore of Long Island. He took possession of a spread of seaside land from a guy who owed him money and who's never been seen or heard from since. Sig built a mansion on the land, spent plenty of cash from the profits of his various enterprises, some of them legal, most of them as dirty as soiled laundry and as bloody as a slaughterhouse. It's how Sigismond Loreale, son of immigrants, grabbed his share of the American Dream, complete with a house in the suburbs. These days, Sig's the biggest of New York's big shots. From a simple muscle-and-bootleg outfit in Coney Island back in the days of Prohibition he's built a web of murder-for-hire, contraband shipments, labor rackets, financial manipulation, and political strong-arm operations. You name it, Sig Loreale is scooping out cash with both hands and amassing the kind of power normally given to tyrant kings and murderous dictators.

He and I have history going all the way back to our roots in Coney, where a young Sig Loreale muscled his way into taking over the rackets and honky-tonks from the old-timers, and I was a kid learning the thieving trade. Over the years, he's helped me, hindered me, trusted me, betrayed me, and hired me to acquire paintings, sculptures, and other treasures for his New York penthouse and his new joint out here on Long Island.

So though I'd rather have a tooth pulled than deal with the guy who holds the life and death of every New Yorker in his hands, my drive along the shore road skirting Manhasset Bay with the top down in my ivory-and-black '54 Buick Roadmaster convertible takes some of the pain off the trip. The early afternoon sun is bright, the crisp September air coming off the bay cools my face and my mood, and the Buick drives sweet and smooth as honey.

I like to be up to date with my cars. You could say they're part of my way of claiming the American Dream. For Sig, it's real estate; for me it's custom-tailored silk suits and cars. I make enough money to trade in last year's model for a new one whenever I want, pay cash right up front. New cars, new suits, the top-of-the-line furnishings in my office, are the rewards of my racket, and if I can't reward myself for risking my life while poking my finger in the Law's eye, what the hell is the money for? The Law hates me, so the hell with the Law.

Sig, though, has his own special brand of allegiance to the Law because he owns the Law, or at least a good chunk of it. He's got cops and judges and politicians in his very deep pockets. They take his money, pass him inside information, protect his interests, and he makes them rich in return. None of them ever have second thoughts or a twinge of conscience; none of them ever balk. If they did, they'd be dead, along with their family and their household pets.

Turning off the shore road, I pull up to the big, shiny steel gates guarding Sig's property. I lower the brim of my cap to shield my eyes from the glare shooting like knives off the steel, reach out to the intercom at the edge of the driveway, press the button, and announce, "Cantor Gold to see Sig."

We're not on the best of terms lately, Sig and I, not since he welched on a favor he owed me, a favor that might've ended the suffering of the woman who mattered to me more than life itself. I wanted to kill him for holding out on me. But killing the most powerful guy in town is a dead-end idea. His thugs would come after me, tear me limb from limb, and the police—especially Huber—would just laugh. And anyway, a dead Sig is a useless Sig, and I need Sig's power and access to information. So here I am once again at the door of the guy who's been over my shoulder since I was a milk-fed thief burying my trove of stolen trinkets under the Coney Island boardwalk. I sweat out wondering if he'll grant me an audience.

I also wonder how many guys with guns are patrolling nearby, unseen in the thick stand of cedars on either side of the steel gates. A big shot as careful as Sig Loreale doesn't trust his safety to just sticks of steel and a piddly little intercom at the side of the driveway. If I want to find out how many gunmen are in the bushes, all I have to do is make one wrong move.

I leave my hands on the Buick's steering wheel.

The big steel gates swing open. I'm tempted to wave as I drive through, but think better of it.

I have to hand it to Sig; his seaside place isn't the usual fantasy Gothic castle or fussy fake Rococo, Georgian or Beaux Arts palace most of Long Island's grandees built for themselves. Sig's place, on a grassy slope above the sea, is a Modernist tour de force. Approaching it along the long driveway, the clean lines and geometry of the pale blue-green multilevel massed forms rise as testaments to clear thinking, the kind of thinking ruthlessly practiced by the crime boss who lives inside.

Sunlight off the bay glows gold on the sleek windows as I drive into the circular driveway in front of the house. Sig's security thugs aren't hidden in the bushes here; they're right out front— two bulky guys in coats and fedoras patrolling the area, two other bulky guys at either side of the walkway to the front door. I park the Buick next to the walkway.

I recognize one of the guys guarding the place, an assassin named Mike Mulroney. He recognizes me. As I get out of the car, Mulroney looks me over with annoyingly pale blue eyes that have no business being in the face of a brutal killer. His look is a silent command to hand over the gun he knows I'm carrying. I don't argue. There's no point, since it's an argument that would end with me roughed up and splayed out on the driveway. And anyway, I know I'll get the gun back when I leave. It's all part of the ritual.

"Cantor," is all Mulroney says as I pull my .38 from its rig under my suit jacket. Sunlight glints on the gun's three-inch barrel and blued finish.

"Mike," is all I say in return, and start for the house.

A gardener in khakis and tan apron is busy trimming the low hedges along the walkway. He gives me a side-eye as I walk toward him. I know that look: slightly baffled, more than slightly disgusted at the sight of a dame in a gentleman's black coat and tweed cap. I smile at him and open my coat to give him a good look at the full picture: my pale gray suit, white shirt, gray and green tie. "Good afternoon," I say as I walk past him. Such moments are always fun.

Less than a minute after I ring the doorbell, a butler opens the door. Anyway, he looks like a real butler. He's trim as a steel rod in his butler's getup, but I'd bet even money there's a .38 nestled neatly inside his livery. "Mr. Loreale will see you in the living room. Please follow me."

I follow the guy through a wide, stone-walled vestibule, the stone a warm, sandy color made brighter by the sun streaming through big plate glass windows. The vestibule empties into the large living room, its sloped, beamed ceiling ending in a curved wall of paned glass facing the bay. Bookshelves and a built-in television set line a side wall, an even paler version of the seaside blue-green of the exterior. Early twentieth-century Modernist paintings hang on the opposite wall. I supplied three of the paintings: a wildly colorful landscape of the French seashore by Matisse, an aggressive image of a train by the Italian Futurist Gino Severini that an English financier had to get rid of with no questions asked, and an early Picasso sketch of a horse.

Seated in a big club chair, reading the sports pages of the *Daily News* in the midst of all this elegant design, is the man whose chilly presence defies the warmth of the pumpkin color upholstering on the modern chairs and couches: Sig Loreale. Even his lord-of-the-manor casual attire of brown trousers and roomy pale blue shirt open at the collar can't soften the menace in his steely gray, heavy-lidded eyes in his fleshy face, his jowls thickened into less forgiving regions of later middle age.

He doesn't bother to get up when I walk in. He just puts down the newspaper, nods to the butler, who discreetly scrams. Sig looks at me like he's trying to look through me, then says in that slow, overly articulate way of his that gives me the creeps, "Why are you here, Cantor?" His cold, guttural voice has all the charm of ice cracking. Sig never indulges in small talk, not even a hello, or asking if I'd like a drink or a cuppa coffee, not even an invitation to take my coat off and sit down.

If you didn't know the guy, you'd never guess that the hard-eyed, steel-souled crime boss seated in his big chair was once a lovestruck suitor who'd had his heart broken. You might even think he hasn't got a heart. I guess he had one long ago, but I figure he lost it when he lost the love of his life to betrayal and violence on his wedding night. So I guess you could say we both had a love that was stolen from us; we both have a wound that will never heal, though the idea of sharing an emotional experience with a guy like Sig makes my stomach tighten. We already share a Coney Island past. That's all the sharing with Sig I can handle.

I take my cap and coat off and sit down in the chair opposite him. "I'd like some information," I say. "There isn't a killing in New York you don't know about, and the police are trying to throw two of them into my lap."

The stare he gives me is one that's pinned me many times over the years. Cold, probing, slightly annoyed as if I've interrupted

41

his day. I used to shrivel under it when I was a kid. Now I just wait it out, even light a cigarette to establish my own place in our tête-à-tête.

And then he does something that makes my skin crawl, has always made my skin crawl since the first time I saw him do it when I was a kid no taller than his belt. His mouth opens, his eyes crinkle, and his head tilts back in a silent laugh.

It's always a relief when that laugh is done and he reverts to his comfortably icy self. "Your life is a joke, Cantor," he says, every word like a scythe slowly cutting me down to size. "Your problem is you don't know how to stay out of trouble."

"I wasn't looking for it, Sig. It found me."

His hand moves as slow as his speech as he opens a humidor on a small square steel and glass table next to him and takes out a cigar and a cutter. He snips the end, puts the cigar in his mouth, takes a lighter from his pocket, and lights his smoke. I'm sure I've aged a year by the time he says, "One of those deaths wouldn't be Eve Garraway's, would it?" The words come through puffs of smoke that halo his face as if he's the Lord of Hell.

I stop myself from saying, "You heard about the Garraway killing?" because of course he's already heard about it. I just nod.

"And the other worked for that shyster, Otis Hollander, am I correct?"

I nod again, marveling at how deep Sig's information goes, how wide his net. Lorraine Quinn wasn't important enough to get Sig's notice. So it's probably Hollander who's on his radar. If the lawyer is having a gangster like Johnny Tenzi followed, you can bet Sig will know about it.

He takes another puff of the cigar, the red tip sending a glow up to his eyes, making him even scarier than usual. "So, am I to assume you were doing your normal business with Eve Garraway," he says, "which is why you were at her house?"

"That's right."

"And the Hollander dame?"

"Yeah, Lorraine Quinn."

"What was your business with her? Or was it business at all?"

Sig's lopsided smirk is even scarier than his laugh. His thick lips part just a little at one side of his mouth, showing a thin line of teeth. Makes me wish I had a stiff scotch to blunt its bone-chilling effect.

But I don't have any scotch. All I have is my cigarette and my determination to get the information I came for. A long drag of my smoke gives me the seconds I need to get out from under Sig's cruel humor and bring the conversation back to business. "Tap Tenzi might be involved," I say. "Hollander's tailing him on behalf of Tenzi's wife, Alice. Used to be Alice Lamarr. I think Lorraine Quinn might have set up the tail."

"And in your opinion, Tenzi killed Quinn for—what—vengeance? Spite?"

"Could be. Tap's just stupid enough to think that putting Quinn away would help his case by getting her off his tail. But that leaves the Garraway killing still dangling. I can't see where Tenzi might be part of that."

"Does he hate you enough?"

The question seeps through me, slow but sharp, like acid corroding my bones down to my marrow. I haven't had a lot of dealings with Tap Tenzi, just now and then through the threads of our shared criminal world. But we have one connection, one intimate, beautiful, treacherous connection: Alice Lamarr.

They say the two favorite motives for murder are love or money. Add jealousy under the love heading. Maybe Tap's jealousy is vengeful enough to come after me for my carnal knowledge of Alice.

But where does Eve Garraway fit in?

Is Tenzi stalking me? Framing me?

Sig's voice comes through my tangle of thoughts. "How many other people hate you, Cantor?"

Time spent with Sig always leaves a bad taste in my mouth, like I've just swallowed gunpowder. The powder burns even deeper today because Sig's question eats right through to my gut. Sure,

43

the Law and all its lackeys—cops, judges—hate me, and so do all those upright citizens who jeer at my love life.

But all that is abstract, just a chill air that hovers around me but which I ignore. Sig's question is full of heat, a red-hot branding iron with my name on it. Sig's question, *How many other people hate you, Cantor?*, makes the hate personal, a fire in my soul that even the sea breeze can't cool as I drive back along Manhasset Bay.

How many other people hate me? Who hates me enough to commit murder and toss the bodies at my feet, set me up for the handcuffs and the Sing Sing chair? Who the hell is stalking me?

Maybe nobody. Maybe two killings in one morning has simply rattled me. Maybe the deaths of Lorraine Quinn and Eve Garraway have nothing to do with each other, and I'm just the unlucky sap to be around for both. And maybe, for once in his bitter life, Lieutenant Huber will be a good detective and slam the cuffs on the actual guilty parties.

That fantasy's about as comforting as cold coffee.

There is one comforting thing to come out of my trip to Long Island, though: Sig agreed to look into the Quinn and Garraway killings. Not that he's doing me any favors. He's doing himself a favor. He doesn't like loose ends, and two murders thrown at the feet of someone he's done business with, me, are more than just loose ends. It's a fraying knot. If that knot frays loose, it could expose all those dirty cops, tainted judges, greedy politicians and corporate thieves Sig's been tying up for years in his web of cash and corruption. They'd all go down, and some of them might be stupid enough to try to take Sig with them.

Having Sig Loreale against you can bring doom to your business, your career, your life. But having him on your side is second only to having God in your corner, and frankly, God's never done me any favors.

Chapter Six

There's a downtown saloon along the East River docks, Oyster Charlie's, where tugboaters grab a plate of oysters, a quick beer, or a cup of coffee between runs. They don't get drunk. The busy waterways of New York won't let them.

The saloon's the kind of place where dockside gossip and baseball stories about Yankee Stadium's Bronx Bombers, Brooklyn's Dem Bums, and the Polo Ground's G-Men are traded across bar stools and at wooden tables darkened by years of spilled drinks and calloused hands stained with soot. Charlie, the original proprietor, has been dead for at least fifty years. The current owner, Charlie's grandson, goes by the name of Gus. His daughter's name is Pauline, a sweet kid just old enough to work the bar, which is what she's doing when I walk in a little after two-thirty in the afternoon. I take my cap off and nod to her in greeting. Pauline cocks her head toward a table in the corner. She knows who I'm looking for, who I meet here when he's not on the water.

Red Drogan's at the table, enjoying a cup of coffee and a jabber with an old salt I don't know. Seeing me, Drogan says something to his pal, gets up, and waves me over to an empty table.

"Cantor," he says in greeting, his throaty rattle making my name sound like a storm at sea. Red's got a friendly face, deeply lined and crusty with smarts. We've worked together for a long time, made many a midnight run through the harbor on his tug. We trust each other with our lives. He trusts me with his money.

So he doesn't get all showy when I hand him an envelope he knows contains twenty-five hundred cash, his cut for slipping me and the little Sumerian votive figure into port. All he says is, "You want coffee? How 'bout a drink?"

"I could use a stiff one," I say. "I just came from a meeting with Loreale. That's enough to make anyone want to get blotto." I signal Pauline to bring me a double scotch, no ice, no water. "Listen, Red, something's probably going to hit the afternoon papers. The client for your twenty-five grand, Eve Garraway, she's dead. Knifed. I was there when it happened. Didn't see it, but Huber wants to hang it on me. He'll likely question everyone I ever shook hands with, so he might find his way to you."

Pauline brings me my drink, then scurries away. Eavesdropping has been thoroughly bred out of her saloonkeeper family's blood-line.

I take a pull on the scotch, take out my pack of smokes, and light one up. The whiskey's not my preferred Chivas Regal, not in a dockside joint like this, but it's sharp and strong, and the alcohol will help focus my thoughts, while the smoke will keep the conversation easy.

Drogan says, "If Huber comes around, hell, I ain't never heard of no Eve Garraway." His wind-bloodshot eyes twinkle and crease over a smile full of sly amusement.

"Never doubted you, Red. I just figured I'd warn you so you can be ready if Huber comes at you."

"If he's smart, he won't start askin' no questions along the docks. He'll get nothin' but the big silence."

Now it's my turn to be amused. "Who said he's smart?"

There's another angle I should take a look at. One that has nothing to do with Lorraine Quinn but might get me a line on Eve Garraway and her collection of treasures. And there's one person in town who knows who's got what, what's moving around, who's moving it, who's stealing it, and who's paying.

It's a short drive from the downtown East River docks to the

Lower East Side neighborhood of Esther Sheinbaum, known to one and all in the underworld as Mom.

I pull up in front of her Second Avenue brownstone, but don't get out of my car. Instead, I flip the switch to put the Buick's convertible top up, and when it's in place I lock it down and just sit quiet in the driver's seat, leaving the window open. I take a minute to breathe in the comforting scents of tangy pastrami and corned beef wafting from the neighborhood's delicatessens, catch the shouts of kids playing stickball in the street, the squeals of girls playing potsie on the sidewalk, and the singsong spiels of the last of the neighborhood's pushcart peddlers, a disappearing breed still hawking vegetables, kitchen knives, used clothing, and old books. These ancient sensations help me keep my fingers from clenching and my jaw from tightening at the idea of dealing with the mountainous old woman who lives in the brownstone.

Mom Sheinbaum is the most successful fence of contraband goods in New York, and has been since the twilight of the horse and carriage days. She taught me a lot when I was still a kid lifting trinkets in Coney Island and trying to sell them on the streets of Manhattan. She taught me the difference between the good stuff and schlock. When I grew up, she introduced me to New York's high and mighty: its politicians, their pockets stuffed with cash; high society types who want to hoard the world's treasures; social climbers who want to buy their way into the city's better circles; all of them my pool of future clients. Mom taught me how to deal with them, how to flatter them, never to trust them, and how to pry their money from their tight fists. Yeah, you could say she mentored me; you could even say she was like a second mother to me, the outlaw mother for an outlaw kid. She was all that to me until a few years ago when I heard from her own lips that I was just business, and unpleasant business at that. Mom likes my racket, my smarts, the money I make, but she gags on my preference for gentlemen's suits and that I take women to my bed.

Nothing's changed. We still do business, underworld family members who can't be rid of each other.

I finally roll up the window, get out of the car, and climb the front stairs to Mom's door.

I use the time after I press the door buzzer to straighten my tie and make sure the buttons of my black wool coat are lined up, the lapels flat, my gray tweed cap on straight. Mom may not approve of the way I dress, but I'll be damned if I'm going to meet her sloppy.

The door opens, and I'm met by a boulder of flesh in a sensible blue cotton dress whose belt accentuates her bulk. The waves of Mom's silvery hair around her puffy face catch the afternoon sunlight, creating an aura fit for the city's Empress of Crime. Her tiny green eyes pin me with suspicious surprise. "I was not expecting you, Cantor," she says in the singsong accent of the old neighborhood, the syllables of my name coming across as *Kentuh*. "You have goods for me?"

"How about if I come in? Let's not talk on the stoop about why I'm here."

She looks at me as if I'm a disappointment which might yet measure up, though doubtful. "Yeah, sure," she says with a cock of her head and a wave of her pudgy hand, her jeweled rings flashing in the light. "C'mon in."

I follow her into the house, through the vestibule and into a parlor where a console television set looks out of place in a room still furnished in the overstuffed style of the gaslight days. Beyond the parlor we arrive at our usual place for conversation, the dining room. The house, as always, has the nostalgia-sweet aroma of honey cake because, as always, there's a loaf on a tray on the dining table, the mahogany polished to a mirror shine.

Mom takes her place at the head of the table. She settles herself into a chair, exhaling a throaty sigh of age, weight, and effort. She pours herself a cup of tea from the floral pot next to the tray of honey cake. "If you want some tea," she says with a shrug, "maybe a slice of honey cake, go get your own cup and saucer and a plate from the kitchen."

"I'll pass," I say and head for the liquor cabinet in the sideboard, an ornately carved mahogany affair as regally old-fashioned as everything else in the house, including Mom. "I need something a lot stronger."

Mom says, "Bad day, Cantor?" through a laugh that has all the geniality of a spit in the eye.

I pour myself a big belt of Chivas, take a pull, let the good scotch smooth out the rotgut that singed my throat at Oyster Charlie's. "Murder always makes a bad day," I say.

"Depends who's dead," Mom says. "Listen, *mamaleh,* if you're getting me mixed up in some murder, you can turn right around and go back outside. I don't need the aggravation."

"I'm not getting you mixed up in anything," I say. "I came here to root around in that all-knowing brain of yours. What do you know about Eve Garraway?"

"Boss John Garraway's kid with the *fency-shmency* collection of goods? You do business with her and you don't tell me?"

"It wasn't a fence job, Mom. And it doesn't matter now, anyway. Eve Garraway's dead. Knifed. You'll probably read about it in the afternoon papers. But maybe you can tell me if anyone had any interest in the Garraway stuff besides me and the usual crowd of museum people and collectors. Maybe you heard something about someone making a play on Garraway's collection? You pick up any noise about any threats to her?"

"There's always talk about her goods," Mom says with a *tsk* and a wave of her hand. "She hoards her *tchotchkes* like food during a plague. But threats? Nah. Not that I heard. Not a word, not a peep. Why you want to know all this, Cantor? She get killed before you got paid? You lookin' to collect from whoever shivved her?" This last rides on a chuckle as she takes another sip of tea.

"I'm looking to stay out of the electric chair," I say. "You remember Lieutenant Huber?"

Mom lowers her teacup slowly, the porcelain barely making a sound when it comes to rest on the saucer. Her small eyes tighten under a frown of anger and misery. It was Huber who viciously grilled Mom right here in this room on the night of her daughter

Opal's murder five years ago. It was only through a discipline fine-tuned over years of playing it smart with cops that Mom didn't strangle Huber with her bare hands then and there.

It was the same night Opal was supposed to marry Sig, the same night Mom spilled what she really thinks of me. It was a lousy night all the way around.

"Huber wants to pin me for the Garraway killing," I say.

The old woman's frown softens, recedes, as she slowly returns to the here and now. She picks up her teacup again, looks at me as she takes a sip. If I didn't know better, if I hadn't heard from Mom's own lips of her less than loving regard for me, I might believe I see worry in her eyes. "Why?" she says as she sets the cup down again. "What's that *mamzer* got on you?"

"I was there," I say. "I was still in the house when Eve was knifed. It probably happened when I was on my way out the door. I heard about it from the Garraway butler, Desmond Mallory. You remember him? Worked bank jobs in the old days. I was still on the street when he came outside and waved me back into the Garraway house."

The mention of Desmond Mallory gets Mom's attention. Even makes her smile, though it's a surprisingly chilly one. I figured Mom and Desmond go way back, crossed paths in the old days, came up through the old ways. "Sit down, Cantor," she says. "Tell me what's what."

The way she says it has an *if you know what's good for you* tone under it. So I refresh my scotch, take a seat near Mom at the dining table, and give her the whole story, Lorraine Quinn included. I spend the next fifteen minutes spilling the goods, from finding Lorraine dead on my doorstep with Huber hovering over the body to delivering the little Sumerian to Eve Garraway, to the arrival of Vivienne Parkhurst Trent, and finishing with Huber's arrival at the Garraway place and his threat to take me in for two killings. "If it wasn't for Vivienne's clout with the top brass, Huber might've hauled me to the city lockup and wrapped a death sentence around my neck."

If Mom's, "Lucky you," was any drier, sand would come out

of her mouth. "So you're telling me that the only person who was in the house when the Garraway woman got killed was Desmond. Am I right?"

"And the killer. Or if you're saying Desmond killed Eve, uh-uh. Old Man Garraway took him in when no one else would touch a broken, washed-up bank robber. Desmond's been loyal to the Garraways ever since."

Mom's *tsk* and dismissive wince accuse me of wasting her time. "What's the matter with you, Cantor? Didn't you learn anything since you were a kid schlepping your bundle of *tchotchkes*? Didn't I teach you? Dogs are loyal. People are another story."

I could tell her I know all about mistaken loyalty, learned it from her the night she skinned me alive, but I'm not here to talk about my hard knocks education. I just stick to business. "I don't buy that Desmond had anything to do with Eve's death, but even if he did—"

"It wouldn't be the first time he's killed," Mom says through a snort of a laugh. "You know that story about the guy he knocked off years ago? A guy who'd hired him for a stickup job, no less. Yeah, he's real loyal."

I get a kick out of Mom's use of the old-fashioned term *stickup job*. Haven't heard those words since I was that kid schlepping that bundle. "Like you say, Mom, that was years ago. And anyway, Desmond's only connected to Eve Garraway. He's got nothing to do with Lorraine Quinn. And Quinn, by the way, worked for Otis Hollander, the divorce shyster."

"Some company she kept," Mom says with a shrug and a sip of tea.

"It gets worse," I say. "It seems Quinn set up the tails on cheating spouses. Otis Hollander is representing Alice Lamarr. She's divorcing Tap Tenzi."

"So who'd be stupid enough to marry a no-good like Tenzi? Guess she finally wised up. You think maybe Tenzi killed Quinn for tailing him? Wouldn't put it past him. Spiteful little shit. He was always *a kleyn denker*, a small thinker."

"Yeah, spite's right up Tap's alley. I heard he once sliced a guy's

51

hand just because the guy beat Tap in a poker game. Even Sig figured—"

Mom snaps, "You spoke to Sig?"

"I was at his place on Long Island a little while ago."

"Me, I never been out there." There's a trace of bitterness in Mom's voice, a wince she can't quite cover up. She's never forgiven Sig for putting her daughter Opal in danger by romancing her. Mom worked hard to keep her precious American-born bundle of joy out of the criminal life, and then Sig came along, fell in love, and swept Opal off her feet. Mom's hopes for her precious, American-born daughter was a future with an upright, square-jawed, blue-eyed dreamboat whose place in America was unquestioned. Those hopes died the minute Opal and Sig laid eyes on each other. "So what did the high and mighty Mr. Sig Loreale have to say?"

"He thinks someone hates me enough to frame me."

"For both killings?"

I answer with a nod, then say, "That's why I need to get ahead of Huber, see if I can separate the Quinn and Garraway deaths. That's why I need to know if you can get a line on any activity around Garraway's collection, see if anyone planned to make a play."

"And what do I get for my trouble, Cantor?"

"What do you want that I haven't already given you over the years?"

Her smile is knowing, sly, greedy. I've seen it a thousand times. It used to amuse me. "You say you got paid for the Garraway job?" she says and extends an arm across the dining table, rubbing her thumb and forefinger together.

Now it's me who's smiling. It's not a friendly smile, no warmth in it, no joy, no pleasure. It's just my move in the emotional chess game Mom and I play.

I take out the envelope of cash from my coat pocket, peel out a grand and slide it across the table.

She wraps her finger around the bills. "I'll be in touch."

Two blocks west of City Hall, on a loud, gritty stretch of Chambers Street, Otis Hollander occupies a fourth-floor office in an Italianate building whose white façade and fussy pedimented windows are stained from fifty years of soot. It's a pretty good announcement of the dirty side of the legal racket where Otis Hollander does business. The other law firms in this building aren't any cleaner. They're either the ambulance chasing type or the cheating spouse type. Strictly gutter trade.

Inside Hollander's pea-soup green outer office, a receptionist at a battered desk abruptly stops typing when I walk in. The look she gives me could straighten her hair, a shiny cascade of brown waves coming to rest on the shoulders of her fuzzy pink angora sweater, which I notice fits her very nicely. Framing her shocked hazel eyes is a corn-fed face, mascaraed, rouged, and lipsticked to pass for big city savvy. "Can I—may I help you?"

I decide to have some big city fun with her. I give her my most chivalrous smile. "Well, that depends," I say, making a big show of looking at my watch. "It's nearly four-thirty, almost your quitting time. You busy after work?" Yeah, sure, I know, I'm being a cad again. But once in a while it's fun to pull society's leg. They want to jail me; I want to kid them.

"I think you'd better leave," she says. "We don't do—"

"Oh yes you do. Otis Hollander's sleazy law office does business with all kinds. And by the way, why aren't you crying?"

I guess the corn-fed girl has been in New York long enough to develop some savvy after all. A hard-edged twin emerges through the shocked sister. The corn-fed face disappears behind the mascara and lipstick.

I lean over the desk, put my face close to hers, put my hand under her chin to stop her from looking away. My next words are a gamble. "I guess Miss Quinn's murder means nothing to you. There isn't even a hint of a tear in either of your pretty eyes."

There's no surprise on her face either, which tells me that the police have already been here, already traced Lorraine to her place of employment. The only expression on the receptionist's face is boredom with a sideswipe of contempt. "I won't shed any tears for Lorraine. She isn't worth crying over. She'd stab you in the back as sure as I'm sitting here. And I said so to that detective, too."

"His name wouldn't be Huber, would it?"

"Yeah, that's him. Nasty sort. Looked at me like maybe I killed Lorraine."

"Maybe you did. You could have done it before you came to work."

That does it; she's had enough, and she swats my hand away. "I didn't kill her, but I'd like to send flowers to whoever did."

"Is that so? Why? What was your beef with Quinn?"

She turns back to her typing, the color in her face gone flat, her skin as pale as a sheet of paper. "You'll have to ask Mr. Hollander."

"That's exactly what I came here to do. Tell Otis Cantor Gold is here to see him. And by the way, what's your name?"

"You'll have to ask Mr. Hollander that, too." She presses a button on the intercom on her desk, speaks into it, announcing me to Hollander.

There's a silence behind the hum of the intercom, until Hollander's iron hard, "Send her in."

With a tip of my cap to the receptionist, I saunter over and open the door that has Otis Hollander's name emblazoned on it in flaking gold letters.

The décor in his office is what you might call Low Rent Attorney Traditional. The walls are painted forest green, but the woodwork isn't classy walnut or mahogany or deep cherry. It's just plain old pine wainscoting painted brown. The expected pair of brown leather overstuffed chairs, the leather cracking, face a big desk painted black, the surface cluttered with folders and papers and a cheap brass ashtray that needs emptying.

Otis Hollander, a balding guy of about fifty with a clipped salt-and-pepper mustache and wolfish gray eyes in a round face, gets up from his desk to greet me. His office may be at the edge of shabby, but his crisp white shirt, navy-and-red striped tie and navy blue pinstripe suit aren't, which gives you an idea of where Otis Hollander likes to put his money. He's not interested in impressing the desperate, love-forsaken people who come to his office. He cares about impressing the people who see him in court or in the nightspots about town, usually with a buxom number on his arm.

"Hello, Otis," I say, extending a hand.

"Cantor, always a pleasure," he answers, taking it. He nods for me to have a seat in one of the leather chairs.

I take out my pack of smokes when I'm seated. Hollander takes out a silver cigarette case from his inside jacket pocket. We both light up, eyeing each other as smoke drifts around us.

He says, "What brings you here, Cantor? I'm pretty sure you don't have marriage problems." He says it to be funny.

"I'm here about Lorraine Quinn. She was knifed at the front door of my apartment building."

Hollander takes deep drag of his smoke, lets it out slowly, his eyes on me while he deals with what I just said. "The police didn't mention that it happened at your place," he says as matter-of-factly as if he's talking about the weather.

"They don't know you and I are acquainted, Otis."

"Aren't we lucky."

That's worth a shrug and a lazy, "Uh-huh," from me.

"Any idea what Miss Quinn was doing at your building?" he says.

"Leaving."

There's a slight crinkle at the edges of Hollander's predatory eyes and a barely perceptible twitch of his mustache over a small smile. The smarmy pleasure in the smile comes from his dawning awareness of how I know Lorraine was leaving my building.

His smile snaps into something darker, a cynical leer oozing suspicion. "Did you know she worked here, Cantor, when you two were—well, doing whatever the hell it is you do?"

The way he's looking at me now, eyes slightly narrowed, probing, amused, I'm sure his imagination's running wild, running sleazy bedroom scenarios he can't quite figure out but is having fun trying. I'm not about to enlighten him. I just say, "I had no idea she worked here, Otis. She never mentioned it. We didn't have that kind of chatty relationship. So you can relax. She took your law firm's secrets to the grave."

He stubs out his smoke and settles back in his chair, his composure as undisturbed as fresh snow. But his deep breath gives the game away: he's relieved. "So what do you expect to get from me?"

"Alice Lamarr."

Now his smile is genuine, appreciative in an underhanded way. "You've done your homework," he says. "So I guess you also know Miss Quinn arranged a tail on Tap Tenzi. It paid off. We got enough goods on him to make the soon to be ex-Mrs. Tenzi a moderately rich woman. The photographs nailed him."

"Tailing Johnny Tenzi is dangerous business, Otis. Dangerous even for you. Alice must be paying you big time for you to risk your law firm, not to mention your life. So what's the story, Otis? Why risk everything on this case?"

He doesn't like the question, hesitates to answer, but my stare won't let him off the hook. Wincing, he says, "It's not the money. Alice doesn't have a lot of money. Let's just say Alice has had an interesting life. It's best to treat that life carefully."

I need to tread easy. If I press too hard, whatever's making him nervous about Alice will get the upper hand and he'll clam up, toss me out of the office. I need to massage him back to safer conversation. "I guess Lorraine got more than she bargained for by shadowing Tenzi."

"You think Tenzi killed Miss Quinn?" he says.

"Do you?"

He answers with a shrug that lets me know it's crossed his mind. "From what Alice told me, Tenzi could be a vindictive son of a bitch, even murderous when crossed. If he had it in for Quinn, and he tailed her to your place, you might be in his crosshairs, too, Cantor."

"No kidding. I'm already in Lieutenant Huber's crosshairs. Does he know about Tenzi? Did you tell him about Alice wanting a divorce?"

"Just the outline, not in detail. I can't give him specific information about Alice's divorce case. That would violate attorney-client privilege."

For the first time all day, something is finally playing my way. "Well, I already know about Lamarr and Tenzi, so you won't be breaking any privilege if you give me her current address. I'll find it out sooner or later anyway, Otis, so why don't you save us both a lot of time, and maybe our necks, by helping me get ahead of this thing. I need to talk to Alice. Where is she holing up since she left Tap?"

Lawyers don't like to be outfoxed, don't like to divulge information, but I've left him no wiggle room to object. Reluctant but giving in, he takes up a pen and a pad of paper from his desk, writes the address, tears the sheet from the pad, and hands it to me. "Miss Sawicki will see you out," he says, eager to be rid of me and the trouble I bring.

"Oh, that's her name," I say with a chuckle as I get up from the chair. "She said I'd have to get it from you. She also said you'd know why she hated Lorraine Quinn."

The glint in his wolf-eyes and the smile slowly spreading on his face says it all, as if he's sharing a dirty secret he mistakenly thinks I'll appreciate: the selfish pleasure of ditching one woman for another.

He's more of a cad than I am. But from what I've seen, most guys are.

But whaddya know, Lorraine Quinn played both sides of the street. Things she learned on one side she brought to the other, to my side, where last night I indulged my pleasure in her experience.

Now that pleasure haunts me.

Chapter Seven

The Collier Hotel on East Thirty-Eighth Street off First Avenue is several cuts below the Waldorf but a reasonable number of cuts above shabby. It's the kind of hostelry where you can be fairly sure the sheets are clean, but the stain on the rug might keep you guessing. In the last light of the afternoon and the creeping arrival of evening, the exterior of the place, fifteen stories of brick with limestone trim, speaks of the building's once grand past but is now content to be merely useful.

The lobby, a red and brown dowager with chandeliers dimmed by dust, is busy with budget tourists with fussy children, and traveling salesmen lugging sample cases. Here and there, a tourist or a salesman gives me the side-eye. A harried mother in last year's hat and dull plaid coat quickly pushes her apple-cheeked little girl of about twelve years old behind her, protecting her, I guess, from the dangers of seeing the likes of me. The girl doesn't seem afraid of me, though. Just curious. When she pokes her head out from behind her mother for a better look, I give her a friendly wave. She waves back. Give the kid ten years and I won't be surprised to see her at the Green Door Club.

The newsstand near the elevators has copies of the late-afternoon editions, and sure enough the story about Eve Garraway's killing is front page news. *POLITICAL PRINCESS MURDERED!* shouts the *Post*'s banner headline with photos underneath of the Garraway house and the murder scene complete with a chalk outline of Eve's body. *GARRAWAY HEIRESS KILLED* is the *Journal-American's* less flamboyant one-column headline, the story nudged aside by a prominent photograph of Marilyn Monroe with current husband Joe DiMaggio.

I pick up copies of both papers, scan their stories about the Garraway murder while I ride up the elevator. Huber was mentioned as the detective on the case, but I was glad to see that Vivienne and I were left out of it. Huber's playing his cards close.

Neither paper has anything on Lorraine Quinn. I guess compared to the killing of a New York nabob like Eve Garraway, a dead secretary doesn't rate.

I get out at the tenth floor, drop the papers on the hall table, and head to room 1016.

It's been almost five years since I last saw Alice. She was one of the showgirls at the Copa at the time, decorating the floor show in gold lamé and plenty of leg. We'd meet after the last show, grab a two a.m. cold supper at Toffenetti's or one of the other all-night show biz hangouts on Broadway, then go back to my place, where I'd enjoy more parts of Alice than the Copa audience did. Our fling was sizzling but short, barely a couple of months. She'd figured out quick that she was just another bandage on my unhealed wound. I can't blame her for tossing me over. But I'd never have guessed she'd jump into the more conventional arrangement of putting dinner on the table for a husband, even a husband as unconventional as Johnny Tapioca Tenzi. Of all the men she could have had—if that's really the new thrill she wants in her bed—why a lowlife like Tenzi?

I knock on the door to room 1016.

A few seconds later, the door opens with a smiling Alice saying, "You're early," before she realizes I'm not the early bird she's expecting.

She's in a black negligee that exposes more than it covers, and what it exposes could get a person arrested just for having an imagination. Her baby doll smile is a cross between a simper and a kiss. Her short, wavy auburn hair dares you to run your fingers through it, and her dark brown eyes hint at stories she'll never tell you.

"You're the last person I'd expect to see," she says. In the years since I last heard it, the come-hither lilt in Alice's voice has added a darker tone under it, a sultrier tone that slides around in her throat like warm booze. "What are you doing here, Cantor? And how did you find me? Tell me fast, and then get lost."

"You used to invite me in when I knocked on your door."

"I have other plans tonight."

"C'mon, Alice, it's cocktail hour. Invite me in for a drink."

"You'll want more than a drink. You always did."

"I still do. Only now what I want is just conversation. Tell me what I need to know and I'll be out of your way before your evening plans arrive."

She steps away from the door to let me in, not because she's agreeable, but because I've got my hand on the door, making it clear that I'm not leaving until I get what I came for.

When we're inside, Alice takes a sheer black chiffon robe from the bed and slips it on. It doesn't do much to hide what the negligee exposes, but blurs things just enough to cool the urge to reach out and touch all the round places inside it.

"You still drinking Chivas?" she says on her way to the two bottles of whiskey on the bureau. "Too bad. I don't have it. I've got a standard scotch and a standard rye. Take your pick."

"Make it scotch."

She pours the whiskey into one of the glasses on the bureau, hands it to me, and pours a rye for herself. "Okay, Cantor, make it quick. What do you want?"

"Let's talk about Lorraine Quinn."

Her eyes widen a little in surprise, her lips part and pucker as if she wants to say "Who?" but it takes only a second for Alice to think better of the lie. Our affair might have been short but it was fiery enough to burn away any sham. We saw the truth of each other. Looks like we still do.

Alice ditches the idea of giving me a phony story and gives me a savvy smile instead. "You still work fast, don't you, Cantor? So

I guess you already know I married Johnny Tenzi and now I'm divorcing the louse. And yeah, the Quinn girl in Otis Hollander's office set up the tail on him. Got some juicy photos, too, or so Hollander says." A sip of rye lubricates her satisfaction at having the goods on her cheating husband. "Was it Otis who told you where to find me?"

I nod my answer.

"What did you do, threaten him? Or does he just have a big mouth? Never mind. I don't want to know. But why do you want to talk to me about Lorraine Quinn? She's just an employee. She does what Otis tells her to do."

"*Was* an employee. Now she's dead. Knifed on her way out of my apartment building this morning."

There's a couple of chairs in front of the bed. Alice sits down in one of them, the faded pink damask upholstery an eye-catching contrast to her black robe and negligee and the flesh inside them. It takes me a minute to notice the look Alice gives me, an *I've-got-your-number* look. She's on to what Lorraine was doing at my place, and she's enjoying throwing it at me. But her expression of cheap pleasure slowly changes as the hard facts of Lorraine Quinn's murder sink in. Alice Lamarr is no fool. She sees the danger, and it scares the hell out of her. "If it was Johnny . . . if it was Johnny . . . if he was angry at being tailed . . ." It's a chant of terror.

Good. Let her be scared. It might loosen her tongue. "Listen, Alice, we have to figure this thing if you want to save your neck from Johnny and I save my neck from the cops. A bloodhound of a lieutenant named Huber wants to hang Quinn's murder on me, and another killing, too. A woman named Eve Garraway, knifed in the back. Ever hear of her?"

"Mm, maybe. Sounds familiar."

"Daughter of an old-time big deal politician. Look, I need to know Tenzi's movements. I need to know if he was stalking Quinn and just wound up at my door, or if he's stalking *me*, killing women I deal with and putting the frame on me. What's he got against me, Alice?"

61

The way she slithers up from the chair would make a snake admit defeat. The sheer robe ripples against her body as she walks toward me, her auburn hair catching light, her dark eyes taking me in as if I'm easy prey. "*You*, Cantor," she says and slides her fingertips up the lapels of my coat. "He hates you."

I grab hold of her wrist before her hand reaches my face. I say nothing, but Alice knows how to read me, and right now she reads that we'll be locked here together, her wrist in my grip, until she comes across with the goods on Tap Tenzi.

"So many scars," she says, her voice low as if rolling up from the gutter. "Your face didn't have so many, once upon a time. Once upon our time."

"Tenzi, Alice. What's the story with Tenzi?" I tighten my grip on her wrist.

She doesn't wince, holds her pain in check, savoring her little victory over me. But it's an empty victory. She's not free of my grip, or my smile, a chilly grin that presses her to tell me what I want to know.

One of the things that made me fall for Alice was her taste for giving as good as she gets. It was sexy five years ago, and it's sexy now. She's giving it good, matching my hard smile with her baby doll grin that dares me to hurt her more because she knows I won't. She knows I don't hurt women, that I'm merciless on those who do. "Johnny hates you," she says, almost spitting it. "He hates you because I made him hate you. I told him all about you one night when he came home drunk and made an ass of himself in bed. When I told him to get off me, you know what he did? He slapped my face, that's what he did. But you know what *I* did? I laughed. I told him you were a better lover than he could ever be, that all of the women who'd been in my bed were better in the sack than Johnny Tapioca Tenzi."

"Why the hell did you marry him, Alice?"

Her laugh comes out slow, its tone heavy and dark. "You jealous, Cantor? Does it bother you knowing that a man's hands roamed around where yours once did?"

If I touch that question it could set off the dynamite inside it, explode in my face and rip deep into me. So I toss the stick of dynamite back at Alice. "I don't care who touches you, Alice. I just never figured you for a wife, and certainly not to two-bit sewer slime like Tap Tenzi. So why him?"

"Because he has money."

"So did I."

"Because he promised to give me anything I wanted."

"So did I."

"Because I didn't have to hide in the shadows with Tap. He could take me to nice places and not give a damn who's looking. Because he's not you!"

I never saw so much venom in a woman's eyes, or so much fire. The venom stings me, but the fire lures me. With my hand still on Alice's wrist, my other arm seems to have a will of its own, wrapping around her, pressing her hard against me. She doesn't struggle. She kisses me.

We're locked together as tight as we ever were, our old needs awakened, inflamed now by danger and fear and anger. We're not kissing, we're devouring, eating each other alive, trying to sate a lust that can only be satisfied one way.

She doesn't resist when I slip off her sheer robe, then lift her and carry her to the bed. I take off my cap, fling off my coat, kneel onto the bed and pull Alice to me, press my mouth to her neck. My fingers slide the negligee off her breast.

There's a knock at the door.

"Your evening plans?" I say through a rough whisper. "Get rid of them."

A breathy "Yes," and Alice gets up from the bed, slips her robe on, and goes to the door. She opens it just enough to talk to the "evening plans" in the hall. I wonder if they're male or female.

The answer comes in response to Alice's limp story about a headache, and a female voice coos, "Let me soothe it."

It's followed by a gruff, gravelly growl, "Go soothe somebody else, girlie. Scram." Hearing it makes the hair on my neck stand up.

Huber pushes his way through the door.

Seeing me on the bed, his eyebrows slide up and then slide down again in a frown so tight it strains the skin of his bony face. His lips curl into a snarl. It's not hard to guess he's angry that I'm a step ahead of him, that I got to Alice Lamarr before he worked his way to her connection to Lorraine Quinn. His annoyance dissolves into a smirk so foul I swear I can smell it oozing around his teeth. "Well, well," he says, pushing his fedora back on his head as he gives Alice a leering once-over before turning his attention back to me. "Too bad I didn't get here five minutes sooner. I'd have finally been able to bring you in on the morals charge the city code has for perverts like you. I'd ask what you're doing here, Gold, but I guess that's a stupid question." He gives this a potty-mouth chuckle that makes me want to ram a cake of lye soap down his throat. "But the better question," he says at the end of the laugh, "is when will you stop lying to me?"

I get up from the bed, say, "What makes you think I've lied to you, lieutenant?" I'm not looking at Huber. I'm looking at Alice, who looks back at me. There's a slight gleam in her eyes, a hint of a smile at the corner of her mouth. Alice Lamarr might be afraid of Johnny Tenzi but she's not the least bit afraid of Huber. The woman's got spine. Not many people can smile under the tough glare of the cops, only people like me who don't give a damn, or people with money or power, or people with powerful connections. People like Vivienne Parkhurst Trent.

And then I remember what Otis said: that Alice has had an interesting life. Maybe it's that interesting life that gave her the spine to hold her own with cops.

I take out my pack of smokes, offer one to Alice. She takes it. I take a smoke for myself, light both our cigarettes. Smoke rises across our faces, a curtain blurring Huber's view of a world Alice and I share.

He says, "You lied this morning, Gold, when you said you didn't know the Quinn woman."

"You got it wrong, lieutenant. I didn't say I didn't know her. I only said I didn't know she was dead until I got off the elevator and saw her sprawled in the doorway."

"That story stinks more with age, Gold. I didn't believe you this morning and I don't believe you now."

"Believe whatever you like. I don't care. The only thing I care about is finding whoever killed Lorraine because the real killer is still out there. That's why you're here, isn't it, Huber?"

Alice chimes in, "Listen, lieutenant, you know I'm Johnny Tenzi's wife, and you also know that I'm divorcing the SOB. Otherwise, you wouldn't be showing up at my hotel room. And I guess you know that Lorraine Quinn worked for my divorce lawyer, and that it was Quinn who set up the tail to catch Johnny cheating on me. And I bet that made Johnny angry, and I bet you know what Johnny Tenzi does when he's angry. So instead of barging through the wrong door, why don't you go find that murdering bastard before he decides to kill me. Because maybe he's decided already."

It's a performance good enough for Broadway, the kind of performance that makes audiences fall in love and throw flowers at curtain call. I don't have flowers and falling in love isn't in my cards. Best I can do is give Alice a smile and stand beside her so that we face Huber together.

He leans close to Alice, his face inches from hers. She doesn't flinch. "Listen, Mrs. Tenzi—"

"Miss Lamarr. I've taken back my maiden name, Lamarr."

"You can call yourself the Queen of Sheba, I wouldn't believe that either. And I don't care what kind of showgirl name you call yourself. Yeah, I know all about your Copacabana days. No doubt you were quite a number. Sorry I missed your show. But if you want me to find Mr. Tenzi, you'll help me. If you clam up, you're on your own. Don't blame me if he shows up here to rip you apart."

I've always suspected that Huber has no heart, or that if he ever had one it burned up a long time ago. But right now I can't find any sympathy for a cop who takes pleasure in telling a woman she's in danger of being torn to pieces.

Huber doesn't let up. "You're easy to find, Miss Lamarr. If I found you, and Gold found you, your hoodlum husband will find you, too."

That got to her. There's a slight tremble in her hand when she takes a draw on her smoke.

"Back off, Huber," I say. "C'mon, Alice. Sit down, have a drink." I take her elbow, lead her back to a chair. "We could all use a drink. Even you, lieutenant."

"I wouldn't drink with you, Gold, even if I wasn't on duty."

"That's a pity," I say, handing Alice a fresh rye and pouring another scotch for myself. "I bet we'd become pals, trade stories. I bet you have some good ones."

"The only story I'm interested in is how two women wind up dead and you're at the scene of both killings."

"I thought you were interested in finding Johnny Tenzi."

"Let me worry about Tenzi," he says. "But you'll still have two dead women at your feet. That's too much for just coincidence."

"But not enough to fry me, eh, lieutenant? Sorry to disappoint you."

He answers with pinched lips, then turns his attention to Alice. "You have any idea where I can find Tenzi?"

"No. And believe me, I'd tell you if I knew. I'd like nothing better than to see that louse rot in jail."

"You have no idea of his hangouts? Where he drinks his booze?"

"He drinks his booze all over town, so unless you want to hit every saloon, I suggest you try a different tack. Maybe ask his mobster buddies, though I doubt they'd talk. They never do."

Huber's not happy with her answer. The way he snaps his fedora back down I'm surprised he doesn't rip the brim off. "That's all for now, *Miss Lamarr*, or whatever your name is." He turns to leave, but not before he gives me a stare so icy his eyeballs might freeze. He slams the door behind him.

"But first he's got to find you," I tell Alice when Huber's gone. "Pack a bag."

Chapter Eight

Moonlight slices through the back alley and gleams along the fender of Rosie's cab as she drives up to the service entrance of the hotel.

Alice, shivering in the chill night air, rubs her gloved hands together and turns up the collar of her black wool coat. She leans against me, seeking warmth.

"Rosie knows where to take you," I say. "You'll be safe there."

"Will I see you later?"

"Sure. Now get going while the alley's still clear of cops. It won't be for long if Huber thinks you can lead him to Tap and he decides to set a tail on you. He'll have the alley covered as well as the hotel's main entrance."

There's no venom in Alice's baby doll smile now, no fire in her moonlit eyes. Just a fear she's working to keep under control, and a sweetness I'd never seen in her before. "Thank you, Cantor," she says, "for getting me out of reach of the police and hiding me from Johnny." But before I can say, "You're welcome," she puts her arms around my neck and kisses me. It's a different kind of kiss than I'd ever gotten from Alice. Softer.

I notice Rosie roll her eyes.

I pull gently away from the kiss. "It's time for you to get out of here," I say, and put Alice's suitcase into the backseat of the cab. She climbs in beside it, and when I close the door, she turns to the window, smiles a little, and blows me a kiss. The Alice I knew five years ago, the Alice who tempted me into her hotel bed a little while ago, shines through the lingering fear in her smile. It's the Alice who wants me to come see her tonight.

Rosie guns the engine, drives the big Checker out of the alley, its tail lights leaving red trails in the dark.

It's nearly seven o'clock when I exit the hotel by the front entrance. If Huber or one of his badge boys is watching, all they see is me walking along Thirty-Eighth Street to my car, all by myself.

I don't see any cops on my tail in my rearview mirror, don't get that skin crawly feeling of eyes on me. But I haven't stayed alive and out of the slammer this long by being careless, so I do a few maneuvers through crosstown traffic, dodge cabs and buses competing for space outside Grand Central Station, hustle my way to the West Side past annoyed drivers honking their horns, and by the time the neon lights of my Theater District neighborhood streak across my Buick, I'm home free.

And hungry.

If any cops are watching my place, they're in for a long night. I drop into Pete's instead, ready for a bite to eat and Doris's good coffee.

The Tuesday evening crowd is a little livelier than the morning bunch, with out-of-work actors schmoozing over casting notices and endless cups of coffee, musicians charging up for their late-night gigs, their horn or string cases by their sides. Here and there, Broadway beat reporters, theater tickets sticking out of their hatbands, read their program notes while finishing dinner or drinking their coffee. No one gives me the side-eye, which is among the reasons I like my interesting neighborhood.

I give Doris my order for a chicken pot pie, then head for a phone booth in the back.

I figure Judson's gone from the office by now, so I ring him at home. After we exchange hellos, I say, "Got anything for me?"

"Yeah. You've hit the trifecta of dangerous dames. How about I start with Lorraine Quinn since she can't do any more damage."

"A little respect for the dead, Judson."

"Sure, okay, sorry. So, Quinn has a bad history. I told you this morning that she left South Jersey for New York, tried her luck at being an actress. Well, all that's hunky-dory, but she didn't leave Jersey voluntarily. She was thrown out, warned never to come back. Seems she crossed the wrong politicians when she tried to blackmail them with dirty pictures of their escapades with mistresses or pretty boys. But she forgot that Jersey pols are cozy with the Mob. So it was either get out of town or get dead."

Now it's my own respect for the dead that's shaky. I tell myself to be a little choosier about who shares my bed. "Looks like she wound up with the perfect job at Hollander's office," I say.

"Yeah, to a T," Judson says. "Okay, on to dangerous dame number two, Eve Garraway. Twelve years ago, when Eve was a senior at a fancy women's college upstate and old man Garraway was still alive and kicking, he used his political clout to get his darling daughter out of a scrape and keep it out of the papers."

"What kind of scrape?"

"The bloody kind. Miss Garraway shared an off-campus apartment with a college roommate. They were in the kitchen one night when they got into a tussle, and somehow a carving knife wound up in the roommate's belly. Eve didn't call an ambulance; she called Daddy, who took care of things, made sure the mess was cleaned up. And get this: the roommate's name was Fiona Mallory. Now, if you're thinking that Miss Mallory was any relation to the Garraway butler and one-time bank thief Desmond Mallory, you'd be correct. She was his daughter."

The news that Desmond Mallory even had a daughter comes as a shock. The news that she was killed by Eve Garraway raises the hair on the back of my neck.

I've always known that the world could be a dark and deadly

69

place, known it since I was a kid in Coney Island when Sig Loreale was muscling in on the old Coney rackets and leaving bodies all over the place. I wouldn't stay alive in my criminal world if I couldn't deal with its denizens of thugs and killers, mobsters and dirty cops. But the news about the dirty dealings of Lorraine Quinn and the deadly doings of Eve Garraway has darkened even the darkest shadows of my already dark world.

And yet . . .

A shaft of light cuts through these shadows, a light that shines in a direction other than mine. Quinn's and Garraway's crimes might be well in the past, but revenge can fester for years.

"Judson, use your most tight-lipped connections to get this information across Huber's desk. I don't want him to know where it came from, understand?"

"Got it. Now, ready for dangerous dame number three?"

There's only one name it could be, and it will break my heart. "Tell me."

"It seems Alice Lamarr's hands are dirty as a coal miner's. Listen to this: the only part of her name that's real is the Alice part. The name she was born with in Lincoln, Nebraska is Alice Letherby, but she's gone by Alice Leander, Alice Lorrie, Alice McKenzie, and now Alice Lamarr, which seems to be the one she finally settled on. All those other names wore out their welcome when Alice was pegged in three states as a con artist specializing in jewelry investment scams. She did eighteen months in Indiana Women's Prison for a con that went bad. Evidently that ended her taste for the racket, and she came to New York a little over five years ago, landed a spot at the Copa as a showgirl."

And met me.

And now that Huber's found Alice, it won't be long until his cop's mind gets curious, sends him digging around for Alice's story, if he hasn't already. He didn't use Alice's past at the hotel. Maybe he's holding it for later if he needs to tighten the screws.

And now I know what Otis meant by Alice's interesting life. Maybe he figured once a con artist, always a con artist, and he might be her mark if he doesn't do right by her in her divorce case.

"Anything on Tap Tenzi? Like where to find him?" I ask Judson.

"Zip. Guy's a shadow, but I'll keep digging around."

I tell him okay, we hang up, and I head back to the counter for my pot pie dinner, but I've lost my appetite.

I walk out of Pete's and into a heavy rain. Ordinarily I like the way my neighborhood looks on a rainy night. Everything glistens. The glow from the neon signs is softer. Their colors shimmer on the wet pavement, wash along rain-slicked umbrellas and wet faces. The beauty of the city on a wet night has been known to refresh my spirit as thoroughly as the rain refreshes the streets. But tonight the rain and its pleasures are no match for the bad news about Lorraine and Eve and Alice poisoning my mood.

It's only a short walk up the block to my place. I turn up the collar of my coat, pull my cap down low, and dodge puddles.

"Gold!" The shout comes from a green '52 Plymouth sedan parked in front of my building, the car's bulbous body streaked with rain and streetlight, its whitewall tires splashed with gutter grime. Mike Mulroney, the thug who took my gun at Sig's seaside place this afternoon, gets out of the car and galumphs over to me, his coat collar up, his fedora dripping rain. "Mr. Loreale sent me over to sit on your place until you showed up. He wants to see you. Get in the car. No arguments."

An invitation from Sig is never going to come with a "please" in front of it. And his invitations are never turned down, not if you value your well-being. But I'm happy to take him up on this one. Maybe he's got something for me on the Quinn and Garraway killings.

I follow Mulroney to the Plymouth. He opens the back door, but grabs my arm before I can get in. "Gimme your gun," he says. There's no point in arguing, so I pull it from my shoulder rig and hand it over. Same ritual as when I drove out to Sig's place this morning. Mulroney slides my .38 into his pocket, then cocks his head for me to get into the car. I get into the backseat, but I'm not alone. Another of Sig's galoots, a ham-faced guy with big ears that hold up his hat, is next to me. His greasy pink cheeks shine in the sedan's overhead light. When Mulroney gets into the driver's seat and the car doors close, the light goes out and the guy next to me turns into a dark blob silhouetted by streetlight.

I settle in for the long ride to Long Island, but Mulroney's turn south on Broadway and a left turn a few blocks later onto Fortieth Street tell me that Sig's not in his seaside place but in his penthouse here in town.

We park in front of the sleek black brick tower Sig calls home. His penthouse, whose four-sided terrace is a Gothic confection of gilt arches and pinnacles, sits above twenty-two stories of offices Sig rents to legit businesses. By day, the building's golden crown shines in the sunlight. At night, when the black brick dissolves into the darkness, the gilded penthouse, glowing like a royal crown, seems to float above the city, a fitting residence for the crime lord whose power reaches across the city and down to the streets below.

It's still raining when we get out of the car. Mulroney places himself in front of me, and Ham Face comes up behind me as we make our way to the soaring bronze-and-glass entrance to the building. Inside, the black-tiled lobby is a dim and shadowy cavern barely illuminated by the few wall sconces still lit after business hours. It's the kind of place that makes the powerful feel important and belittles everyone else.

I take off my cap and coat, shake off the rain.

"Hey," Ham Face says, "you're messin' up the floor."

"I'm sure Sig can afford to hire someone to mop it up," I counter.

Mulroney says, "Shut up, Gold."

Our friendly little exchange echoes up into the vaulted ceiling and dissolves in the darkness rising three stories above our heads.

At the bank of elevators, Mulroney puts a key into a lock for the elevator at the end, Sig's private car. When the doors open, we all step in, the same parade that marched into the building: Mulroney in front, me in the middle, Ham Face bringing up the rear. This arrangement sorts itself when the doors close and we ride up to the penthouse.

"Thanks for the protection, boys," I say. "You never know what goblins might leap out of the elevator walls and kidnap me."

I get another, "Shut up, Gold," from Mulroney.

At the penthouse floor, the elevator opens onto a green marble hallway that has the warm welcome of a mausoleum. At Sig's big black door, Mulroney presses the buzzer. A moment later, a maid opens the door and our little parade walks inside.

The maid takes our wet coats and hats.

Mulroney says, "Mr. Loreale's waitin' for you in his den."

I have to go through the living room to get to the den. Despite its surprisingly homey décor for a guy for whom assassination is just another way of doing business, the living room is a haunted house of memories for me. Around the walls, many of the eighteenth- and nineteenth century landscape paintings—which reinforce Sig as lord-of-all-he-surveys—were supplied by me. A small granite Egyptian Eighteenth Dynasty statuette of the god Osiris that I smuggled out of Cairo is on the coffee table, and a twelfth-century jeweled chalice I lifted from the Louvre is on the mantle. It was here in the living room that I handed Sig an Athenian Geometric period vase and he handed me fifteen thousand dollars. And I was here the night that Mom's daughter Opal died, the night she was going to marry Sig in this living room.

I don't linger in this chamber of recollections. I walk out of the living room and through the hall to Sig's den. My knock on the door is answered by Sig's slow, gravelly, "Come in." It drills through the wood.

He's reading a file of papers and smoking a cigar at his desk, a sleek burled maple number that matches the burled walnut walls of the den. The desk lamp, the only light in the room, leaves the upper part of his face in shadow but picks out his mouth and the curves of his jowls. The burning tip of his cigar sends a red glow around his eyes. Completing this portrait of the Lord of Hell are tendrils of cigar smoke coiling along his cheek and into the darkness.

"Sit down, Cantor," he says, waving his cigar toward the pair of gray leather club chairs that face the desk. "I have information for you." He's smiling. I wish he wasn't.

But Sig's just handed me the possibility of the first bit of good news I've had since Lorraine Quinn slammed the door of my apartment this morning. Maybe my lousy day is finally turning around. "Let's hear it, Sig."

"Well," he says, taking a torturous stretch of time before continuing, "it seems City Hall has an interest in the Garraway murder." It comes out slow as a dirge, the spaces between each word just as deathly.

"Not surprising," I say. "Eve Garraway was the daughter of one of the most powerful politicians ever to swindle the State of New York. Our own city pols probably owed old man Garraway their careers. They'd likely remain loyal to his daughter."

Sig's, "Naturally," rides on a sigh that's as good as a wagging finger accusing me of being stupid. He leans back in his big chair, his face now completely in the shadows. "You are not seeing the big picture, Cantor." All I see is the burning tip of his cigar in the darkness.

"Oh? And what picture is that? Enlighten me."

"There are certain facts in Miss Garraway's past which City Hall would not like brought to light."

"If you're referring to that little incident with the knife and the dead college roommate, where does City Hall come into it?"

When Sig smiles, even a smile of approval, your first instinct is to run for your life. And when the smile comes through shadows tinted red by the glow of his cigar, as it does now, you remember that adage about abandoning all hope. "That boy of yours," he says, "what's his name? Judson? Yes, Judson. He certainly does his homework. You were very smart, Cantor, to take him on." He lowers his cigar to flick ash into a polished chrome ashtray on the desk. His face is in full darkness now, and only his voice comes through. "Yes, that unfortunate college girl incident is the issue. But your Judson likely does not know the rest of the story, and it's the rest of the story that the mayor and various

74

members of the city council would like to remain hidden. They are concerned that any investigation into the murder of Eve Garraway would dig up that old dirt. It could expose a number of them as complicit in helping John Garraway make the scandal go away."

"Are you telling me City Hall wants Lieutenant Huber to lay off?"

"That is what I'm telling you." He takes another pull on his cigar, the glowing tip burning through the dark.

Scary as that sight is, I like the news it rides on. I can't squelch a smile, and I don't want to. I'd give anything to have seen Huber's face when word came down from the higher-ups ordering him to let go of a headline-grabbing, career-making murder case.

Sig says, "I wouldn't smile just yet, Cantor. Naturally, the lieutenant was not happy about it. No policeman likes to be pulled off a case by his superiors." The word *superiors* comes through on a hiss. There's probably a sneer under it, hiding back there in the shadows. "Now, I have it on good authority—well, let us not beat about the bush—I heard it from the mayor himself that Lieutenant Huber offered what he believed was his ace up his sleeve. He told them he would give them a killer they'd approve of. He told them he would give them you."

My joy at Huber's just desserts just went out the window.

But Sig answered the question he threw at me this afternoon: *How many people hate you, Cantor?* Right now I can think of one: Lieutenant Norm Huber.

"I suppose I'll have to watch my step," I say.

"No need," Sig says as if dismissing something of no importance. "I have secured the guarantee of the mayor and the police commissioner that Lieutenant Huber will not pursue you in the Garraway matter." He finalizes the statement with a deep puff on his cigar. It sends a red glow around his eyes again.

I should feel relieved about Sig getting Huber off my back. Instead, it's making every nerve in my body do somersaults. Sure, Sig has the power to call off the dogs, but he wouldn't do it unless it has something in it for him. And what's in this for him seems to be *me*. He's not handing me to the cops; he's handing me to *him*. "To what do I owe your generosity, Sig?"

"The politicians may be content to let the Garraway matter drop," he says, "but I am not. Having a killing take place that I did not sanction, especially the murder of a prominent person such as Miss Garraway, is a loose end I cannot let dangle. Independent operators are pests. They bring unwanted attention, which interferes with the smooth running of my business. So I want the Garraway murder solved, I want her killer found, and I want you to do it, Cantor. You can pursue the case more quietly than the police."

"Wait a minute, Sig. Okay, I understand why you want the Garraway killing cleaned up. But why me? You can blanket the town with your army of operatives and thugs who'll make people talk. They'll get results a lot faster than I will."

"Don't underestimate yourself, Cantor. You have excellent contacts in Eve Garraway's world."

"I'm not especially well connected to politicians. That's your department."

"I'm speaking of your art people. Your clients, your collectors. Your curators. Miss Parkhurst Trent, for example."

That somersault-y feeling just turned into a cold grip on my spine.

It's pointless to ask how he knows about Vivienne. He knows because he's made it his business to know about the lives and associations of everyone he deals with. He probably knows everyone I've ever said hello to, every woman I've ever smiled at or slept with.

Vivienne doesn't deserve Sig's icy breath on her neck.

Denying I do business with her, though, is a losing move. I'd never get away with it. Better to play the cards Sig's dealt me and stay in the game long enough to figure how to win it. "Okay, sure, Miss Parkhurst Trent could be helpful," I say with a shrug. I take my smokes from my pocket, light one up as a show of ease I don't feel.

76

"Good," Sig says. "I leave you to deal with her. Maybe someone among Miss Parkhurst Trent's contacts or among Miss Garraway's acquaintances or employees is our killer."

"Eve's acquaintances, possibly. Employees, I know of only one: her butler, Desmond Mallory. And if you know about the college girl killing, then you know the dead coed was Desmond's daughter. Revenge is a pretty good motive for murder."

That gets me a scolding *tsk*. "Then why wait twelve years? You disappoint me, Cantor."

"Wouldn't be the first time," I say.

"But I've always expected better of you. Mallory, if you remember, was a professional in the rackets. Yes, he would have the discipline not to rush into things, but twelve years is a long time to wait to do something he could have done the minute John Garraway was no longer around to control him. And he would certainly know enough to pick a better moment to commit murder than the one this morning, when you were in the house." Sig sits on that for a minute before he says, "Still, we cannot count him out. But you should look elsewhere, too. When you identify Miss Garraway's killer, you will either bring this person to me or let me know where I can find them. Is that understood, Cantor?"

You bet I understand. Sig will be judge and jury, the death sentence already decided, the quiet disposal of the body arranged. City Hall will be happy to have the matter quietly disposed of without their involvement. The only question is the manner of execution. My imagination can't even come close.

Sig says, "And you will have plenty of time to pursue the Garraway matter, Cantor, because you will no longer involve yourself in the Quinn killing."

"Did you get Huber knocked off of that case, too? Fine by me. Give it to a cop who doesn't have me in his gun sights."

"Lieutenant Huber will remain on the case."

That gets my head up. "It seems that I have to watch my step after all. You know Huber wants to fry me for the Quinn murder.

If you want me to work on the Garraway killing, Sig, you've got to get Huber off my back. I can't snoop around about Garraway if I'm in jail."

He leans forward, his jowls catching light. His smile is small, its chill matching the amusement in his eyes, the kind that likes to pull the wings off flies or tear the limbs off people. "Then I suggest you be very careful. In the meantime, you will stop asking around about the Quinn woman, and that goes for your young Judson, too. That is all, Cantor. Good-bye." His hand slides under his desk. A second later Mulroney comes into the den. "Cantor is leaving now, Mr. Mulroney. Please take her downstairs to the front door."

My bookending thugs ride down in the elevator with me. I'm glad Mulroney and Ham Face aren't the chatty type. I don't need conversation clogging up my thoughts about my meeting with Sig. I try to figure what Sig is up to, why he's protected me in the Garraway matter but thrown me into Huber's teeth in the Quinn case. But I can't figure it, because as usual with Sig he treats information as a commodity he owns and you don't.

I'm on my own.

At the ground floor, Mulroney and Ham Face march me across the lobby to the front door of the building.

I say, "My gun, if you don't mind, Mulroney."

"Oh yeah, sure." He takes my .38 out of his pocket, hands it over with a juicy grin that makes me glad I skipped dinner.

Outside, the rain's let up to a cold drizzle, the sort that stings your face and neck. There's no respite until I go down the subway stairs at the corner of Fortieth Street and Sixth Avenue. I shake the water off my cap, but can't shake the chill I feel deep down in my gut. It's not from the rain; it's from Sig's frosty smile when he said good-bye.

Chapter Nine

Back home in my apartment, a hot shower takes some of the chill from my bones. A change of clothes into a pale green pullover and a navy suit anchors me again after Sig's double-dealing with my life. A cup of strong coffee with a hefty dollop of Chivas steadies my thoughts.

It's a little after nine p.m. when I pick up the phone and dial Vivienne.

"Oh hello, Cantor. I hoped I'd hear from you."

I like the words. I try to catch if there's anything more than just business behind that velvety voice. There isn't. I'm surprised at my disappointment. "I take it you have information about Eve Garraway?" I say.

"I do. And you know, I almost feel sorry for her. Oh—my—I guess that's in poor taste, considering she's dead. One can't feel much sorrier about something than that."

"No, I guess not. What's your news, Vivienne?"

I hear sounds of a lighter snapping shut and an exhale of breath before Vivienne says, "As I suspected, the wives higher up on the social ladder despised Eve. They considered her a social upstart, a woman whose money could buy her fine clothes and good diction but could never give her genuine class. They treated her carefully, though, since a number of their husbands were indebted to her father for various favors, some of them involving money, some involving making scandals go away. They couldn't

79

chance angering Eve in case her father passed his secrets to his daughter."

"Any indication she turned the screws on any of them?"

"You mean blackmail? Not that I know of. At least no one would admit to being blackmailed. But none of the wives I spoke to or heard about were the least bit sorry that Eve is dead, even if they found the manner of her death, well, distasteful."

Only a crowd with nothing more to worry about than what jewels to wear to dinner would consider murder merely distasteful. "Did any of the wives find it less distasteful than the others?"

"Actually, yes. Dierdre Atchley. She's the wife of—"

"Brooks Atchley? The Park Avenue banking family Atchleys? They have a son—what's his name? James?—an officer of the Atchley banking interests and a big deal in yachting. According to the gossip columns, the son even lives on his yacht."

"Yes, that's the family. The Atchleys are very old money, very old lineage. Brooks traces his family all the way back to the English taking over New Amsterdam from the Dutch and renaming it New York. And Dierdre's maiden name was Haddonfield. The Haddonfields are connected to English aristocracy. Landed gentry, I believe, with a pile of stones that dates back to the Tudors."

I make a mental note that the next time I'm in England I'll see about purloining some of the Haddonfield family heirlooms. I don't mention it to Vivienne. "What's Mrs. Atchley's beef with Eve Garraway besides social climbing? What did Eve have on her?"

"It's not what Eve had on Dierdre; it's what Eve was doing to the family. Even after old John Garraway died, Eve still had influence with the politicians and legislative committees that oversee the state's banking concerns. It wasn't in Brooks's interest to cross her. But maybe things came to a head, because it seems Eve has been quietly arranging proxies to buy big blocks of shares in the Atchley banking empire. Her acquisitions put Brooks in danger of being forced out of a firm his family ran for nearly three hundred years. I understand she was days away from gaining enough shares to make trouble. She really had it in for Brooks."

"Any idea why? What did he ever do to her?"

"He didn't marry her."

"She wanted him to divorce his wife?"

"No." I hear it through what sounds like an exhale on her cigarette. "Brooks was single at the time. Dierdre is his second wife. They've been married about five years. Dierdre's first husband, Archie Westerton, died early in their marriage. Inoperable cancer, I believe. Very sad. James is her son by Westerton, though the family had his surname legally changed to Atchley in order to keep the dynasty going. Brooks was a widower, too, when he romanced Eve."

"Aren't they all," I say. That story is as popular with cheating spouses as the *My wife doesn't understand me* song and dance.

"It's not funny, Cantor. Brooks's first wife died in an automobile accident. Drunk driver hit her. That was about eight years ago. Brooks was despondent. It took him a long time to get back to himself, and I'm not sure he ever really did. He took up with Eve about a year after his wife's death. But he would never marry her. Even her political power couldn't make up for belonging to the wrong social class."

Bingo. There they are, those two favorite motives for murder: love and money. Only this time it's a vicious foursome: love, money, jealousy, and revenge. The Garraway-Atchley melodrama has plenty of all of it.

"Still," I say, "even if Eve succeeded in forcing Atchley out of power, he was hardly a candidate for the soup kitchen. I'm sure he could retire more than comfortably."

"Yes, of course," Vivienne says, "but socially the family might not have survived the humiliation. The air's pretty thin up where they live, Cantor. A scandal could suffocate them. They'd be snubbed at the city's better clubs, their memberships canceled. Influential people might turn their backs, and social invitations would stop coming. Suitable marriage prospects for their son could dry up." The way Vivienne says the word *suitable* means that poor James might have to settle for a bride whose only listing might be a tony address in the phone book, not the *Social Register*.

"I need to talk to them, Vivienne. Can you arrange something?"

Another exhale comes through the phone. It's a long exhale, giving Vivienne plenty of time to answer my question. It's a habit of hers, dangling what I want of her, making me wait for it. She finally says, "I can't let you badger them, Cantor. Dierdre is a friend of mine. She doesn't know I've gathered this information about the family. If she knew, it would put me in the doghouse with her. I can't let that happen. The Atchleys are major donors to the museum."

"Why, Vivienne," I say, putting a heavy spoonful of honey into it, "you know how chivalrous I can be. I promise to put on my smoothest silk gloves before I stroke Mrs. Atchley's cheek."

"Very funny," Vivienne says. "Let me think about it." She hangs up.

"Don't take too long," I say anyway.

I take a dry coat, a brown one, and a gray cap from the hall closet, slip them on. Where I'm going, I like to look sharp.

The rain's stopped but the night air is cold and wet. I pull my coat collar up, pull the brim of my cap low, and walk down the block to where I parked my Buick. The street's busy with people making the rounds of the neighborhood's nightclubs, everyone's shadow sliding around them on the pavement below the street lamps. I'm just another pedestrian and another shadow in the crowd, New York's most protective overcoat.

I've got a headful of thoughts as I weave through the throng, thoughts about women, but not my usual delicious daydreams about that beautiful sex. Tonight my mind's tangled up with thoughts of dangerous women, women with secrets, women with reason to kill.

The Green Door Club, a nightspot for women of my romantic persuasion, is downstairs in an alley off Tenth Avenue near Fourteenth Street. It's nearly ten-thirty when I walk in, give my coat and cap to the adorable blonde in the checkroom, and make my way to the bar.

A slow tune from the band winds through the mix of chatter and laughter in the room. Conversations, some intimate, some trying to be, are whispered in red leather booths lining the walls and at white cloth'd tables around the dance floor where couples sway. Light from amber-shaded wall sconces and small lamps on the tables glints off necklaces, bracelets, earrings, lipstick and polished nails. The light sends a sheen along colorful satin dresses and the lapels of suits. A new addition, a jukebox bright with candy-colored lights, stands next to the bandstand, ready to take over when the band, an all-female three-piece combo in green organza, takes a breather. Behind the bar, bottles sparkle, promising paradise.

I claim a bar stool, put a buck on the bar, enough to cover a drink and a tip. The bartender, Peg Monroe, pours me two fingers of Chivas without even bothering to ask. She doesn't have to.

Peg's a big woman with a big heart, liquid brown eyes in a light brown face, and plenty of smarts. That big heart will go the distance for you when you're in trouble, and her smarts will burn your lies right off your tongue. Her "Good evenin', Slick" is as mellow as a warm Southern night through her trace of a Georgia drawl. Her strong hands in her crisp white shirt move with sureness and grace as she pours drinks and maneuvers glasses to customers along the bar.

Coming back to me, she says, "She's upstairs. Trouble in a purple dress."

"She giving you problems?"

"No, but there's plenty of trouble hiding in those brown eyes. She's got cobra's eyes, Slick. They size you up before she decides to eat you. How long you planning to stow her here?"

"Not long, I hope. I have to get her out from under some bad business. Listen, you remember the woman I left with last night, Lorraine Quinn?"

Peg gives me a mocking laugh that only a trusted friend can get away with. "What's the matter, Slick? You slippin'? You didn't get her phone number?"

"I won't need her phone number. She's dead."

Peg's laugh dries up fast, replaced by a look that questions me without uttering a word.

"Knifed this morning," I say, "right outside my building."

Peg leans on the bar, leans in close to me, speaks low, "And now the Law wants to tie you up in it?"

I nod my answer, then ask, "What do you know about her, Peg? I hadn't seen her here before last night, but that doesn't mean she's never been around. You got anything on her I can throw to the cops to send them in another direction?"

"She came in once in a while," Peg says with a shrug. "Sometimes on the arm of some sharp dresser, sometimes alone. But she didn't stay alone long. Not surprised she took up with you, Slick. You're her type," she kids, fingering the lapel of my suit jacket.

"Any of those sharp dressers stake a claim on her?" I ask.

"You mean follow Lorraine around? Huh, couldn't say. Why you asking? You think maybe some Jealous Jackie followed her to your place, waited until she left and shivved her?"

"You have any Jealous Jackies in mind?"

Peg glances around the room, stops here and there for a look at who's wearing sharp threads, who's in a well-chosen tie, who has the style to finish things off with a pocket square. Lorraine's type. "No one's ringin' that bell, Slick. But I'll think on it. Meantime, what about the lady upstairs? How's she tied into this Quinn thing?" Peg's smarts are right on the money.

I give her a smile, lift my glass in toast to her sharp thinking. After I drain the scotch, I say, "That's what I'm trying to find out."

"Well, find out fast. I can hold her here for a while, but not too long. You know the risks."

"Uh-huh. If it ain't the Mob, it's raids, cops, morals raps, jail, the nuthouse. Nothing we can't survive. We always have."

She leans over to me again. "Listen, Slick, ever think maybe it's time to do more than just survive?"

"Every day, Peg. Every day."

"Maybe it's time you didn't do it alone."

"I'm my own best protection," I say with a discreet pat to the gun under my suit jacket.

"What are you gonna do, Slick, shoot a cop? Shoot a judge?"

"You got a better idea when the cops rough you up and throw you in the paddy wagon? What are *you* gonna do, Peg?"

"Sue 'em."

Leave it to Peg to give me a much needed laugh in my otherwise lousy day.

I finish my drink, pull a fiver from my wallet for the rest of the bottle, take it with me to the end of the bar and through a door marked Employees Only. It takes me into a hallway of storage rooms, a washroom, a janitorial closet, the club's office, and a stairway.

There's only one door at the top of the stairs. I knock on the door, say, "Alice, it's me, Cantor."

I hear the click of the lock. Alice opens the door. She's wearing the purple dress. Peg didn't mention that it's velvet, or that it fits Alice like a second skin, except where the bodice reveals plenty of Alice's own skin. She's smiling like she's happy to see me, and then confirms it by sliding her arms around my neck, pressing her body against mine and lifting her face to kiss me. It's a helluva kiss, deep and probing, like she's trying to find the taste of anyone who's ever kissed me before and replace it with only the taste of her. I like the way she tastes, and I like her body against me, like her heat, but I know too much now about the con artist Alice Lamarr *née* Letherby to trust that the taste won't turn sour.

I pull away from the kiss, walk past Alice and into the small room Peg's tricked out with a bed, a hotplate on top of a small white metal cabinet next to a refrigerator, a white kitchen table, and a couple of chairs covered in yellow vinyl. The shaded lamp on the bedside table throws a weak arc of light along the cracked and faded peach-colored walls. Peg uses the place sometimes after the club closes. She has her reasons, and I don't ask.

Alice says, "What's wrong, Cantor? You look like you'd rather kill me than kiss me." There's a laugh in her voice, but it's a nervous one.

"I don't want to kill you, Alice, not unless you give me an excuse."

"If you're trying to be funny, it's not working."

"All right," I say, taking two glasses from the cabinet, "let's both stop joking." I bring the glasses to the table, pour shots of Chivas into each glass. "Have a seat, Alice. I'm going to ask you some questions. You're going to give me straight answers and I'm going to try very hard to believe you."

Alice doesn't sit down in the chair as much as she slithers into it, a cobra's supple body to match what Peg called her cobra's eyes. I barely see her eyes in the dim light of the bedside lamp, but the waves in her auburn hair glimmer in the light like roadside danger flares.

I take a swallow of scotch. So does Alice. When she puts the glass down, I see a hint through the shadows of the baby doll smile that slew me five years ago and again this afternoon. I wonder now if it's natural to her or one of her ways to soften up her prey.

Tempting as she is, I don't soften. "First question," I say. "What do you know of any connection between Tap Tenzi and Sig Loreale?"

"Oh my," she says, "you've been a busy little beaver today."

"Answer the question, Alice."

"I have a question first. What are my answers worth to you, Cantor?"

"My freedom, which you probably don't care about, and your life, which you do. If you want my protection, Alice, you'll stop playing games and come across with the truth. You do still know how to tell the truth, don't you, Miss Lamarr? Or is it Miss Leander or Miss Lorrie or Miss McKenzie? Or how about Letherby?"

Two things happen when a con artist's jig is up. First, they shrink inside their skin, even imperceptibly, and then they breathe deep, fill their lungs along with their nerve. I watch it happen to Alice, watch her shrivel and then take that breath, fill her rather attractive chest while she readies whatever challenge she has in mind to what I just said. But the challenge fizzles. The breath leaves her body in a long, sad stream of defeat. "You really have been a busy beaver today. If you know all that about me, then you know I gave it up after I got out of the Indiana lockup. You were never a mark, Cantor."

The catch in her voice seems real enough, but after all I've learned about Alice, what's real and what's a con is up for grabs. "Then don't con me now," I say.

"Or what, you'll kill me?"

"I won't have to. I'll just leave you to Tenzi, or maybe Loreale. He's involved in this mess, isn't he, Alice."

She takes another swallow of scotch, drains the glass. As she puts it down, the lamplight catches the rim. The glass is trembling in her hand. "How did you know? What gave it away?"

"Never mind how I know. But you're going to tell me how Tenzi is connected to Loreale. What would a two-bit sometime hired gun for the Mob have to do with the most powerful boss in New York?"

Her slow nod carries the weight of fear, fear of no escape, fear for her life. Even in the faint light of this dingy room I can see Alice's shoulders tighten, an attempt to fortify her against the danger she's in. I'm her only lifeline, and she knows it.

She finally faces me, then looks away, runs her hand through her hair, doing everything she can to avoid a story that scares her, until she can't avoid it anymore. "I think—I'm not sure," she says barely above a whisper so threadbare it hardly has any human sound at all, "I thought Loreale might have told Johnny to kill the Quinn woman. But now I think it's something else. I think maybe Johnny's on the run from Loreale."

And my tryst with Lorraine Quinn got in the way. *I* got in the way. That's why Sig warned me off. Huber is Sig's instrument to find Tap Tenzi, and the poor sap of a cop doesn't even know it.

But that's only the end of the story, not the beginning, not the Once Upon A Time that set the story racing toward Lorraine Quinn's death. And why the hell was she killed on my doorstep?

"Alice, what was Tenzi's connection to Sig in the first place? Sig has an army of killers at his command. Why deal with small change like Tenzi?"

"Yeah, Johnny was small change, all right," she says with a bitter laugh. "But all of a sudden he was sure he could climb up from the small time and make the big time by getting in with Loreale's operation. The crazy thing is, our divorce gave him the goods to make that play. It seems Quinn's camera work might have caught something Loreale didn't want revealed and Johnny knew it."

Which made Lorraine Quinn and her pictures what Sig hates most: loose ends. And now Tenzi is a loose end. And Alice is a loose end. If Sig finds out Otis Hollander has photos of something Sig wants kept secret, Otis will be a loose end. And if I find out what it is Sig wants hidden, I'll be a loose end. He warned me off the Quinn case so I'd stay alive to look into the Garraway killing. But I don't kid myself. If I become a loose end, I'll become part of Sig's possible cascade of murder along with Tenzi, Alice, and Otis Hollander.

So I think twice before I ask, "Do you know what Tenzi had on Sig?"

Alice waves off the question. "No, and I don't want to. Safer that way. But Johnny called me and told me not to go through with the divorce because he was setting up this big thing with Sig Loreale. It could keep us in the chips for life, he said. But if I insisted on the divorce it would be the end of me. That's when I scrammed out of our apartment and took a room at the Collier Hotel. Only my attorney knew where I was, until you found me."

"And the police found you."

"Yeah, and the police." She says the words as if they taste bad.

I pour her another drink, then pour another for me. We both need it.

Alice takes a deep swallow. It restores her enough for her to say, "So what about those other questions, Cantor?"

"Just one," I say, easing into the subject that's stood between us since I walked into her room at the Collier. "Why did you marry Tenzi? And don't give me the same song and dance you gave me this afternoon about showering you with money and taking you to popular hotspots. Johnny Tenzi never had the kind of money you wanted, and living in the open isn't all it's cracked up to be. And besides, the shadows are your natural territory, Alice."

I guess it's another subject she wants to avoid, because she gets up from the table and wanders near the bed, turning her back to me.

I get up from the table, too, walk over to her, stand right behind her, close, close enough for her to feel my breath on her neck. "Why did you marry Johnny Tenzi, Alice?"

"I—" she starts, shivers, then starts again. "A few weeks after you and I were through, I started seeing another girl at the Copa, a showgirl like me. We'd get together on the quiet because the management would toss us out if they knew. Well, it was around that time that Johnny started coming to the club. He and his lowlife Mob buddies. The Mob guys would sometimes come backstage after the show, take the girls out for drinks. One night, Johnny asked me out. One of his gangster thugs was standing right next to him. I felt trapped. You don't say no when a Mob guy wants your company. So I went. After that, Johnny came around every night. He thought he owned me now, thought I was his girl. The girl I was seeing got scared that if Johnny or his mobster friends found out about us they'd kill her, or maybe both of us. So she scrammed, left town. Anyway, pretty soon Johnny asked me to marry him. I tried to, y'know, laugh it off, keep things light between us. I told him that things were okay the way they were. But he wasn't having it. He said that if I didn't marry him, I'd be sorry. You know what that means, Cantor."

Yeah, I know. It means Alice would never be seen or heard from again.

"So I married him."

Everything she said rings true. You don't cross the Mob. You don't say no to killers. So why is my skin tingling? Why is there an itch at the base of my skull? A question creeps up on me. "And you weren't afraid to divorce him?"

That turns her around. The light of the bedside lamp catches the fear and fury in her eyes. "Of course I was afraid. I'm still terrified! But I couldn't take being swatted around anymore. I couldn't take his drunken rages. And I couldn't take . . . couldn't take . . ." She's crying now, soft tears of exhaustion and agony. "I couldn't take . . . his touch."

That's the first thing Alice has said that I fully believe. Maybe the rest of it is true, maybe it isn't, but I know Alice's body, know what it wants, what it needs, and I know Johnny Tenzi wouldn't have a clue. No man could.

Lamplight brushes Alice's face. Tears glisten in her eyes, tears and something else. What Alice's eyes are telling me is that the shadows are my natural territory, too.

The bed is shadowed. We sink into it. We're where we belong.

Alice whispers my name, groans my name as my mouth, my fingers, claim her body. I groan her name when her mouth takes me in, her hands rocking me even as I shout my ecstasy.

We doze, we wake, we take each other again. We're in our territory of shadows.

We're jolted awake by a rumble of music, loud and thumping, with a guy shouting about rocking around a clock. The music's coming from the club downstairs. It's that new music, rock and roll, blasting from the jukebox.

Chapter Ten

More thumping, no, not thumping, not as loud, just something knocking in the darkness of my sleep.

"Cantor?"

My name wiggles into my head from somewhere outside of sleep. The knocking's coming from outside now, too.

"Cantor?"

The call of my name finally tugs me awake. I know the voice, know who's calling me. It's Peg. She's at the door.

Alice, groggy, turns over. She shields her eyes from the light of the bedside lamp. "What's—"

"Shh," I say. "It's just Peg."

I pull on my trousers and undershirt, open the door.

Seeing me half dressed, Peg looks over my shoulder, gets the picture of what's been going on. "You never learn, do you, Slick. It's been one mistake after another since—"

"Stop right there, Peg. Don't say it. Don't say her name. What do you want?"

"Rosie's downstairs at the bar."

"She knows I'm here?"

"Uh-huh. She's been looking for you. Finally ended up here. Now get yourself dressed," she says with a friendly laugh as she heads down the stairs, "and come down to the bar."

I call after her, "What time is it?"

"Two-thirty. We close in a half hour."

"Cantor?" This time it's Alice calling my name. "Everything okay?"

"Everything's fine. Go back to sleep. I have to go downstairs."

She stretches her arms out to me, says, "Come here," in a way that promises a garden of pleasure and sins of the gutter, twin temptations I'd love to roll around in.

But if Rosie's come looking for me at the Green Door Club at two-thirty in the morning, it's not because she's in the mood to dance.

I tell Alice, "I have to go."

The three-piece combo is playing a sweet Gershwin ballad, "Someone to Watch Over Me," for the last dance. Peg's already dimmed the lights, leaving the swaying couples in a dreamscape of shadows and glimpsed swirls of colorful dresses rippling against silhouettes in suits.

Rosie's at the bar. Peg's showing her something in a magazine. My coat and cap are already on a bar stool.

I greet Rosie and ask Peg to pour me a Chivas.

Rosie says, "I've been looking all over town for you. Even checked Drogan's tug."

"Yeah? What's up?"

"You can't go home tonight, Cantor. You can stay here," she says with a shrewd look in her eye and a little twist of a smile at the corner of her mouth, "or I can put you up tonight. But you can't go home."

"Why not?"

"Look, I drove over to your place when I got off shift at midnight—"

"I thought you had plans." I could kick myself for saying it, even as the words tumble out of my mouth. Rosie doesn't deserve cheap digs from me.

"Plans change," she says, her tone flat, not letting the hurt in. Rosie's finished being hurt by me. "Never mind my plans. Just listen to what I'm telling you. You can't be seen coming back to your place. I saw a couple of guys, maybe cops, maybe even nastier sorts of fellas, parked out front, watching the door to your building. I circled the block a few times and every time I came around, they were still there."

"What kind of car was it?"

"Pontiac, recent model, maybe '53, '54. Dark blue, I think, hard to say at night. But definitely a Pontiac. It had those chrome stripes down the center of the hood."

"Then it wasn't cops. The department usually outfits them in Fords or Plymouths."

"Okay, then it's bad guys, really bad guys, Cantor. So what do you want to do? Stay here, or come to my place?"

The combo's stretching out the final bars of "Someone to Watch Over Me," letting the swaying couples enjoy a last embrace. "I'll go home, Rosie."

Peg says, "Don't be a fool, Slick. You could be walking right into a whole heap of trouble. And haven't you had enough trouble for one night?"

"You can save the tender loving care," I say. "I'm not the hiding type. I can't let the bastards think I'm afraid of them."

There's a hand sliding along my shoulder. I turn around to see Alice. She's back in the purple dress. Her hair's a little disheveled, but the swirls of dark red look good on her. So does the dress. "I doubt you're afraid of anything," she says. "Hello, Rosie. Thanks for ferrying me over here."

"Any time," Rosie says, friendly enough, but just.

I slide Alice's hand from my shoulder, hold her hand between mine. "I have to go home," I say.

She's disappointed, but soon the disappointment in her eyes is crowded out by the same lure her eyes sent me earlier: the lure of shadows. "Take me with you," she says.

"Too risky. I don't know who's out for me, and I might not be able to keep you safe. I'll come by tomorrow."

I feel a tug on the sleeve of my suit jacket, hear Rosie say, "If you're gonna go, then let's go, Cantor."

93

"Yeah," Peg says. "Get going. I need to close up. I'll make sure Alice is safe."

I give Peg a nod, give another nod to Rosie.

I slip into my coat and cap, walk beside Rosie as we move with the crowd leaving the Green Door Club.

Outside in the alley, Rosie says, "No chance I can talk you out of going to your place?"

"Save your breath," I say. "Look, I appreciate the offer, really I do, but I don't like being pushed around. I have to go home and face these guys. Nobody's going to keep me from going where I want to go."

Rosie says, "Funny, Peg was talking to me about the same thing. She gave me this magazine." She takes the magazine from under her arm, shows it to me in the dim light of the alley. Not a bad-looking cover from what I can make out, with a drawing that plays to my taste: two women in classical Greek dress against a Greek vase called a *lekythos*. "There's poetry in here," Rosie says, "and articles and stuff about people like us getting together to come out of hiding and push back against the creeps that want to throw us in jail."

"I push back every day, Rosie."

"Yeah, but if everybody pushed back together, maybe the creeps would stop."

"And then what?"

"And then, I don't know, I guess they'd let us lead regular lives."

"Now why would I want to do that?"

Rosie grabs my arm, turns me to her, runs her finger along my lips and cheek. "So that you don't get any more scars on your face?"

I have no answer to that.

Even at nearly three in the morning, my Theater District neighborhood never goes dark. Actors took their bows on Broadway's stages hours ago, but the theater marquees still glow bright, blazing the names of big-time stars like Joan Fontaine in *Tea and Sympathy* at the Barrymore on Forty-Seventh Street, and John Raitt singing his heart out in *The Pajama Game* at the St. James on Forty-Fourth. Not to be outshone by the live stages, the movie houses light up Hollywood's famous names and faces on gigantic billboards. Marlon Brando lords it over the Astor at Broadway and Forty-Fifth Street in *On the Waterfront,* a movie about the dockside Mob that I have it on good authority the real dockside Mob does not care for. The gorgeous Grace Kelly and the lucky James Stewart are ogling murder in *Rear Window* at the Rivoli on Broadway and Forty-Ninth. Closer to the ground, neon lights from nightclubs and jazz joints float their colors on hats and coats and across faces in the crowds still lingering on the streets after their last nightcap.

I spot the Pontiac parked in front of my building, see the silhouettes of two guys in fedoras and bulky coats in the front seat.

I walk up to the car. The guy in the passenger seat sees me, opens the door and gets out. He doesn't need the bulky coat to prove that he's built like a linebacker, and his fedora can't hide the stone-cut angles of his big face. "You Gold?" he says. His voice is gritty, like he just swallowed a gravel pit.

"And you are . . . ?"

"I'm the guy who's telling you to get in the car." He opens the back door.

"We can talk out here," I say. "We won't get arrested for talking on the street."

"We're not here to talk, Gold." He makes his point by pulling a snub nose .38 from his coat, camouflages it with his sleeve, out of sight of passers-by. But I see enough of it to know it's aimed right at my gut.

He calls to the other guy, who's still behind the wheel, "Get over here, Marv, and check her for a gun."

Marv's another linebacker, but his face is more waxy than stony.

I save him the trouble of searching me for my .38 and just hand it over. Besides, I don't want his hands on me.

He pockets my gun, goes back around to the driver's seat.

The other guy's never taken his eyes off me. "Now get in the car," he says.

What was it I said to Rosie about not being pushed around, not told where to go?

The guy with the gun can't figure out why I'm chuckling when I get into the backseat of the Pontiac. I bet these guys are taking me somewhere I really don't want to go.

Either Marv and the linebacker sitting next to me are stupid, or it doesn't matter if I see where we're going. They didn't blindfold me, didn't put a bag over my head, so I guess they figure they're taking me on that good old one-way ride. For the time being, at least until we get to wherever the hell we're going, and despite the linebacker's gun in my ribs, I'm more or less a tourist taking in the nighttime glow of tugboat and freighter traffic on the East River as we make our way uptown.

I have kinship with the crews of tugs and freighters. Like them, I do a lot of business on the river in the dead of night. They're even helpful in letting their boats hide me in their shadows. Some of their captains know it, some of them don't, and even if they do, they'd never talk. The waterfront doesn't belong to the Law. It wouldn't be as profitable or as much fun.

At a Hundred-Twentieth Street we pull away from the river and head up First Avenue to the Willis Avenue Bridge connecting Manhattan to the Bronx. The bridge is an old iron truss job that swings open for passing marine traffic on the Harlem River.

When we're across, Marv drives us through residential neighborhoods whose rowhouses try their best to keep their scruffy dignity. At this hour, the area's hardworking inhabitants are all tucked up and asleep.

The Pontiac keeps going. Rowhouses with the pride of well-swept stoops give way to the big brick warehouses and industrial behemoths of Hunts Point, dark now for the night.

Marv drives into an alley behind a small two-story factory—

the High Style Tie & Handkerchief Company, the painted sign says—on East Bay Avenue. It's the kind of seedy joint that pays their employees pennies for piece-goods work. I make a note never to buy anything made by the High Style Tie & Handkerchief Company.

A single light glows through a dirty window on the second floor. Marv parks the Pontiac by the back door.

The linebacker with the gun in my ribs says, "Get out slow, Gold. Don't try to run, don't try anything funny or you'll have bullets in your kneecaps."

"Wouldn't dream of it," I say, and get out of the car.

Marv takes a key from his pocket and unlocks the back door of the factory. Inside, he turns a light on in a dingy hallway, the air scratchy with dust. The big steel sliding doors to our left probably open to the factory floor.

Since we're not here to make ties or handkerchiefs, Marv leads the way up the stairs. The linebacker with the gun follows behind me.

Upstairs, the second-floor hallway is dark except for a line of light seeping under one of the doors. Marv gives the door a knock. A guy's voice answers, "Yeah?"

Marv says, "We got her. We got Gold."

The guy inside says, "Bring her in."

Marv opens the door, hauls me inside, and closes the door behind him. We're in an office cluttered with stacks of ties, fabric samples, order books and other paperwork strewn on a gray metal desk and shelves lining the walls. Seated behind the desk, smoking a cigarette and reading a girlie magazine, is the answer to my prayers.

"Well," I say, "this saves me the trouble of trying to find you, Tap. And by the way, when did you go into the tie and hankie business?"

He puts the magazine down, says, "It's my cousin's place. And I didn't bring you here for your benefit, Gold." Tenzi has what you might call a sweet-talk voice, smooth as a middle-of-the-night saxophone. The voice is completely at odds with the thrust of his square jaw in his pockmarked face, and the gray eyes that lack all warmth, humor, or any sign of brains. "I brought you here to put the fear of god into you," he says. "So sit down."

Marv and the linebacker push me down into a lumpy, green vinyl-covered chair facing the desk. Before I get the chance to thank them for their assistance, they use a couple of ugly neckties to secure my wrists to the chair's wooden armrests. When I'm all trussed up, the two goons stand at my sides like lazy soldiers.

Tenzi gets up from behind the desk. His eyes stay on me as he takes off his suit jacket—a gray double-breasted number that didn't come from a Fifth Avenue tailor—and places it on the back of his chair. His pinky ring, a showy thing with a bunch of little rhinestones pretending to be diamonds, flashes light as he rolls up the sleeves of his white shirt and loosens his tie, a red one with gray chevrons. I wonder if he stole it from his cousin's factory.

He comes around to the front of the desk, takes the cigarette from his lips, drops it to the floor, and stubs it out with his foot. "Now," he says, "you're gonna tell me things. But first I'm gonna give you a reason to talk to me." His reason arrives with the back of his hand and a wallop across my face, his pinkie ring tearing the flesh at the corner of my mouth.

I don't know which annoys me more, the sting on my face or the blood dripping onto my pale green pullover. "Any more reasons like that, Tap, and you'll break my jaw. I won't be able to tell you a thing. So why don't you just say what's on your mind?"

He twists a fist into the palm of his hand and says, "On my mind? All right, I'll tell you what's on my mind. Gettin' rid of you, that's what's on my mind. You're sick, Gold, sick and twisted. You've brought your sickness into my life twice now, and that's two times too many."

He wallops me again because I'm smiling. I'm smiling because I've heard this song before, heard it from men who want to punish me because some woman they've had their eye on turned out to be more interested in me then them, heard it from restaurant

98

owners and maître d's who've refused to serve me, from cops who'd sooner beat me up over a parking ticket than protect me from attack by irate straight-backs. I've heard this song before and laughed at it before, and the only thing that's stopping me from laughing now is Tenzi's next wallop across my face.

"So tell me, Tap," I say, able to at least smile through the wallop's sting and more drips of blood, "is all this about Lorraine Quinn or about Alice?"

Taunting him about Alice, riling him up even more, is probably not a good idea if I want to avoid more wallops, but I enjoy it anyway.

"Sure, go ahead, joke all you want," he says, then bends to me and grabs the lapels of my coat. "You do understand you're not gettin' outta here alive."

"Y'know, Tap, when they were handing out brains you must've been in the wrong line, the one where they were handing out toilet paper. Why would I tell you anything if you're going to kill me anyway?"

He lets go of my coat, stands up, gives me a wide, toothy grin that crinkles the pockmarks on his face into squiggling worms, which pretty much sums up his personality. "Boys," he says to Marv and the linebacker, "this pervert wants to know why she's gonna tell me stuff. Whaddya think, Eddie?" he says to the linebacker. "Should we tell her? Or are we gonna let her figure it out for herself?"

Eddie says, "She don't look too smart to me. Smart people don't get dragged to the Bronx in the middle of the night."

"Uh-huh," I say, "I get it. I can either go out fast and easy, or hard and screaming. So let's just get on with it, Tap. What the hell is this all about?"

He walks back around the desk, sits down and lights another cigarette, the rhinestone pinky ring flashing its cheap sparkle. "It's about you, Gold. It's about you snoopin' around. Why are you snoopin' around about who killed the Quinn woman?"

"Because she was murdered on my doorstep this morning—well, I guess by now it was really yesterday—that's why. I don't

99

like blood and bodies on my doorstep ruining a sunny Tuesday morning. And I don't like the cops that blood and bodies attract."

"Then you shouldn't be fooling around with weasels like Quinn." The grin Tenzi gives me oozes disgust. "You're revolting, Gold. And that Quinn woman was revolting. Y'know, it's funny how it tied up. If I hadn't followed her to that club and saw her come out with you and then go home with you, I'd never have figured she even knew you. If I'd known she was a pervert like you . . . hah . . ."

"You could've used it against her? Threatened to expose her if she didn't turn over the pictures of you with some sweetie so Alice wouldn't have grounds to divorce you or couldn't take you to the cleaners if she did? You wouldn't have had to kill Quinn if you had those goods on her? That's what I mean about you getting in the wrong line for brains, Tap. Killing Quinn would bring cops, sure, but killing her in front of my place would bring the kind of cops who already have me in their hunting sights. Didn't you think I'd do everything I could to keep their hungry eyes off me and point them someplace else? Like finding the real killer of Lorraine Quinn?"

Tenzi's not exactly squirming in his chair, but he's not at ease in it either. So I keep pressing, try to find the spot that changes his mind about killing me. I know it's a long shot, but with my wrists tied to the chair and two bruisers on either side of me, it's my only shot.

"And another thing," I say. "Quinn's murder annoyed Sig Loreale. It attracted attention, which Sig doesn't like. And he knows Quinn was tailing you for Otis Hollander. Oh yeah, he knows. So Sig, being a smart guy, puts two and two together, figures maybe you're good for the Quinn killing because he knows what a vindictive, hair-trigger son of a bitch you are. In Sig's eyes, the Quinn murder makes trouble and makes you a loose end, which means whatever deal you'd hoped to make with him went right down the toilet. And now he's on your tail, Tap. And he'll find you."

I don't need to finish that scenario. Tenzi's clenched fists and the tight line of his lips say he gets the picture. Whatever torture he has in mind for me couldn't come close to what Sig's people could do to him. "So whaddya want, Gold?"

"Besides getting out of here alive? I want you to leave Alice alone."

"And just how does that help me get out from under Loreale?"

"It doesn't," I say with a shrug. The action pulls the ties around my wrists but doesn't loosen them, just digs them deeper into my skin. "Leaving Alice alone gets *me* off your back, though, Tap. That's one less hunter coming after you."

He thinks that's funny. "You can't come after me if you're dead."

"Sure, yeah, I see your point," I say. "But a bunch of people will miss me, people who know I've been looking for you. Maybe they'll figure I found you, or you found me first, but either way you knocked me off. You don't want to annoy those people, Tap. One of those people will be Sig. You'll never see the others."

When Marv and Eddie first dragged me in here, Tap Tenzi was just a man on the run. Now he's a desperate man on the run. He parks his cigarette in the corner of his mouth, fidgets with his ring, squints through the cigarette smoke lapping at his eyes, killing his play to stare me down. He gives up and takes the cigarette from his mouth, waves away the smoke and quickly gets back to his tough guy attitude. But this time there are cracks in it. Maybe I can sneak through the cracks and get the hell out of here.

"I tell you what, Tap," I say. "Let's make a deal. I've got a question for you. If you give me an answer I like, I won't come after you if you let me go. And I'll sweeten the deal by not telling Sig I saw you, or that your cousin owns this place. He won't be able to sweat your cousin for information on your whereabouts if he doesn't know about him. But you'll have to leave Alice alone. If you come after her, I'll make sure Sig finds you. If I were you, I'd think about leaving town. They say Tasmania's nice this time of year."

He chews on that idea like he's chewing gum, his mouth and jaw working things over. Then he says, "What's your question?"

101

"What do you know about the Eve Garraway killing?"

"Who the hell is Eve Garraway? Wait a minute. Isn't she that politician's kid I read about in the afternoon paper?"

"That's the one." The expression on Tenzi's face is suddenly as innocent as a curious baby's, just uglier. But it tells me he had nothing to do with the Garraway killing. The idea that Quinn's killer and Garraway's killer are the same person and that they're out to frame me is a dead end. Eve's killer is still out there.

Maybe I'm an inch closer to Tenzi letting me go, but maybe not. My wrists are still tied to the chair. Marv and Eddie are still at my sides. They have their guns. Marv has my gun. All I have is my wits. I search for another avenue of escape, come up with flattery, betting that Tenzi's the type who falls for it. "By the way, Tap, smart move to shiv Quinn instead of shooting her. Quieter, neater that way, less likely to attract attention until you're gone from the street. You probably had a car waiting at the curb, too."

"Yeah, well, y'know, I'm a professional," he says with sleazy pride. "Bullets are evidence. I don't like to leave evidence. After I shivved Quinn, I just pulled the evidence out and had Marv drive me away. Neat and—"

Tap's boast is drowned out by the smash of the door and a gravelly, "Hello, Tenzi," from Lieutenant Huber. His gun's out. So are the guns of the two blue boys with him.

If anyone had told me I'd ever be grateful to see a cop, especially Huber, I'd have made a reservation for them in the nuthouse. Instead, I say, "Well, congratulations, Lieutenant. That entrance was worthy of a smash hit on Broadway. Perfect timing, too. How the hell did you find this place? Not that I'm not glad to see you. Have one of your boys untie me, will you?"

He doesn't answer me, just nods to his blue boys to put the cuffs on Tenzi, Marv and Eddie, who all look as if they've just eaten rotten meat.

Huber's cops march their snarling captives out, presumably to waiting cars or a paddy wagon outside. Huber and I are alone.

He pushes his hat back, smiles at me with far too much pleasure for my taste. "Now that's how I like to see you, Gold. Tied up and helpless."

"Who knew you have such gaudy fantasies, Lieutenant? Too bad I'm the wrong object to satisfy them, but I can set you up with—"

"Shut up, Gold. So you didn't kill Quinn, but you're still in the picture for Garraway as far as I'm concerned. Too bad Tenzi didn't spill for that one, too."

"You heard his confession?"

"What do you think I was waiting for? I've been outside that door hoping that either he or you would confess. I hate to say it, Gold, but you would've made a good cop, the way you made him spill."

"You wouldn't like who I'd arrest and who I wouldn't. But how'd you know to come here?"

"I got a call. Some dame said she saw you pushed into a car with two thugs. She got the plate number but didn't give me her name, just hung up."

Rosie. She must've followed me back to my place.

Huber says, "After your little episode—" the word *episode* comes out through a smutty smile—"with Tenzi's wife today I had a hunch he might have been back of grabbing you. So I put out an APB on the car's plate after I got that phone tip, and whaddya know, here you are."

"How long you been out there? You were awfully quiet," I say.

"It's because I'm a good cop, Gold. A patient cop." He looks at me when he says it. I can't miss the implication: he's patient enough to wait until he can cuff me.

He should live so long. With any luck, he won't.

Chapter Eleven

It's dawn on Wednesday by the time I fall into my bed, nearly noon by the time I wake up. Not because I want to wake up but because the phone beside my bed rings itself right into my dreams.

After my groggy hello, I hear, "Cantor? It's Vivienne. You sound like you've—well, never mind how you sound. Your life is your own business."

"And good morning to you too, Vivienne. To what do I owe the pleasure of having your lovely voice rouse me from my bed?"

"You're meeting me for cocktails at five-thirty this afternoon at my house."

"I am?" Funny thing about the upper crust. Invitations are for people they consider their peers. They simply order everyone else around.

Vivienne says, "Well, if you want to meet Dierdre Atchley you'll be there."

"Then I guess I'll be at your house for cocktails. Thanks for setting this up."

"You'll owe me, Cantor."

"Don't I always?"

After two cups of coffee and a bagel at Pete's, where Doris approves of my brown silk suit but not the new gash at the corner of my mouth, I get to my office a little after two o'clock to check in with Judson and pick up a .38 to replace the one Marv took from me and that's now and forever in the custody of the cops. No matter. I've got spares.

Judson's grinning like a Cheshire cat when I walk in. His smile fades a little, but just a little, when he notices the damage at the corner of my mouth.

"What's making you so happy?" I ask.

"You see the morning paper?"

"Not yet. Why?"

He hands me this morning's *Daily News*, open to the page he wants me to see and the story that made him smile. The headline reads, *GANGSTER TENZI NABBED FOR MURDER*. It's a swell story, all the better because there's no mention of my association with Tap's victim, identified as secretary Lorraine Quinn. Huber's given all the glory as the arresting officer in a *"middle of the night raid at a factory in the Bronx."* The story's accompanied by a photo of Tap Tenzi in handcuffs, scowling. I bet he's annoyed he didn't make the front page.

Judson says, "Looks like you're out from under the Quinn rap. But what's with that nasty wound?"

"A gift from Tenzi before he was arrested."

His eyes widening behind his wire-rims, Judson says, "You were there?"

"Uh-huh," is all I say as I walk into my private office and close the door.

I open the safe behind my desk, pull out a spare .38 Smith & Wesson, then dial Sig's number. The receiver's cradled under my chin as I load the chambers of my gun.

One of his flunkies answers.

"Tell Sig Cantor Gold wants to talk to him."

Sig soon comes on the line. "Good afternoon, Cantor," he says in that slow, too careful way that makes even a greeting sound like a death sentence. "What can I do for you?"

"You can thank me," I say.

"Is that so? Have you brought me Miss Garraway's killer? No, you have not. So why am I thanking you?"

"Because it turns out I led Lieutenant Huber to Tap Tenzi, where Huber heard me trick Tap into confessing to Quinn's murder. Now that Tap's in custody, and will soon be in Sing Sing prison, do you think he'll meet his demise in the electric chair, or should I place my bet on something sooner?"

I don't know if he's giving me that creepy silent laugh of his or if he's just giving me the silent treatment. All I hear is dead air through the phone. It makes the hair on my neck twitch until he finally says, "Now that the Quinn matter is resolved, you will have no impediments to taking care of the Garraway business. Lieutenant Huber has been sidelined, so you are free to proceed as you wish. Your methods are your own to decide, except they must result in bringing the guilty party to me. No more involvement by the police, no more loose ends. Do you understand, Cantor?"

He doesn't wait for an answer, just hangs up.

Sig may own a lot of politicians, courtrooms full of judges, whole police precincts, entire Mob outfits, even teenage street gangs, but he doesn't know beans about any of the people he owns. He doesn't see their souls, their contempt for the Law or their fear of it. He sees their failures but not their pride. He has no idea that Lieutenant Norm Huber will never just step aside, no matter how much brass comes down on him.

But I know. And I know that Huber hates me.

Maybe Sig knows that, too.

The Green Door Club has a different feel in the afternoon than it does at night. The crowd's smaller, older, less colorfully dressed, the drinking more relaxed. There's no band; no one's put money in the jukebox. No one's here to find the love of their life or just pick up a night's tumble. During the day, the Green Door Club is a snug spot to find friendly peace and quiet and just be.

Peg's pouring a beer at the bar for an older butch I've seen around now and then, who nods, says, "Hiya, Cantor."

I tip my cap, say, "Hello, Jo. How's retirement treating you?"

"Better than the factory ever did." There's enough dignity in her smile to make the Queen of England kneel, and enough pain to make even a Marine cry.

Peg pours me a shot of Chivas. Noticing the gash at the corner of my mouth, she gives me a "not again" *tsk*. I answer with a shrug, down the scotch, and head upstairs.

Alice throws an arm around my neck when I walk through the door, runs a finger tenderly along my wounded mouth, and then kisses me. Her tongue slides along the torn flesh as if trying to taste my blood. It's a kiss that eats you alive and makes you happy you're on the menu. It's not until she pulls away from the kiss that she says, "Hello," through a smile that's equal parts sweet and seductive. She's dressed in a black sheath with a square neckline that's coy, at least for Alice, with just enough tease to make me kiss her again.

It's my turn to kiss deep, to search and probe every corner of her mouth. I open my coat, wrap us both inside, pull Alice hard against me. Her every curve molds itself to me, sparking every nerve in my flesh, each one triggering in my imagination what I want to do with Alice Lamarr.

My need of her is so deep it scares me, sets off an alarm in my head warning of danger. I don't want to need anyone this much. Not again.

I pull away from the kiss, but gently. Through a smile meant to mask my jitters, I say, "Have you heard?"

She answers with a questioning tilt of her head.

"You haven't seen today's paper?" I ask.

"No, why?"

"Tap's been arrested for the murder of Lorraine Quinn. You're out of danger."

I guess after living in fear of Tenzi's violence for so long, Alice's smile is as nervous as it is happy. "They took him alive?"

"You were expecting a shootout? They only happen in the movies."

Her smile's brighter now, able to enjoy my joke. "I guess he'll get the chair?" she says, not bothering to hide her hope.

"He's got a reservation for a cell on Sing Sing's death row." I don't mention that Sig might remove Tap from this earth before the state does. I bet she wouldn't mind that either. "C'mon," I say, "let's get you back to your room at the Collier."

"And that nice big bed." Her smile is part kittenish, part alley cat, and all temptation.

"I can't stay," I say when we're back in her hotel room. "You might be out of danger but I'm not. There's someone I need to see who could help get me out from under."

"You'll come by later?" She slides her arms around my neck again.

"I'll try," I say, wondering if I mean it. I slip her arms from my neck and head for the door.

"Cantor," she calls after me. "Kiss me good-bye."

I give her a smile from the doorway, then escape before I can't.

The Parkhurst Trent mansion on the swanky Upper East Side, on a block between Fifth and Madison Avenues, is bigger than your common rowhouse but smaller than the New York Public Library. A Beaux Arts confection of European gewgaws, its door is the showstopper of the block. The big walnut slab is carved with tangled forest scenes painted deep red. When the sun hits it, the forest looks like it's burning. At night, in the shadowy light of curbside street lamps, the forest looks like it's bleeding. The door was designed for the house's first owner, Malachi Trent, Vivienne's Gilded Age great-grandfather, the bruiser who bullied his way into a maritime fortune and managed to marry the aristocratic Parkhurst copper heiress. According to Parkhurst Trent family lore, the old scoundrel wanted a house dignified enough to take its place among the mansions occupied by his more pedigreed neighbors but with something to announce the mighty Malachi's arrival into New York's upper tiers of power. The fearsome door was Malachi's billboard.

Inside, though, is another story, a calmer one. Vivienne's been redecorating the house, getting rid of the stuffy nineteenth-century furniture and the remnants of Malachi's safari hunt décor and replacing it with comfortable elegance.

Her butler, George, has been with the family since before Vivienne was born. He's served her faithfully ever after. This isn't the first time he's taken my coat and cap and led me through the house, keeping his disapproval of me tightly wrapped under his butler's stiff demeanor. But it's there in his eyes, his suspicion that I bring disrepute and danger to Miss Vivienne. The newest gash to my face probably isn't improving his assessment.

He's escorting me to the living room. Along the way, my shoes tap on the checkerboard marble floor in the mahogany-paneled hallway. Priceless European Renaissance paintings hang on the walls, masterpieces by bad boys Caravaggio, who was said to have murdered a Roman pimp, and Fra Filippo Lippi, who ran off with a nun. There's a jewel of a triptych of *The Annunciation* by Netherlandish master Jan van Eyck, and drawings by Leonardo. I supplied the Lippi and one of the Leonardos. Getting the Leonardo out of the London townhouse of a drunken British aristocrat was easy. Slipping the Lippi past the Vatican's robed princelings and the zealously vigilant Swiss Guards was an adventure.

Arriving at the living room, George opens the double doors and announces me to Vivienne and her guest, a woman who I'd guess is about fifty but whose money made sure those fifty years treated her kindly. Her tailored gray suit is expensive. Her light brown gray-flecked hair in an off-the-face style of tight waves, topped by a disc of a gray hat, frames a sculpted face that declares the patrician bloodline of its owner, a lineage even more lofty than Vivienne's. Both women, enjoying martinis, are seated on the slate green sofa, its black pillows fringed in gold. The sofa wears well in the handsome room of rich greens, browns and golds, complementing the pale skies and gentle waterways of the sixteenth-century Dutch landscape paintings gracing the walls.

Vivienne's guest looks me over as if making sure I am as advertised. Evidently the danger of my life was part of the advertising, since she doesn't flinch at the sight of my scarred and newly wounded mug. The woman's carefully lipsticked mouth, a shade of red less vibrant than Vivienne's, doesn't move a muscle.

Vivienne, however, flinches, but it's a flinch of exasperation with a dash of worry. That Vivienne would have even a speck of worry about me comes as a surprise. She recovers quickly, though, reverting to her natural state of cultured scholar and high society hostess. When she gets up from the sofa, graceful as a panther, the pleated skirt of her pale rose knit dress, belted at the waist, ripples and swirls as she walks across the room. I marvel again at how easily Vivienne carries the Parkhurst elegance and the Trent savagery in the same body.

"Cantor," she says, taking my arm and leading me across the living room, "you're right on time, five-thirty. Allow me to introduce Mrs. Dierdre Atchley."

Mrs. Dierdre Atchley does not get up, but offers her hand for a light shake. "How do you do," she says. Her mellow voice and articulation roll out in the leisurely rhythm developed through centuries of high-status breeding. "Vivienne tells me that you wish to ask me about Eve Garraway. I understand that you have, well, an interest in her death."

Before I can answer, Vivienne says, "Can I get you a martini, Cantor? Or do you prefer to stick with your usual scotch, neat." She's at the small bar behind the sofa.

"Scotch," I say, and sit down in the club chair across from Mrs. Atchley. "Do you mind if I smoke?"

"Not at all," she says. "In fact, I'll join you."

I take out my pack of Chesterfields, offer her one, but she says, "I have my own, thank you," and takes a silver cigarette case from the alligator bag beside her. She selects a cigarette, places it between her fingers, and looks at me.

I get the message. I pick up the heavy silver lighter from the coffee table between us, lean over and light Mrs. Atchley's cigarette.

All of this, I realize—including our inhales, exhales, and veils of smoke—is our way of sizing each other up. Mrs. Atchley wonders how deeply I want to probe; I wonder what she wants to hide.

Vivienne returns with my drink, then resumes her seat beside her guest.

Lifting my tumbler of scotch, I smile at both women, say, "Well, cheers."

"Indeed," Mrs. Atchley says. Her smile is as guarded as Fort Knox. I'll have to probe with precision if I hope to get at whatever it is she's guarding.

I start slow. "Mrs. Atchley, yes, I have an interest in Eve Garraway's death. Has Vivienne told you of the circumstances we found ourselves in when Eve's body was discovered by her butler?"

"She mentioned that the police officer, a Lieutenant Huber, was convinced you are the guilty party. I take it you disagree."

"Strongly," I say. "Which is why I need to know more about Eve, about the people she knew, maybe anyone she crossed, giving them a motive for her murder. Do you have any ideas along that line, Mrs. Atchley?"

She puts her martini down on the coffee table, takes a pull on her cigarette. After exhaling a long, slow stream of smoke, she says, "Cantor—may I call you Cantor? Miss Gold seems rather inappropriate."

"Cantor will do just fine. Now, what were you saying?"

She gives that a polite smile. "When Vivienne invited me for cocktails and to meet you, she explained who you are and she did indeed tell me about yesterday's tragedy at Eve Garraway's house. Now, I am a woman of considerable resources and influence, and I put those resources to work to look deeply into who you are and what you do. What I learned did not entirely surprise me. It's no secret—well, not a very well kept one—that museums and collectors often acquire their treasures through, shall we say, less than legal means. What surprised me, however, is the life you lead so openly. Frankly, I was, and am, impressed on your insistence on living as you please even at the risk to your freedom."

I'm being played. I'm being massaged and stroked by a woman who's accustomed to believing that a good word from her makes the recipient bow down.

But I can be a player, too. I guess her research on me didn't find that out. She's impressed with how I survive? She's about to learn. My probing knife is about to get a lot sharper. "Thank you, Mrs. Atchley. Kind of you to say so. I'm sure a woman in your unfortunate position can appreciate what it takes to survive in this sometimes cruel world."

"I beg your pardon?"

"Mrs. Atchley, the life I lead, the work that I do, and the associations they bring, provides me, too, with access to information. Information on you and your husband, for instance." At the corner of my eye I catch Vivienne looking anxiously at me. She needn't worry. I'd never rat her out. I keep my attention on Dierdre Atchley. "I understand that Eve Garraway hated your husband for choosing you over her as a suitable wife. She was getting her revenge by moving to acquire enough stock to have your husband kicked out of his own banking institution. If she'd succeeded, I bet the humiliation would have been—"

"Cantor!" It's Vivienne. "I didn't invite you here to insult—"

"It's all right, Vivienne," Mrs. Atchley cuts in, cool as a crisp day. "Cantor is no doubt trying to ascertain if either I or my husband have a motive for murder. Well, of course we do. While we would not have been completely ruined financially had Miss Garraway succeeded with her stock scheme, you are correct, Cantor, that the humiliation would have been difficult to overcome socially. The loss of my husband's financial influence would have reduced our position in important circles, leaving us at the mercy of powerful financial or political interests who may harbor ill will toward my family. Certain doors would have been closed to us. My son's future would have been severely constricted."

Yeah. A lower-tier bride and second-string yachting races.

How would he ever withstand the hardship. "Well then, Mrs. Atchley, did you kill Eve Garraway?"

"I did not."

"Did your husband?"

"He could not have. He's been away in Geneva on banking business for the last month. He's not due back until late tomorrow night."

"What about your son?"

"Of course not. James is a sweet and respectable boy."

James, if I remember correctly from the newspapers, is in his early thirties, well past the age of being considered a boy.

It's the first crack in Mrs. Atchley's polished armor. But that doesn't make her a murderer, and it doesn't make her son a murderer. But it could.

Mrs. Atchley regains her composure by lazily stubbing out her cigarette in the ashtray on the coffee table. "Is there anything else you wish to ask?"

"I'd like to know more about Eve's situation," I say. "I understand that she was not especially welcome in your circles, but that you and the other wives put up with her because her political connections were important to your husbands. Am I right?"

"You are unfortunately correct, yes."

"Does anyone among your crowd harbor something more than simple dislike of Eve?"

"You mean someone with malign intent, and someone besides me?" I have to hand it to her; she actually laughs a little when she says it, enjoying her sarcasm at her own expense.

"Yeah, that's what I mean. Anyone come to mind?"

"You want me to talk out of school about my dearest friends, men and women I've known all my life. That's not particularly honorable of you, Cantor Gold. You want me to be what I understand the people in your world call a rat."

"Let's put it this way, Mrs. Atchley. You and I now have something in common. Lieutenant Huber thinks I'm guilty of murder. And I think you, or your son, make just as good candidates. So if all of us wish to escape frying for something we

113

may not have done, I suggest you get rid of your prissy ideas of honor and come across."

I never knew I was such a comedian, but Mrs. Atchley is laughing again. "Oh my, you can have all the suspects you want! All you have to do is open the *Social Register*. There isn't a New York family in that book who's shedding a tear over the social-climbing viper who was Eve Garraway. Even her little *soirées,* as she liked to call them, were tasteless. Absurd evenings of gaudy food and self-serving entertainment. But as you say, we put up with her and attended her soirées in order to protect our husbands' interests."

"*Your* husband's interest and reputation in particular," I say.

She gives that a chilly, "Yes. Now, if you'll excuse me, I must be going," she says, getting up and putting on a pair of gray kid gloves. "The French ambassador and his wife are coming for dinner, and I have preparations to attend to. Thank you for the martini, Vivienne. And thank you, Cantor, for such fascinating conversation."

Accompanied by Vivienne, Mrs. Dierdre Atchley crosses the room with a firm step but a brittle confidence. I guess I got to her. Time to shake her a little more. Maybe something will tumble out. "I figure you didn't kill Eve, Mrs. Atchley. Looking at you, I'd say you're in damn good shape, but frankly I don't see you stealthily entering Eve's house unnoticed and stabbing her in the back. But I wouldn't put it past you or your husband to hire an assassin. New York has plenty of them, and they're not listed in your *Social Register*. Or maybe they are."

"Good day to you, Cantor Gold."

"Mrs. Atchley."

Once Dierdre Atchley is out the door and in George's practiced care, Vivienne turns and looks at me as if she wants to say something but isn't quite sure what it is. All she can manage is, "Well," which comes out through pursed lips, unfolds into an unexpected and slowly expanding smile, and finally lands in a laugh. "Let's have another drink, shall we?"

At the bar, Vivienne refreshes my scotch and pours herself a martini. After a sip, which she enjoys with gusto, she says, "I think Dierdre's gifts to the museum just doubled."

"No doubt. And so will her donations to the Police Department's widows and orphans collection plate and any number of city and state pols' reelection coffers. Respectability and protection don't come cheap." I don't mention that there's one guy Mrs. Atchley can't buy off, and that he won't give a damn about her money or status if Dierdre Atchley, her husband, or her son turn out to be responsible for Eve Garraway's murder. Sig will dispose of the Garraway problem by disposing of the Atchleys, and the cops and pols he owns won't notice, or pretend not to. City Hall will be silently grateful. The *Social Register* crowd will simply rearrange the seating at the next ball to cover the absence of the no longer available Atchleys.

I don't mention Sig's plan because it might be too much for Vivienne to stomach. I don't know that I can stomach it, either. But if it comes down to Huber making me a gift to the electric chair or Sig exacting his own ruthless justice, I'll make my peace with whatever Sig has in mind. I'd rather stay alive with a knotted stomach than have my stomach and the rest of me burn to death.

Vivienne sits down on the sofa, sipping her martini. "Do you think she did it? Do you really think Dierdre had Eve Garraway killed?"

"She certainly has reason. But it sounds like so do a lot of other people in her crowd. Maybe I should buy a copy of the *Social Register*."

"Don't bother; I'll lend you mine. Drop by my office. I keep it there as a source to tap for museum donations."

"I assume you're in it?"

Laughing, she says, "I am. So according to Dierdre, I might be a suspect in the murder of Eve Garraway, too."

"I won't mention it to Lieutenant Huber," I joke. "What can you tell me about James Atchley? He strike you as the murdering type?"

"Well, he's certainly arrogant enough," Vivienne says with a thoughtful shrug. "But does he have the spine? Good question.

He came along with an upstate hunting group I was part of last season. He managed to bag a deer, but when it came to dressing it"—meaning skinning and gutting it—"he went green as a houseplant. So, knifing Eve at close quarters? I don't know."

"You'd be surprised at what people can do if they're angry enough or scared enough or hate someone enough."

Just yesterday, I saw Vivienne look at me as if I scare her. Over the years, I've also seen her look at me as if I make her sad. Right now both are in her eyes, a combination I've never seen in her before. The confident, brilliant, sometimes haughty Vivienne I've known seems lost somewhere inside herself, in a place maybe she didn't even know she has. "I guess you'd know about all that, what people filled with hate can do," she says slowly, as if trying to understand her own words. "Sometimes I forget everything you have to face, everything the world throws at you."

"I can take care of myself," I say.

"Yes, you can. But for how much longer, Cantor? How much more damage can your face and body take?"

It's a question I try not to think about. I do what I have to do to survive. I can't worry about the damage. "Thanks for the drinks," I say, "and for setting me up with Mrs. Atchley. I'd better get going. Bye, Vivienne."

I'm at the living room door when Vivienne calls out, "Cantor? Was it helpful? Talking to Dierdre, was it helpful?"

"Yeah," I say, over my shoulder, "it was. Thanks again, Vivienne."

"Cantor?" she calls again when I'm in the doorway.

I turn around, see Vivienne standing at the sofa.

She has that troubled, frightened look again, but it dissolves into the sweet smile I haven't seen on Vivienne in a long while, not since our night of carnal knowledge four years ago. Whatever's behind it, it's suddenly giving her the fidgets, and her smile changes again into the slightly imperious one I'm more familiar with. "Oh, nothing," she says, taking a sip of the martini. "Just be careful out there."

Chapter Twelve

I used to enjoy driving in New York. I still do, I guess, but not as much. Since the end of the Second World War back in '45, the city, in fact the whole country, freed from the two knockout blows of the Depression and the war, has gone on a buying binge: television sets, washing machines, kitchen appliances to turn every meal into a quick and easy banquet, and a lot of cars. Out in the suburbs, even in the city's boroughs, every new house comes equipped with a two-car garage, and every ex-GI and his wife have the latest sedan for him and station wagon for her. They add to the clog in New York's streets every time they drive into town. Today's crunch slows me down on my way to check in with Red Drogan, to see if he can fill me in about James Atchley's activities on the water. But the evening is young, the city's trees are silhouetted against a purple-gray sky, and people are going about their business. New York's rhythm keeps going, even if the rhythm of traffic is more syncopated than flowing these days.

There's nothing to do except wait my turn to inch up to the traffic light at the corner of Thirtieth and Lexington. I use the time to think. I think about Dierdre Atchley trying to snow me, think about how deep the vengeance against Eve Garraway might be lodged in the Atchley family's snooty little hearts. And I think about Vivienne and *her* snooty heart, though her heart

117

also has a more plebeian side that keeps her connected to the rest of humanity. I'm thinking about all these things, rolling my Buick slowly toward the traffic light, halfheartedly listening to a news program on the dashboard radio, when a news story almost causes me to crash the car: *"Former showgirl Alice Lamarr was found dead in her room at the Collier Hotel at 6:05 this evening, just under an hour ago. The cause of death, according to the authorities, is an apparent suicide. A gun was found lying by Miss Lamarr's hand, the small caliber matching the shot to her temple. It is believed Miss Lamarr was distraught over the arrest of her husband, gangster Johnny Tenzi. The body was found by a room service waiter delivering Miss Lamarr's dinner."*

I dodge traffic to pull over to the curb, setting off honking horns by angry drivers, the glare from their cars' headlights crisscrossing into the Buick as I lurch across Lexington Avenue.

The only thing stopping me from screaming with rage is the numbness taking over my whole body. My mind, though, is wild, a tangle of thoughts like snakes hissing in my head. But one thought comes through clear as a clanging bell: Alice asked me to kiss her good-bye, and I didn't.

I didn't kiss her, but I saw the look on her face. It was sexy, the best kind of sexy, the kind that has love in it, and hope, and desire, and the promise to show me every shape and shadow of that desire. The kiss Alice asked for wasn't meant as a toodle-oo from this Earth. It was a toodle-oo until later. Alice was counting on there being a later with me, maybe a lot of laters. People don't do themselves in when they've got plans for later. And they don't order a room service dinner and do themselves in before it gets there.

The hissing thoughts start to loosen and untangle. What was that the news guy said? That Alice was distraught over Tap Tenzi's arrest? Who is he kidding? Alice was no more distraught over her soon-to-be ex-husband's arrest than I'd be over the death of a bug under my shoe. She was tickled pink that Tenzi was out of her life, and she'd shed no tears when he'd fry in the electric chair.

The suicide story's a plant, spoon fed to the press by someone

118

with the power to make them swallow it. Someone like police brass who don't want to muddy up the Tenzi case, or someone who doesn't like loose ends. Someone like Sig Loreale.

Alice Lamarr was murdered.

I get out of the Buick, head for the phone booth at the corner, its blue-and-white enamel Bell Tel sign flickering in the blinking neon light of a nearby liquor store. Inside the booth, I flip through the pages of the phone book, hoping the party I'm looking for has a home listing. He does.

I drop a dime in the slot, get the guy on the line. "Otis? It's Cantor Gold. Have you heard the news about Alice?"

"No. I'm in the middle of dinner. What about Alice?"

"She's dead. They're trying to pass it off as a suicide, but that story's not worth the dime it cost me to make this phone call. Someone's cleaning up loose ends on the Quinn and Tenzi cases. If I were you—"

"I'll pack a bag." He hangs up.

I'm tempted to call Huber, tell him to put a protective detail around Tap Tenzi's cell in the city lockup. But if Huber turns out to be smarter than I've ever given him credit for, he's already taken care of it, because Alice's suicide story has likely been rammed down his throat.

I make another call instead, this time to Judson's apartment. It takes him several rings to answer, and when he finally does, his "Hello," is thick, though it's too early for sleep. It's not too early, though, for a different bedtime activity.

"Give my apologies to the lovely lass beside you, Judson, but I need you to look into something. Alice Lamarr is dead. You'll see a phony story in the paper or hear it on the news broadcasts about it being a suicide. It's baloney."

"You want me to look into possible killers?"

"No. I want you to find out if anyone's made any funeral arrangements, maybe arranged by her family back in Nebraska, if she still has anybody there. If no one's claimed the body or no funeral's been planned yet, make the arrangements. Get her a nice coffin. It's on me."

119

I get back into the Buick after the call, just sit for a while, get a handle on my rage, calm it down so my thoughts won't tangle up again. Every bone in my body wants to drive over to Sig's and have it out with him. I want to throw it in his face that I know he had Alice killed.

But that little daydream gets me nowhere except as dead as Alice. Either Mike Mulroney or one of Sig's other thugs will put a bullet in me before I even make it across the lobby, or Sig will do it himself if I manage to get to his penthouse. I wouldn't get any justice for Alice Lamarr.

There will never be any justice for Alice Lamarr.

I start the Buick, pull away from the curb. There's still the matter of justice for Eve Garraway.

Pauline, the barmaid at Oyster Charlie's, told me that Red Drogan's gone to his berth in Brooklyn for the night, which is why I'm back in the Buick, headed across the Brooklyn Bridge. This gorgeous Gothic stretch of steel and stone has tough memories for me. It's where Mom Sheinbaum's daughter Opal, Sig's fiancée, met her death, tossed off the bridge by a jealous hoodlum. It was the night Sig had Rosie kidnapped, her life threatened, his way of forcing me to find Opal's killer. And now he's doing it again. Through his threats and his power, he's forcing me to find the killer of Eve Garraway. Last time, his stake was personal. Now it's just dirty business.

Red's berth isn't the usual waterfront tie-up, with rows of tugs and barges lining the piers. Red likes his privacy, and I like it that Red likes his privacy. It's conducive to our racket.

He berths his tug at the wilder edge of Brooklyn. This clump of the borough is so desolate even rats would find available prey slim pickings, and so marshy a less skillful tug pilot would get his rudder tangled up in this boggy inlet of tall reeds and swampy grasses. But Red Drogan's not just any tugman. He can slip his boat through a chain link fence if he has to and never scratch the sides.

I park the Buick well back from the bog's edge, find the planks Red's laid among the mud and grasses as a path to his berth.

He's sitting on a barrel on the deck of his tug, enjoying a bottle of bourbon by the light of a lantern. He gets up when he sees me, says, "I'll get yer bottle," and disappears into the cabin.

He's out a minute later with the bottle of Chivas I keep on his boat for my visits.

I prop myself onto a barrel facing Red, take a swig of the Chivas. I need it after the soul-crushing news about Alice.

Red says, "Y'look like someone just ran over yer dog, only I know y'ain't got no dog, so what's wrong?" In the light of the lantern, the lines in Red's face carve deeper, his stubble is grittier, his salt and pepper hair craggy as stone. But his eyes betray him. Behind the toughness is an honorable soul, trusted by all the salts up and down the waterfront.

"Another woman's been murdered," I say, "and there's nothing I can do about it. I can't get justice for her."

"This woman, y'cared fer her?"

Another swig of whiskey helps me say, "As much as I could."

Red gives that a nod but no more. He knows not to probe too far into the state of my heart, and he knows why. He just takes a draw on his bottle of whiskey, wipes his mouth with his hand, the calluses scratching across his stubble. "What brings you around?" he says.

"You know anything about a yachtsman named James Atchley? I know you harbor guys keep an eye on the pleasure boat crowd, don't let them tie up the waterways."

Red gives that a hard *tsk* of disgust that twists the lines of his face. "Some of them guys think they own every drop of water around all five boroughs of New York. But a lot of the yacht fellas are good sailors, though, so as a waterman I gotta respect that."

"Is Atchley a good sailor?"

"Damn good, I hear. Really knows how to work the wind and the water."

"What kind of a guy is he? Ever met him?"

"Nah, never met him, only seen him around the water, but I heard stuff. They say he don't like to lose."

"Nobody likes to lose, Red," I say with a laugh, toast it with a draw on the Chivas.

"Sure, but some people won't let a winner win, if you catch my meanin'."

"You mean they'll poison the victory somehow."

"Yup, that's what I mean. I hear yer boy Atchley is one of those."

"Ever hear of him getting violent?"

Another pull of bourbon and a scratch of his cheek helps Red think that over. "Never pulled a weapon on anyone as far as I know, but they say he gave a guy a good punch over somethin' that happened durin' a race. Never did get the whole story, but the guy wound up with a broken nose. Look, if you want, I can run y'over to Atchley's slip. Maybe y'can catch him, talk to him y'self." He volunteers this without asking what my business is with James Atchley. I'd tell him if he asked, but he won't. He never does. After our years together working the smuggling racket, he figures I'll tell him what he needs to know. Anything else is my business.

I say, "Yeah, I hear Atchley lives on his yacht."

"He's a real sea dog, or so they say."

"Start your engine, Red."

The stars in the night sky shouldn't even bother to compete with the lights of New York for sheer wattage. Seen from the harbor, the city's skyscrapers blaze with millions of diamond eyes, greeting arriving travelers with the lure of everything money can buy and greeting immigrants with the hope of dreams come true. The streets might not be paved with gold, but those dreams are, and they're all here, rising as high and bright as your imagination, your will, and your guts can take you.

For some people, though, the riches of New York come without the need of courage to compete for them but a simple birth certificate to claim them. James Westerton Atchley is twice over the recipient of New York's trove of diamonds and golden dreams: by Westerton birth and Atchley marriage. His boat, the *Ambrosia*, is a sleek two-masted schooner that stretches about sixty feet from stem to stern. She's docked at the mouth of the Seventy-Ninth Street Boat Basin on the Hudson, her sails furled and tied to her masts in port. The boat basin's got a great view of the fashionable apartment buildings on Riverside Drive on one side and across the river to the Jersey shoreline on the other.

Light glows in the *Ambrosia*'s shaded cabin windows, so I guess the master of the seas is home. Red pulls the tug alongside.

I know better than to break the code of the waterways and board the vessel without permission, so I tell Red to nudge the *Ambrosia* to get Atchley's attention while I call out, "James Atchley, you have company!"

A shadow moves across a window shade. Its owner emerges onto the deck a moment later. In the glow of Drogan's mast light I can see that even in his heavy wool jacket the guy's as sleek as his boat: trim in the waist, broad at the shoulders, blond as a Viking prince. His cheekbones are so chiseled and his jaw so square he could pass for a marble statue in the park. "Who wants me?" he calls across to the tug.

"Cantor Gold. I had cocktails with your mother this afternoon. I'd like to talk to you, get your side of things. Permission to board?"

"Permission denied. Neither my mother nor I have anything more to say to you. Shove off." He turns to go back inside the cabin, his crepe-soled shoes squeaking on the teak deck.

"Have it your way, Atchley. I got what I came for."

He laughs at that, a tight-jawed condescending cackle, but he doesn't go into the cabin. "Don't try the bluff with me, Gold. I play for very high stakes every day."

"I bet you do. Maybe life and death stakes, too. You look like you could handle it. You're young and strong. You've got a sportsman's build. You've got the strength to overpower someone, and the agility to sneak into their house quietly. The only question is, do you have a killer instinct."

"If I ever see you in a dark alley some night, Gold, maybe you'll find out. Now shove off." He turns to go back into the cabin.

I say, "The talk around the waterfront says you have the killer instinct when you race this boat. And you don't like to lose. Eve Garraway was setting your family up to lose." He turns around again. "Yeah, lose big," I say. "Getting rid of her would mean you'd win the game she was playing. That's more your style, isn't it? Winning? And by the way, where were you yesterday morning?"

He walks to the edge of the boat. The mast light of Red's tug pins his face, reveals his sneer. A braggart's sneer. "If I were you, Gold, I'd leave off that line. My mother told me all about you, about your shady dealings. You and your gangster pals think power comes through the barrel of a gun. You don't know what real power is, the kind that can ruin you, clean out your bank account, run you out of town, even get you sent to prison. I don't need to do violence to win, Gold." He turns to go back to the cabin again.

"Maybe you don't need it, but you could do it. Or maybe you could hire it."

He stops at the cabin door but doesn't answer me, just stands there, his hand on the doorknob. A moment later, he walks inside, slamming the door behind him.

Red says, "Watch y'self with that one, Cantor. Snooty young bucks like him are just slick enough to be trouble."

It's nearly nine-thirty when I'm back at my Buick at Red's berth in Brooklyn. A half hour later I'm across the bridge again and back in Manhattan. It rises in all its glittering splendor, the bright lights a veil obscuring the shadows where dirty deeds are done, where people like Sig Loreale get away with murder and people like the Atchleys get away with everything else, maybe murder, too.

The Atchleys, mother and son, have given me a headache, and the murder of Alice Lamarr hurts my soul. I could use a drink and a little soothing.

Chapter Thirteen

The Green Door Club combo's rendition of "Be My Love" isn't the popular Mario Lanza throat strainer but more in the mood of a candlelight seduction. Couples on the dance floor sway all over each other as I walk to the bar.

Peg pours me a double Chivas before I'm even on a bar stool. "I heard about Alice on the radio," she says when I'm seated. "News report said suicide."

"You believe that crap?"

"About as much as I'd believe a peach tree back home could walk right down to Mr. Sam's fruit stand and shake its peaches into the bin. You got anyone in mind who's good for it?"

"You don't want to know, Peg."

"Afraid you'll have to protect me?" she says through a light laugh.

"Afraid you'll try to protect *me*," I say, through my own chuckle.

Peg pours herself a short bourbon. She takes a sip, then says, "I've been reading about a bunch of our kind of folks who think it's time to protect each other."

"You mean in that magazine you gave Rosie?"

"Uh-huh. Articles in there say it's time to get organized. You know, fight back against the Law and the raids."

"When the war starts, let me know," I say, and finish off my scotch. "Just don't make me wear a uniform."

"The war's already on, Cantor."

"Well, let's postpone it for tonight. I've been fighting for my life all day, and what I need tonight is a furlough. The kind that comes with whiskey and soft shoulders." I put another buck on the bar and motion for Peg to refill my glass while I look around the room. Couples talk and kiss at tables, or sway and kiss on the dance floor where suits and ties press close to dresses and what's inside them.

But the unattached, the uncoupled, are at the bar. Some, lost in loneliness, look only at their drinks, others size up who's who. A pretty brunette in a pale green dress she fills to the brim gives me a smile. I smile back, get off the bar stool, take my glass of scotch with me.

"Hello, what's your name?" I say to the pretty brunette.

"Marjorie," she says in a voice surprisingly flat for such a curvy body and sparkling blue eyes. But I'm not interested in her voice.

"Well, Marjorie, would you like to dance?"

She's agreeable, so I take her arm lightly, lead her to the dance floor. The combo's switched from "Be My Love" to "Tenderly," a swoony number that Rosemary Clooney recorded in a silky rendition.

We start dancing. Marjorie's body fits nicely along mine. A good start to that furlough I mentioned.

We dance, we sway. I start to drift from the ugliness of the day, drift away from guilt over not giving Alice that good-bye kiss, guilt over not protecting her, guilt over giving Lorraine the brush-off. I drift away from seeing a knife in Eve Garraway's back, drift away from Sig's threats and the Atchleys' arrogance. I just drift in Marjorie's arms. Let my body do my thinking, give my mind a rest.

"You must lead quite a life," Marjorie whispers in my ear. "I mean, those scars, and that cut at the corner of your mouth."

Her whisper might as well be a bugle call, waking me from my dreamy drifting, calling me back to my battlefield life.

I stop dancing. "I'm sure you're swell, Marjorie, but yeah, these scars on my face are the story of my life, and right now my life is calling."

"So you're telling me you're leaving?"

"Sorry, yeah."

She shrugs like it doesn't matter, or maybe I don't matter, and walks off the dance floor.

Just as well. The band's taking a break, replaced by a jukebox tune, a rock and roll number with a booming beat and lyrics that sound like the guy's gagging on every word.

The phone's ringing when I walk into my apartment. I pick up the receiver, barely get through "Hello" before I hear Mom Sheinbaum's, "So I've been calling and calling. What, you've been out carousing when a person should be home in bed at this hour? Such a life you lead."

"It has its charms. What's on your mind, Mom?"

"You asked me to noodle around about the Garraway dame's goods. Well, I noodled. And I found out something maybe you should know."

"I'm listening."

"Good. It seems an outta town auction house has been talking to Garraway's lawyers about what happens to her collection now that she's dead. The lawyers said they can't discuss what's in Garraway's will, but they told that shifty butler, Desmond Mallory, to hang around in the house in the meantime. Y'know, like a caretaker."

"Makes sense," I say. "The Garraway collection can't be settled until Eve's murder case is resolved. The stuff could be part of the evidentiary material."

"Sure, okay," Mom says, "but that's not what's interesting. That auction house, it's a Chicago outfit, Sterling Auctions."

"I know them. Very high line."

"Good for them. But it's the money behind them that's the story, Cantor."

My first thought is the Mob. My second thought is some powerful players like the Chicago equivalent of the Atchleys. But before I get those ideas out of my mouth, Mom is already supplying the answer: "It's mister big shot Loreale's money. Yeah, that's right, Sig's the biggest shareholder. Practically owns the place. Cleans up his dirty cash as good as one of those newfangled modern washing machines."

I should be stunned, but I'm not. I should be hopped up on anger at Sig manipulating me, but I'm not. Instead, a small chuckle sneaks out of me. It rolls into a rumbling deep-in-the-gut laugh, a laugh of choking grief over Alice's murder, a laugh of cynical amusement over Sig's sleight of hand.

"Cantor?" Mom says. "This is funny? The guy's running you around and you think it's funny?"

"Funny as a funeral," I say, my laugh twisting down into a tight chuckle. "Thanks for noodling around."

I hang up, pour myself a short Chivas, have an enjoyable if useless daydream of making a midnight run to Sig's place where I wake him up and slap him silly. I tell him I know his game to make me do his dirty work by hunting down Eve's killer while Sterling Auctions gets the Garraway collection on consignment, no questions asked, auctions it off piece by piece, and Sig pockets a fortune.

But it's only a daydream. I just enjoy the scotch instead, and then another, and then I take Mom's advice and go to bed.

I turn off the bedside light. I'm laughing again, choking on it.

I'm on my way out to Pete's Luncheonette for breakfast and Doris's good coffee when Lieutenant Huber shows up at my door. He walks in uninvited, just pushes right past me into my living room.

I say, "Well good morning to you, too, lieutenant. Come to arrest me for anything in particular today?"

His hands are stuffed in the pockets of his brown tweed coat, which flaps like loose tree bark when he turns around to face me, his fedora low on his brow, throwing a shadow across his hooded eyes. He doesn't look happy. Then again, he's never happy to see me. But he looks even unhappier on this Thursday morning, and it's only eight o'clock. If his mood grows any more sour as the day moves along, by noon the guy might be downright homicidal.

He says, "Alice Lamarr didn't kill herself." His gravelly croak through his bad mood is tough to take before I've had my coffee.

I say, "And I didn't kill Eve Garraway. Now that we've gotten those weights off our chests, we can move on to exactly what you're doing here, lieutenant."

He doesn't say anything, just looks at me, purses his thin lips, looks away, then looks back at me. Whatever's on his mind, he came here to dump it in my lap but he's not quite sure how to do it. He says, "I don't like you, Gold," to break the ice, I guess.

"Tell me something I don't know."

His *tsk* pretty much spits annoyance. "It's back talk like that that's part of the reason. And the way you live your life is disgusting, even if you weren't a thief and a smuggler. You know, I could arrest you just for wearing that snazzy blue suit. There's an ordinance against dressing like you do, peacocking around in the wrong clothes. Your whole life is criminal—"

"Okay, lieutenant, you can cut the litany of my transgressions and just tell me why the hell you're here. And by the way, you look like you could use a drink, or a good night's sleep."

"What I need," he says, adjusting his hat as if his head itches, "is for you to leave my precinct. Better yet, leave town. Take your sick life and criminal racket somewhere else. But I guess I won't live to see that wish come true."

"I love you, too, lieutenant." My delivery's flat and dull as card-board. "But that doesn't mean I want you in my house, especially at eight in the morning, and before I've had my breakfast. So what the hell are you doing here?"

"Very cute, Gold," he says through an acid grin. "Look, the Lamarr case is all locked up. Nothing I can do about it." He almost gags on every word. "You and I both know she didn't kill herself, but the brass is sticking to that line. You were, uh, close to Lamarr," he says in a way that makes me want to scrub his filthy tongue with a wad of steel wool, "so maybe you have an idea about why her case is slammed shut with that suicide line?" He looks at me like he's using his eyes to drag an answer from of my throat.

But it's not worth my life to bring Sig's name into it, at least not yet. There's still the Garraway business with Sig, which just added another tangle after last night's phone call from Mom. So my only answer to Huber is to shake my head.

Huber's pinched face doesn't wear a smile well, and the smile he gives me now through his tobacco-yellow teeth makes me glad I haven't eaten breakfast yet. "You're lying, Gold," he says. "You know more than you're telling, but I'm gonna leave that alone. We've got bigger fish to fry."

"We, lieutenant?"

He's got that near-gagging look on his face again. "Y'know, Gold, even though I don't like you, and it's a sure bet you're not too crazy about me, I gotta admit there's one thing we have in common. We don't like being pushed around."

The idea of having something in common with a cop, especially this cop, is about as comforting as having pins shoved under my fingernails. But I can't argue with Huber's point. I don't like getting pushed around, and it doesn't surprise me that an up-from-the-ranks cop like Norm Huber doesn't like it either.

He says, "Maybe we can help each other out."

I give that a grin that has more doubt in it than humor. "Well, that's a new one," I say. "I never thought you'd wave an olive branch in my face."

"I'm not any happier about it than you are, Gold. If I had my way, I'd lock you up for the Garraway murder just to get a wrong-dressing deviant like you off the street."

"That's more like it, that's the cop I know. You'd send me to the electric chair just because you don't like my tailoring."

"Cut the smart mouth, Gold. I can still run you in."

"But that wouldn't help you with whatever it is you came here for. Listen, lieutenant, stop dancing. Somebody's pushing you around," I say, keeping what I know about it to myself, "and you don't like it. Well, I don't blame you. But you said we could help

131

each other. How about you fork over and tell me what the hell you're talking about."

His face takes on the tight look of a guy searching for a last chance to change his mind. Finally, he says, "I don't like having two unsolved murders."

"Lamarr and—"

"Garraway. And you were right about there being no fingerprints on the knife. Whoever killed her wiped that fancy handle clean, or maybe wore gloves."

"So you've dropped the idea that I'm her killer?"

He gives that a sideways smile. "Let's just say I could be convinced. Oh, I still think you could be good for it, but other possibilities have, um, cropped up."

"Such as?"

"Such as it seems Garraway had a nasty past, a hushed-up killing of her college roommate. Funny thing, some interesting dirt landed on my desk. Dirt about Eve Garraway, Lorraine Quinn, and Alice Lamarr. You wouldn't have any idea how it got there, would you?" If his eyes probed me any deeper, they'd come out the other side and burrow into my living room wall.

"I guess someone did some good police work," I say with a not-so-innocent shrug.

"Uh-huh. Yeah, well, if Garraway had one skeleton in her expensive closet, maybe there's others. Maybe there's a skeleton some people don't want dragged out of that closet."

"Powerful people who could squeeze the police brass, who then push you around?"

He doesn't like the sound of that, even makes him wince. It's the first time in the years I've known him that his wince isn't directed at me. This time it's directed at whatever anonymous powers are pushing him around.

If he only knew.

He says, "I've had the Lamarr business shoved down my throat, and now the Garraway business is getting shoved under the rug. Strings are being pulled, Gold, strings I can't see, but maybe you can. It's too late about Lamarr, but maybe not about Garraway. Somebody, or maybe a lot of somebodies, wants the case to just disappear. That annoys my cop's soul."

I want to say *I didn't know you had a soul,* but insulting the guy could bring what's turning out to be an interesting conversation to an end. So I say instead, "What's my part in all this, Huber?"

"Could be all that art in her collection is at the center of this. That's where you come in. You have connections in that world. You can nose around there, see if anyone wanted her out of the way to get to her stuff."

"C'mon, lieutenant," I say as if he tried to kid me and failed, "you know it's not as simple as that. If someone killed for it, they'd have to move vast amounts of art and artifacts from Eve's vault and move it through her house on the sly, which would be a helluva job. And everyone in the art game would hear about the heist, know the stuff was stolen, so it would be hotter than a five-alarm fire. Without a prearranged buyer, the thief or thieves couldn't unload any of it. But like I said, you already know that."

"Sure, I know it, but I also know that not every thief is as slick as you, unless you're telling me it can't be done."

"Sure, it can be done. Anything can be done, as long as you make smarter arrangements."

"Okay, then use your connections to find out if someone is either stupid, or made those smarter arrangements."

I give him a thoughtful, "Uh-huh," with more than a dose of distrust under it. "Okay, suppose I take you up on it and snoop around. That's only half of our Devil's bargain, lieutenant. You said you could help me out. What's your end?"

"I could get you off the hook for Garraway's murder."

"I'm already off the hook," I say.

"For the moment."

That's the problem with making a deal with cops. You can't trust deals with people who have the power to take your freedom.

I feel my smile harden and my eyes narrow. But I force a more accepting expression. It may be a Devil's bargain, but having

133

Huber's gun and badge in my corner is better than no bargain at all, and Sig won't know a damn thing about it.

Meanwhile, I need to know just how much Huber knows. I need to hear anything he has on the Garraway killing. "How deep have you dug into Eve Garraway's life?" I ask. "Maybe figured any enemies besides the crowd involved in the college roommate cover-up?"

"The daughter of Boss Garraway is bound to have enemies," he says as if that's an old story. "I'd be working that list all the way to my retirement. You have something to narrow the list?"

"Could be. You know the Atchleys?"

"The banking family?"

"The same. Word has it they had a beef with Eve Garraway."

Huber lifts his chin, tilts his head back, his hooded eyes under the brim of his fedora narrowing to penetrating slits. "What kind of beef, and where'd you hear about it?"

"Let's just say I heard it around." There's no way I'm selling Vivienne out, not in this lifetime or any lifetime I might stumble into. "And the beef involves that favorite quartet for murder: money, power, jealousy, and revenge. Y'know, hell hath no fury like . . . well, you know the rest."

"You telling me Eve had a fling with the Atchley boy?"

"Wrong Atchley."

It would surprise me if Huber looked surprised, but he doesn't, because cops, like outlaws, have seen a lot and heard almost everything.

"By the way," I say, "I had a chat with James Atchley last night. He docks his yacht at Seventy-Ninth Street. He's pretty protective of the Atchley name and interests, and the guy's got a temper to boot."

"I'll look into it," Huber says, and moves to the door. "And I'll have a look at the college roommate angle, too. The dead girl was the Garraway butler's daughter, right? Maybe his grudge caught up with him."

"I'll work the Garraway collection, get a line on any players," I say to his back as he opens the door. And I'll take my time figuring whether to lead Huber to Sig's interest in the Garraway killer. I wouldn't mind if either Huber or Sig devoured the other, and I don't care which one. That would be one less son of a bitch with his claws in my hide.

Chapter Fourteen

Vivienne's butler George takes my coat and cap and leads me to the dining room. Vivienne is reading *The New York Times* while having breakfast at a polished walnut dining table where the crowned heads of Europe wouldn't be embarrassed to dine, which pretty much describes the ambience of the whole room. Vivienne's peach silk blouse and slender dark green skirt contrast nicely with the dining room's pale blue walls and dark blue drapes held open with gold cord. Light from the tall windows bathes the whole place in a soft, golden sunlight that comes with the moneyed neighborhood's real estate.

"Good morning, Cantor. What brings you around today?" she asks, then adds, "George, please bring a cup and saucer for Cantor. And some eggs and toast?" She's looking at me.

"Scrambled is fine, thanks," I say and take a seat near Vivienne at the table.

She says, "So, Cantor, any news?" She takes a sip of coffee, looking at me over the rim of her cup, a late eighteenth-century beauty of white porcelain with dark blue bands and gold trim. It goes well with the room and Vivienne's green eyes. But everything goes well with Vivienne's eyes.

"What do you know about Sterling Auctions?" I ask.

"The Chicago firm?"

"That's the one. Any chatter among your museum set about Sterling competing for the Garraway collection?"

"I haven't heard, but it wouldn't surprise me. They handle top of the line items, so the Garraway hoard would find interest among their clientele. Why? Are you linking them to Eve's murder? If you are, you're really barking up the wrong tree. I've known the Sterling people for years. They can tell you all about fifteenth-century Italian stilettos but none of them have the nerve to use one."

"Just a thought," I say, as if tossing off an idea of no consequence.

I know she's not buying it because of the way she sits back in her chair and looks at me through a half-smile that would make great-grandfather Trent proud of his descendant's gutter savvy. "Bringing up Sterling Auctions out of the blue is more than just a thought, Cantor. There's something you're not telling me."

I'm a sucker for smart women. Whether they come from the streets or more lofty regions, women with brains are the sexiest creatures on earth. And right now Vivienne Parkhurst Trent is very sexy. Too sexy for her own safety. Her intelligence, her curiosity, not to mention her involvement with me, could put her in danger, and that scares me to death. It scares me that she could join the company of Lorraine Quinn, Eve Garraway, and Alice Lamarr, because all three of those women had two things in common: me, and the notice, even sideways, of Sig Loreale.

I'm damned sure Sig is responsible for the death of one of them, but his power hovered over all of them.

Spilling the beans about Sig's involvement with Sterling Auctions could put Vivienne in his crosshairs. I can't let that happen.

"Well?" she says, looking at me with the Parkhurst arrogance mixed with the Trent back-alley rawness that floors me every time. But the look changes to something softer, sadder, even tender. It's the same look Vivienne gave me yesterday after the meeting with Dierdre Atchley. Maybe I'll explore what's behind that look someday. But maybe not. Something about me scares Vivienne. Something about getting close to Vivienne again scares me.

"Cantor?" she presses again.

She's not letting go, stubborn as a dog with a bone. She's already figured there's more to the story. I have to give her something. She's earned it by setting me up with the Atchleys, but if I want to keep her safe I have to hold tight to the string.

"Three women are dead," I finally say, the pain of it deep in my gut. "Three women who've crossed my path. Two of them—well . . ." I let that drop before I get twisted up again about giving Lorraine Quinn the brush-off and failing to protect Alice. I just say, "I think it's safer to keep you out of things, Vivienne."

"Don't treat me like a child," she says. "You know I'm not a shrinking violet. You know I can handle myself."

"Sure, when you see what's coming at you. But—" I'm cut off by George bringing in a cup and saucer and a plate of eggs and toast, which he places efficiently before me and just as efficiently leaves the dining room.

I pour myself a cup of coffee from the silver pot on the table, refill Vivienne's cup, then take a sip of the rich brew. Vivienne can afford the most expensive and exotic beans, but I'll take Doris's street-strong cuppa anytime.

"Thanks for breakfast," I say, taking up a forkful of perfectly scrambled eggs.

"You're welcome. Now, about Sterling Auctions."

I put the forkful of eggs down. "The less you know, the safer you'll be."

"The less I know, the less I can help you find Eve Garraway's killer." She's looking straight at me, dares me to look away, dares me to defy the steely Trent backbone behind those aristocratic green eyes.

"Look, if it puts your mind at ease," I say, "I doubt anyone from Sterling Auctions came all the way from Chicago to sneak into Eve's house and put a knife in her back."

"So why the interest in them? Are they connected to the Atchleys?"

"Not that I know of," I say after a forkful of eggs. "Y'know, George really knows how to whip up scrambled eggs."

"I'll be sure to tell him. No doubt it will make his day. Cantor, don't you understand? I want to help you."

"You've already helped me. You set me up with the Atchleys. By the way, I talked to James Atchley last night. He's one slimy article."

"Don't change the subject. Tell me why you asked about Sterling Auctions."

I have to get Vivienne off this track.

An idea occurs to me, a dicey idea, but yeah, Vivienne knows how to handle herself. I know it, too. I've seen it. "You really want to help me?"

"I said I did, didn't I?"

"Okay. Then come with me to the Garraway house. Let's have a talk with Desmond. Did you know he's an old thief from way back? He also killed a guy, or so they say."

Her face lights up with the excitement of a kid on a Coney Island thrill ride. "Really? I had no idea. Did Eve know?"

"Probably. Her father knew. The old man took Desmond in, gave him a second chance and a roof over his head after he got out of prison. Desmond trusts me—"

"Sure. Rogue to rogue," Vivienne says with a mischievous laugh.

"Which is why he'll talk to me, tell me who's come around, who's maybe been pushy about getting the Garraway collection."

"Okay, but what's my part in this?"

"Just be yourself," I say. "You're the art expert, even more than I am. You can ask the right questions and spark his recollection of any pieces in the collection that triggered more interest than others. You know as well as I do that people's taste in art says a lot about them."

Vivienne's in her element now. Cool as a huntress with her finger on the trigger and prey in her sights, she says, "And maybe something in the Garraway collection caught the eye of a killer."

Desmond's ditched his butler's duds in favor of brown slacks, tan shirt, and a brown cardigan, all of it hanging on his skinny frame like laundry hung out to dry. His eyes are red and watery, maybe

139

from crying, maybe from drinking, or maybe just from the cigarette smoke.

We're all in the living room, a heavy room of overstuffed furniture and dark woodwork, the kind of room made for brandy and fine cigars. I can picture Boss John Garraway enjoying both in this room while making shady political deals and twisting powerful arms.

Desmond, Vivienne, and I are having coffee and cigarettes. Desmond is seated on the sofa. Vivienne and I are in big chairs, our coats draped over the backs. My cap's in my lap. Vivienne still wears her hat, a close-fitting number of swan feathers dyed peach to match her blouse.

"I really miss her," Desmond says through his wisp of a voice. "Miss Garraway was very good to me. Generous at Christmastime, too. Always a nice bottle, and extra cash in my pay envelope."

I say, "Maybe you'll get lucky, Desmond, and she'll be generous to you in her will."

"Well, we'll see," he says. "So what's on your mind, Cantor?"

"Just thought we'd drop by. See how you're holding up."

"I'm okay. This house feels empty, though. Only memories here now. I swear, Cantor, sometimes I think I hear old man Garraway's voice in these rooms, y'know? Asking for his nightcap? And I can hear Miss Garraway's laughter when she was just a wee thing. Tell you the truth, I'm glad you dropped by. For the company, you understand."

"Haven't the police been back around?"

"Not since they took the body away. The lawyers have trooped through here, though." There's an edge to his breathy, old man's voice when he mentions the lawyers, like a knife blade gone to rust. "They took Miss Garraway's papers, and the ledger listing all the stuff in her art collection."

"Yeah, lawyers can be nosy that way," I say. "Listen, Desmond, before Miss Garraway died, when she was dealing with people who wanted her collection, was there anyone who seemed, well, off to you? You know, maybe pushier than they should be?"

140

His face folds into a crunch of wrinkles, his nose crinkling as if he's caught a bad smell. "They were all pushy, if you want my opinion. Greedy bunch, thinking they're so classy with all that art talk—oh, no offense, Miss."

Vivienne taps into her Parkhurst heritage and gives him a truly classy smile, but it's the Trent side of her that's working. "None taken. My profession can be as cutthroat as any scoundrel's."

He likes Vivienne's sassy attitude and uptown smile. He gives her a smile in return. I can't say I blame him. Vivienne's smile could raise heat in even the coldest heart. It's winning Desmond over, which is what Vivienne had in mind.

Warming to her, Desmond sits up straighter on the sofa, leans forward in her direction. He says, "And let me tell you, Miss Garraway saw right through those snooty people. She really was her father's daughter. Couldn't pull the wool over her eyes nohow!" He says it through the type of laugh so stuffed with memories there's more sadness in it than joy.

I say, "Yeah, Eve was no fool. Was there anyone among the suitors for her collection she especially didn't like?"

He takes a final puff of his cigarette, stubs it out in the ashtray on the side table, sits back against the sofa cushions, as relaxed as if he owns the place. "Hard to say. She once told me that she thought all of them a bunch of thieves. We had a laugh about that. And you know what else she said, Cantor?"

"I'll know when you tell me."

"Well, she said the only thieves she trusted were you, me, and her father." This makes him laugh again, a jollier laugh than the first one.

Vivienne says, "Did she ever mention a Chicago firm, Sterling Auctions?"

My eyes slide over to Vivienne. Hers are on Desmond.

"Sterling. Sterling," he says as if trying to recall the name. "Nope, doesn't ring a bell."

For the moment, my end of the bargain with Huber—playing the art angle—is going nowhere. Time to take another road. I'll decide later whether to give Huber anything new I pick up. Huber's still a cop and I'll always be his target, Devil's bargain or not.

I say, "What about people outside the art crowd? Anybody have it in for Eve?"

Desmond's face lights up like someone's just told him he's won the Irish Sweepstakes. "Well," he drags the word out, "I don't want to tell tales outta school . . ."

"C'mon, Desmond," I say, "if it helps find Eve's killer, you'll be doing a service to her memory."

"Her sainted memory."

"Okay, her sainted memory. Now come across."

"Well," he drags the word out again, enjoying the spotlight, "she wasn't a woman to be trifled with. If you crossed her, she could be as tough as her old dad. He taught her to be loyal to her friends and to destroy her enemies and folks who make the mistake of doing her dirty. Those politicians on the city council or up in Albany, they knew to stay on her good side. More than one of them has lost an election or didn't get a law passed because they didn't dance to her tune."

"Any one of them threaten her?"

"Nah. They knew better. As long as they played ball, she let them be. But there was one fella," he says, really warming up now, "who she particularly had it in for. Not a politician, a banking fella, a Mr. Atchley. She was really playing with fire there, and I told her so. Those big money people are more powerful than politicians, and slimier, too. They get away with everything, don't they, Cantor. They can even get away with murder."

"You're talking about Brooks Atchley?"

"Yeah, he did Miss Garraway wrong."

"And Brooks Atchley threatened her?"

"No, not him. The son. A hoity-toity sort, thinks he's better than everyone else. He came around, oh, I don't know, maybe a month ago, told Miss Garraway to lay off, or else."

Vivienne says, "Or else what? Or else he'd kill her? Or come after her money? Her reputation? What?"

142

Desmond doesn't like the question. "What do you think?" he says, snippy as a bratty schoolgirl.

But Vivienne doesn't back off. "He said he'd kill her?"

Desmond sits back in the sofa, calm again, the quiet calm that made him a champion bank robber with steady hands and even steadier nerves. "He didn't have to say it. Miss Garraway wound up with a bruise on her arm, an ugly red thing where he grabbed her. Boy's got a temper."

That fits with Drogan's story about James.

Desmond keeps talking. "Yeah, I bet it was him. Now I think about it, I bet it was him who killed Miss Garraway. Hope they give that high-and-mighty punk the chair."

We're all quiet after that: Desmond with satisfaction, Vivienne with a worried look for the possible downfall of her friends and museum benefactors, the Atchleys, and I'm tossing around the idea of handing James Atchley to either Huber or Sig. If James is the killer and I give him to Huber, he'll likely die in the chair. Juries love to stick it to high society snobs even more than they like to fry cheap gangsters like Tap Tenzi. And after a humiliating trial, James will have an agonizing wait on death row. Months, maybe years of appeals to sweat out. Maybe Sig's way is more merciful. It's certainly faster.

I take a good look at Desmond. I've always liked the guy. Maybe it's because he made the best of his second chance with the Garraways, or maybe, as Vivienne said, he and I deal with each other rogue to rogue. But I'm having a hard time liking him now. There's a look on his face I've never seen before, a sort of cat-that-ate-the-canary satisfaction, but meaner. If Desmond's the cat, then James Atchley's the canary, and Desmond's enjoying the meal too much.

Maybe it's time to look at something I didn't want to look at, something that risks breaking the old bank robber in half. "Yeah, families," I say. "They'll do anything to protect each other, or if someone wrongs them, they'll make them pay, no matter how long it takes. Isn't that right, Desmond?"

He looks at me like I just stepped on his foot, but he's too stunned to say *ouch*.

I'm about to press the issue but Vivienne grabs the conversation. "Just a minute," she says, "let's not jump to conclusions. It sounds like you have good reason to point a finger at James Atchley, Desmond, but I'm not satisfied that the Garraway collection didn't play a part in Eve's murder. Some of the people in my world play rough to get what they want, or keep others from getting it. So I want to ask you again, was there anyone else, anyone from the museums or galleries, who was, let's say, aggressive in their pursuit? And I'd like to have a look at the collection. I'm familiar with the catalogue. I want to make sure the collection is intact. If anything's missing, that could lead to another suspect in Eve's murder."

"Miss . . . Miss Trent, is it?" Desmond says.

"Parkhurst Trent."

"Miss Parkhurst Trent. You wouldn't be implying that I—"

"Oh, of course not," she says, turning on her irresistible charm. "Your devotion to Miss Garraway is clear. You would not do anything to besmirch her name or her memory. No, I'm referring to outsiders. Anyone come to mind?"

"I'll have to think on it," he says, "though I think young Atchley is still your best bet. And anyway, if you want to enter the vault, you'll have to ask the lawyers. They have the combination."

"Eve didn't share it with you? Her trusted retainer since childhood?" Vivienne's smile could melt the North Pole.

Desmond's smile could freeze the tropics.

Chapter Fifteen

It's nearly twelve-thirty when I drop Vivienne off at her museum, and just after one o'clock when I get back to my office after I pick up a chicken sandwich from Pete's. Judson tells me he's had Alice's body released from the city morgue and taken to the Harris Funeral Parlor on Sixth Avenue. "Funeral's tomorrow morning, Flushing Cemetery, ten o'clock," he says and hands me four messages: three from clients who want me to risk my life to get them some treasure or other to decorate their walls or add to their museum's prestige, the fourth is a message from Sig to call him back.

I take a bite of my sandwich and dial another number first.

When the desk sergeant gets Huber on the line, I say, "Anything new, lieutenant?"

"You first." He doesn't bother to hide his distrust of me or his dislike of our arrangement. His gravelly voice only makes it worse.

"Okay, then," I say. "So far, the art angle isn't coming up with anything useful. I had a talk with Desmond Mallory, figuring he might remember some of the more aggressive suitors for the Garraway collection. The guy didn't have a kind word for any of them, so that's a wash for now. But he was touchy about his loyalty to Eve Garraway."

"What do you mean, touchy?"

145

"He gave Vivienne the big freeze when she plucked a nerve about Eve's loyalty to him."

A snide, "Who the hell is Vivienne?" comes through the phone.

"Really, lieutenant? Don't tell me you've already forgotten your charming chat Tuesday morning over Eve's body. The lady was Vivienne Parkhurst Trent."

"You brought her along to see Mallory?" he snaps, almost growls. "Bad enough I'm dealing with you, Gold, but bringing amateurs into an investigation stinks."

"Vivienne's no amateur when it comes to art, lieutenant, and she's no amateur when dealing with butlers. She was raised with one, and everyone she grew up with has one. She was able to get right down into Mallory's marrow."

Huber's silence is so thick it clogs my ears. He finally says, "I've been looking into the death of Mallory's daughter and the Garraway woman's part in it. But I'm running up against a wall. Somebody's clamping down on every scrap of that old case. And they want me clear of it."

"Protecting the high and mighty from getting dirt on their shoes," I say but keep to myself that Sig Loreale is doing a lot of the protecting.

"And protecting the Garraway reputation." Huber sounds so disgusted he's almost sniveling. "Hell, even from the grave old John Garraway's still got City Hall and the State boys by the balls. I'll keep my eyes on Mallory. I'm also keeping an eye on James Atchley. I had a talk with him at his Wall Street office after I left your place this morning. Seems he has no one to back up his alibi for the time of Garraway's murder. He says he was at his office Tuesday morning, but his secretary stumbled all over herself when I asked about it."

I say, "And then there's Mrs. Atchley, the matriarch of the clan. She looked so far down her nose at Eve Garraway she could barely see the top of Eve's head."

"You think she's capable of murder?"

"I think she's capable of anything. She could probably run a country. But she had Eve's vengeance to deal with, and that could drive anyone to murder. Did the secretary tell you about that?"

"Sure," he says, sounding annoyed again, "the secretary spilled about the trouble Eve Garraway was making, threatening the Atchley family's control of the firm. But I guess you knew that before I did. This is why I don't trust you, Gold. You keep secrets."

"Keeping secrets keeps me alive, lieutenant."

"Keeping secrets from me could land you in handcuffs. I don't know where you get your information, Gold, and maybe I don't want to know, if your sources are so dirty that a judge would throw the stuff out of court. But if you keep information from me, I'll end this little arrangement so fast—"

"Yeah, yeah, you'll cuff me and toss me."

"And the entire police department will cheer." It's the happiest he's sounded since I picked up the phone.

"Well, that sends my help with the Garraway murder down the drain," I say.

"Maybe it doesn't matter. I've got four good suspects for the Garraway killing," he says. He still sounds happy.

"Four? I count Mallory, James Atchley, and Dierdre Atchley. Lemme guess: you still count me in."

"Always, Gold. I always count you in." He hangs up.

I sit back in my chair, put my feet up on my desk and finish my sandwich before I call Sig. I need to let the chicken settle after that irritating threat from Huber and before whatever threats Sig throws at me.

And I need to think.

Eve Garraway. James Atchley. Dierdre Atchley. All three of them with vengeance in their bitter hearts. Maybe Desmond took his revenge, too, though I can't shake the feeling he wouldn't wait twelve years to avenge the death of his daughter. But who knows? Maybe his loyalty to the Garraways wasn't loyalty at all. Maybe it was an "or else" grip, first in Boss Garraway's fingers then in Eve's, until Desmond decided to snap those bones. But Tuesday morning, when Eve was expecting visitors, seems like a chancy time to commit murder. An old pro like Desmond would know better. Or should know better.

Vengeance. It's a fire in the veins. I know. I've felt it burn my blood. I felt it when I couldn't save the woman I loved from a living hell. I still feel it when Sig tries to twist me in his grip. I've learned to cool it down because vengeance eats at the mind, and I need clear thinking when dealing with Sig, and to stay alive in my outlaw world.

Who knows what a festering vengeance drove Desmond to do? It certainly drove Eve's plan to ruin the Atchley family. Maybe it drove the Atchleys to murder.

And James Atchley has no solid alibi for the time of Eve's death, maybe even lied about it. Maybe that's the arrogant twerp's slip-up. But if James Atchley or even Dierdre Atchley was Eve's killer, how the hell did they get into the house? I didn't see anyone go in before or after me. And the back garden is two floors below the office where Eve was killed. James is probably athletic enough to reach the office window, but I don't think he's stupid enough to make the climb in broad daylight. And the idea of the stately Dierdre climbing up the wall gives me a laugh.

A slug from the bottle of Chivas I keep in a desk drawer helps settle the chicken sandwich and stiffens my spine to deal with Sig.

I dial his number. The maid answers. "Cantor Gold returning Sig's call," I say.

Sig's, "Hello, Cantor," when he comes on the line has all the warmth of a dark night in a hard winter. "I am not pleased with recent developments."

"I'm not too pleased with them, either," I say. "Three women are dead, murdered." I don't doubt for a second Sig's caught my accusation about the phony suicide of Alice Lamarr.

"And if I am not mistaken," he says in that slow way that makes my bones turn to dust, "all three women are connected to you. But let's not dwell on such unpleasant matters and their possible consequences for you."

"Suits me," I say. "So what have I done this time to make you unhappy, Sig?"

148

"You have done nothing to make me unhappy that I'm aware of. I am unhappy with Lieutenant Huber. He has not heeded the orders of his superiors. He continues to look into the Garraway matter. I will consider taking steps to stop him."

That dark night in winter just became a freeze along my spine. Sig's threat could mean anything as inconvenient to Huber's career as having him demoted or thrown back in uniform, or it could mean a headline in tomorrow's paper, *COP FOUND DEAD ACROSS THE RIVER IN NEW JERSEY SWAMP*, though that last one's a stretch. Killing a cop brings too much heat. Even Sig knows to avoid it.

Sig says, "In the meantime, have you learned anything new about Miss Garraway's death? Anything to lead you to her killer?"

"If I did, would that make you happy?"

"It will make me even happier when you bring the killer to me, as instructed."

"Hold on to that happiness, Sig. Let it soothe you until the picture gets clearer. You wouldn't want me delivering the wrong person, now would you?"

"You will not deliver the wrong person, Cantor. You will deliver the guilty one."

Chapter Sixteen

Huber was right about one thing: I don't like being pushed around. Not by cops, not by the laws they enforce with their billy clubs, not by a goody-two-shoes public who thinks my love life is a sin, and not by Sig Loreale. I get around the first three by sticking my finger in the Law's and the public's eyes by living life my way. It's time to do something about the last item. It's time to get out from Sig Loreale's grip.

I put a plan in motion by calling my lawyer, Winston "Winnie" Maximovic. Winnie's about as well connected as a lawyer can get, with people in high places who owe him favors and people in low places who owe him their freedom. I phoned him because I need to talk to Tap Tenzi, and Huber's keeping quiet about where he's stashed him. And even if I'd known he'd stashed Tap in Brooklyn's Raymond Street jail, the chances of me just waltzing in and having Tap brought to a visitor's window are slim to none. Cops in Brooklyn don't like me any better than cops in Manhattan, and Tap wouldn't want to talk to me anyway, since it's my doing that landed him in jail. But Winnie plucked the right strings to find out which cell bars Tap is currently behind. He also put a word in the ear of some political hack to grant us visitation and make sure Tap shows up.

We're driving there now.

Winnie's car, a '54 Lincoln Capri sedan, black with chrome accents and white interior, is a rolling tuxedo. The big but graceful car suits the big but graceful man driving it. That's the thing about Winnie; his three hundred or so pounds is all class, with a melodious voice and elegant speech to go with it. That's the Winnie the public, the press boys, the politicians, and the courtroom crowd see. What they don't see are glitzy gowns the size of tents in his bedroom closet, or the handsome young men he wears them for.

He parks on Willoughby Street at the corner of Raymond. The neighborhood's the sort where bobby-soxers hang out at drug store soda fountains, kids play jump rope on the sidewalk and ride bikes in the street, and housewives hang laundry on lines stretching from the back of one rowhouse to the back of another.

The Raymond Street jail, an old Gothic graystone building that could pass for a church, a castle, or the setting of a Frankenstein movie, looms next to us. Before we get out of the car, Winnie says, "Are you quite sure you want to do this, Cantor? Mr. Tenzi is not apt to be cooperative with you."

"I have to try," I say. "He has information which could get me free of Sig."

"You are coming perilously close to blackmailing Mr. Loreale. This frightens me, Cantor. I can help you escape the police, and I can keep you out of jail, but even my most deft legal maneuverings cannot save you from Loreale's vengeance."

"Let me worry about that."

"And you should worry. But if I can't talk you out of this unwise enterprise, at least put your gun in the glove compartment. They won't let you into the jail with it."

I put the rig with my .38 into the Lincoln's roomy glove compartment and get out of the car.

The shadows cast by the mesh-screened window separating us from Tap carve the pockmarks in his face even deeper. His square jaw is clamped tight, his gray eyes hard as pavement. He is not happy to see me.

He's still wearing the same white shirt and suit pants he had on when Huber arrested him at the High Style Tie & Handkerchief Company last night. I guess he won't get his prison stripes until he's sent up to Sing Sing after his trial. The flashy rhinestone ring is missing, though. It's probably gracing the finger of a jail guard's wife, or more likely the guard's outside-the-house amusement.

Tap says, "Why are you here, Gold?" in his smooth, middle-of-the-night voice. "And who the hell is the mountain of blubber you brought with you?"

Winnie says, "My name is Winston Maximovic. I am an attorney."

"I already got a shyster."

"I'm not here to represent you, Mr. Tenzi. I am here to accompany Cantor."

"Yeah? So why is she here?"

I say, "How would you like to help me take down Sig Loreale?"

I've caught Tap's attention but not his pleasure. He works his jaw as if he's gnawing on the idea I just tossed him, but he looks at me as if he's disappointed I'm not dead. "Now why would I want to help you with something?" he says. "You're why I'm in these deluxe accommodations, Gold."

"If you need a reason," I say, "okay, here's one: Alice."

Everything on his face slowly tightens. His lips pucker, his cheeks suck in, stretching and reddening the pockmarks. "What about Alice?" he says, spitting it. "The little tramp, and a sick one at that, screwin' around with you."

There's no sadness at the mention of her name. "You haven't heard?" I ask. "Don't they give you newspapers or a television or even a radio in this joint?"

"Heard what?"

"Listen, Tap, Alice is dead. They put out a phony story that it was suicide, but I say it's a sure bet Sig had Alice killed. She was a loose end."

There's no expression at all on his face now; even his shoulders have gone stiff. But his eyes tell another story, one of creeping grief.

It's Winnie's cue to press the point, use his courtroom skills the way he gets a hostile witness to change sides. His fleshy face takes on an expression of such kindness and tenderness the angels would weep. "And you will be next, Mr. Tenzi. Mr. Loreale will either allow the state of New York to execute you, or if the state declines, or takes its time, he will see to the matter himself. Perhaps here in this jail, or perhaps later when you are upstate."

I jump back in, keep the pressure on. "Listen, Tap. When you tried to make a deal with Sig, he sent you away like you were the wrong lunch order. Or maybe he didn't even bother to see you at all. That's where he made his mistake, didn't he, Tap. You saw something he didn't want seen, and he had no idea Lorraine Quinn had caught it on her camera. I bet even Lorraine didn't know. Otherwise Loreale might've saved you the trouble of killing her. But he just ignored you. You never got your chance to make a deal with him, your silence for a spot in his operations. Well, here's your chance to get even, Tap. Here's your chance to take Loreale down, just like he slapped you down. Look, you're a dead man and you know it. But at least you can go out laughing, get the last laugh on the guy who slapped you down."

Tap doesn't move a muscle. I swear, I think the guy is barely breathing. He just stares at me through the mesh screen, doesn't even blink. But I finally notice that his lips aren't completely still. His mouth is opening but so slowly I feel like it's next year when he finally says, "I loved Alice. She thought I didn't, but I did. Having her on my arm was everything. But you—you and your sick ways, your disgusting ways, and she, and you and Alice—" He runs the back of his hand across his mouth as if trying to wipe off something bitter. "Loreale wants to kill me? Let him. I don't care. Like you say, I'm already a dead man. And dead men don't do favors. Get out of here, Gold."

"Well, it was worth a try," I say when we're back at Winnie's Lincoln.

"I hate to say it, my friend, but Mr. Tenzi may have just saved you from a foolish and dangerous adventure."

153

"No more dangerous than being pushed around by a crime boss who thinks you're born to do his bidding."

When Winnie purses his lips, his whole face moves like a leather satchel opening and closing. "And do I need to know just what it is Mr. Loreale is bidding you to do?" he says as we get into the car.

My silence gives him his answer.

"Just be careful, Cantor. As I told you earlier, I can keep you out of jail, but I cannot save your life."

Back in Manhattan, I had Winnie drop me off on Chambers Street. After the washout with Tap Tenzi, I fall back on that old idea that if you want a job done well, do it yourself.

Which is why I'm stepping off the elevator on the fourth floor of the sooty Italianate building housing the law office of Otis Hollander. It's just a little after four o'clock in the afternoon. I assume the office is still open.

Miss Sawicki, tightly encased in another fuzzy angora sweater, this one turquoise, is at her reception desk. Seeing me, she quickly puts down the *Photoplay* movie magazine she's ogling, its cover featuring a shirtless Rock Hudson. "Mr. Hollander isn't here," she says.

"I know. I came to see you."

"Well, I don't want to see you. You wear trouble as easily as you wear a coat. And besides, you're—"

"Not your type?" I joke as I sit on the edge of her desk.

"Not even close. I'm no sicko. Now get off my desk and go away. I have work to do." She shoos me away like she's brushing off cracker crumbs.

I put a finger on the *Photoplay* magazine. "Helped by hunky Rock, no doubt. I tell you what," I say and slide off the desk. "I'll make a deal with you. You help me with what I need, and you'll never have to see me again. How about it?"

"Is that a promise?"

"I never lie to a lady."

She leans back in her squeaky desk chair and eyes me like I'm an odd vegetable she'd never consider buying but wonders why some people like the taste. "Well, what do you want?"

"Lorraine Quinn's photographs of the Tenzi surveillance."

"No can do. They're locked in Mr. Hollander's current case files in his desk."

"And you don't have a key?"

"No, I do not have a key. I'm just the receptionist, not his private secretary. Hey, you can't go in there!" she shouts at my back as I walk to Otis's office. Miss Sawicki trails me.

The file drawer in Otis's desk is locked, and I don't have my lockpicks with me. But the lock looks like a standard drawer job, nothing a little finagling with a couple of paper clips can't handle: one curved into a hook, the other as a pick.

"Give me two paper clips," I say to Miss Sawicki.

"What for?" she says, but she knows damn well what for.

The hard stare I give her finishes her naïve act, and she gets two paper clips from the desk drawer and hands them over. I twist them into a hook and a pick and go to work. In less than a minute, I feel the click of the lock and I open the file drawer.

I run my fingers along the row of files until I find the one labeled LAMARR and pull it out, then have a seat at Otis's desk. I say to Miss Sawicki, "Maybe you shouldn't be here for this. There might be something in the pictures that could put whoever sees it in danger."

"What kind of danger? Maybe I don't mind a little danger," she says, trying to cover a taste for nosiness with a brave front.

"This danger's the bad kind," I say. "The life and death kind. The Lorraine Quinn and Alice Lamarr are already dead kind."

Her corn-fed cheeks go pale under the powder and rouge. "I'll . . . I'll be at my desk if you need me," she says. "But do me a favor and don't need me. And don't take long anyway. It's almost five o'clock, my quitting time." She escapes to the safety of the reception area.

I open the file. A bunch of papers are on top: depositions, lawyer's notes, notations of billable hours. Behind the papers are Lorraine's photographs, each one stamped with a date and time.

Lorraine was good at her job. Stealthy and skilled. No invasive flash bulbs for her, no sudden bright light catching her prey but scaring them into stopping their miscreant activity. Lorraine was skilled enough to use the kind of film that can take pictures even in the low light of streetlights or the lights of motel parking lots at night. The film makes grainy pictures, but clear enough to identify who's in them, clear enough to catch Tap Tenzi cheating on Alice Lamarr.

My first reaction is to laugh. There's Tap, days and days of him acting like Don Juan, romancing a series of women, entering or leaving cheap motels in New York's outer boroughs or across the river in Jersey.

The photographs would nail him in court. Alice would get the divorce. A judge, seeing the photos, would give her everything Tenzi'd socked away, including the socks he stashed it all in.

And then I stop laughing. I almost feel sorry for Tap, because all the women in the photographs bear a passing resemblance to Alice.

He told me at the jail that he loved her. I guess I have to believe him.

I take a closer look at the photos, look for whatever it is that Lorraine caught on camera that Sig doesn't want seen. I don't find anything. It's just picture after picture of Tap and various women and his DeSoto and a motel. Lorraine was a thorough documentarian. Each picture is stamped with the day, the hour, even the minute.

But then I do see something, not something that's there but something that isn't. There's time unaccounted for in a sequence taken on Wednesday, August eighteenth. At 9:32 p.m., there's Tap and a woman getting out of Tap's DeSoto in the parking lot of the Hi-Ho Motel in Astoria in Queens. At 9:33, they walk into the office, and at 9:37 they walk out again. At 9:39 they approach room 603. At 9:40 they enter. The sequence jumps to 10:12 p.m. with a handwritten note attached: *Investigator Quinn exited her vehicle at 9:40 p.m. to take up a position outside the window of room*

603 *of the Hi-Ho Motel. Mr. Tenzi and the unidentified woman were heard laughing in room 603, followed by sounds of sexual activity.* The note sets up uncomfortable images in my head of Lorraine crouching outside the motel window, a stalker with a predatory camera. But she'd set herself up to get the photo that would get Alice a profitable divorce. At 10:26 p.m., Lorraine got the prize-winning shot through a slit in the room's window curtain of Tap and the woman naked, Tap's torso wrapped in the woman's legs. There's another note: *Mr. Tenzi and the woman remained in room 603 until 11:54 p.m.* The next shot shows them walking out the door at that time.

It's the next photo, stamped 12:01 a.m., that raises my hackles. It's the back of Tap's DeSoto. Seen through the rear window are the backs of two heads—Tap's and the woman's—as he eases the DeSoto into traffic on Northern Boulevard.

Lorraine's surveillance, through photographs and handwritten notes, accounts for every minute on the night of August eighteenth. She stayed as tight on Tap's ass as a lioness chasing its next meal. She'd never look away; she would not drop six minutes of activity of her prey. There's six minutes in that motel parking lot unaccounted for. At least one photograph is missing.

I close the file, put it back into the drawer, and go out to the reception area. I ask Miss Sawicki, "Did Otis say where he can be reached?"

She's not happy to see me and even less happy about the question. "I can't tell you where he is because I don't know where he is."

"But he left you a phone number, yes? He'd need to stay in touch with you, find out if any clients called, what court dates are coming up. And you'd need to reach him in case of emergency, legal or otherwise."

"Well, sure, but I'd lose my job if I—"

"C'mon, I just saved your life by keeping you out of trouble about those photos. Return the favor."

Suggesting that someone's life could be on the line always

does the trick. Miss Sawicki's hand shakes as she writes a phone number on a slip of paper and hands it to me.

I say, "You never saw me, you understand? If anyone besides Otis asks, if any cop or stranger asks, you never saw me. And you never saw those photographs."

Outside my living room window, early evening drifts down on the city. Lights come on in the apartment house across the street. Streetlight filters up from the sidewalk. Neon signs tint the air with a rainbow of colors. It's a perfect New York evening, the kind of evening that teases with the possibility that your big city dreams might come true or shatter like cheap jewelry on the pavement. Dream big, die trying. The thrill of living here.

I'm in a favorite club chair. The phone's in my lap, the receiver against my ear, and a glass of Chivas at my side. The number Miss Sawicki gave me rings four times before the line's picked up and I hear Otis say, "Yes?" He sounds as if he's wondering if he should've answered at all.

"It's Cantor," I say.

"Cantor?" He says my name like he's relieved it's me and not someone who might kill him. "How did you get this number?"

"Your receptionist thought it was a good idea to save her life, maybe yours, too. Look, Otis, I won't ask you where you are—"

"And I wouldn't tell you. It's best for both of us," he says. "And I won't be at this location much longer anyway."

"Uh-huh, moving around for a while. Probably a good idea."

"Yeah," he says with the bleak conviction that getting killed might be the only other alternative. "So what's on your mind, Cantor?"

"I had a look at Lorraine Quinn's photographs of the Tenzi surveillance."

"You what? How? That drawer is locked, and Miss Sawicki doesn't have—oh. Never mind," he says through an amused snicker. "I just remembered how you make your living."

"Then you know I didn't break the lock," I say with a friendly little laugh. "But I needed to have a look at those pictures. I'd hoped they could help get Sig Loreale off my back. Yours too. Look, Lorraine's surveillance was first rate, every minute accounted for. So it's all wrong that there's a gap in the August eighteenth photographs. Six minutes of activity is missing. Lorraine wouldn't have been that sloppy. What happened to those six minutes, Otis?"

My question brings only silence. I wait a little bit, give the guy a chance to collect his thoughts or his courage. When he doesn't come across, I say, "Otis?"

A few seconds of more silence, then, "There were two pictures," he says as if all the air in his lungs has been squeezed out. "I burned them both. The negatives, too."

"Okay, but you saw them. What was in them?"

"Listen, Cantor, when I saw those pictures, I knew they were explosive; they could get me killed if Loreale ever got wind of them, so I burned them. The other pictures already gave me enough on Tenzi for Alice's case, so I didn't need those two. I thought that was the end of it until you called and told me Alice Lamarr was dead. Now drop it, Cantor. Please. I don't want to die, and neither do you. Just let it go."

"I can't," I say. "What happened during those six minutes might be my only leverage when dealing with Sig. I want to know what was in those photographs, Otis"

"I won't tell you, Cantor. With Alice dead and Tenzi in jail, the divorce case is moot. The surveillance doesn't matter anymore."

"It matters to me."

"Well, make it unmatter," he snaps. "I don't know what kind of game you want to play with Loreale, but if he knows you saw something he didn't want seen, he'd want to know how you know about it."

"I'd never rat on you, Otis."

He gives that a sullen laugh. "I'm supposed to rely on your integrity, huh? You know as well as I do, better probably, that

159

Loreale has ways of making even the mute talk. You'd talk, Cantor. You'd talk, and then you'd never be able to talk again." He hangs up.

Barely a second after Otis slams the phone down in my ear there's a buzz at my door.

I take the glass of Chivas with me. When I open the door, there's a gun in my face.

Chapter Seventeen

The face behind the gun is cool and calm, the head beneath the small round green hat aristocratic, the eyes behind the netted hat veil steady. "It's your fault," Dierdre Atchley says.

"It usually is," I say. "Why don't you come in, and we can talk about whatever it is that's my fault. And if you shoot me, at least the neighbors won't have to deal with blood spattered all over the common hallway."

She keeps her revolver aimed at my face as she walks inside. She doesn't look around, doesn't take in the furniture, doesn't admire the art on the walls. The body inside the sealskin coat moves with the single-minded fortitude of a soldier.

I say, "Now suppose you tell me what's my fault. May I take your coat?"

"I'll keep it if you don't mind. I wouldn't trust you not to steal it."

"Pelts are not my line. Didn't your sources of information tell you that?" I take another pull on my scotch, keep my sights on Mrs. Atchley over the rim of the glass.

Her chiseled face of careful breeding quivers ever so slightly at her mouth and chin. She's fighting hard to control it, and she's got the spine to carry it off. "James has been arrested," she says. Her usually mellow, moneyed voice has a hard edge to it. "Your Lieutenant Huber seems to think my son killed that upstart Garraway woman. He had the gall to go to James's boat with two police officers and arrest my son like a common criminal."

161

"Murderers are not common criminals," I say. "They're their own special breed."

Mrs. Atchley is not amused. The look she gives me slices right down to the bone. She pushes her gun closer to my face. "Our family attorney was able to secure his release into my custody until trial," she says. "But there were news people at the jail when he was released. His picture will be all over the papers and the television news. My family will be humiliated beyond repair, and we will have you to blame. You set that detective on us, Cantor Gold, and you will pay for it."

"By killing me? I have no doubt you have the stuff it takes to pull that trigger, Mrs. Atchley. There's nothing deadlier than an enraged momma. But you'd be better off using that gun to protect your son. And maybe spend some of the Atchley fortune to hire an army of bodyguards, too, because your son is in danger. As soon as those news stories hit the streets, maybe even sooner, your son is a dead man."

The line deepening between her brows says it all. An unfamiliar sensation is insinuating itself into Mrs. Dierdre Atchley: fear. Fear of things foreign to her gilt-edged world of society balls and private clubs, fear that she can't save her son from the deadly side of a New York she doesn't live in and that even her money and social position can't control. "Why is he a dead man?" she says.

Her gun hand trembles just a little bit, but it's enough for me to move fast to knock her hand and grab the gun away. The shock on her face overtakes the fear, but not for long. The fear seeps back. Behind the net veil of her hat, her eyes tighten, and the furrow at her brow deepens. "Why is my son a dead man?" she says again.

"Because there are people who want the Garraway case to go away. Powerful people, and brutal people."

She looks at me as if I'm speaking gibberish. "Who are such people?"

"You'd know that better than I would," I say. "Some of them are people in your world, up where the air is thin and reputations fragile. The Garraway case has tentacles that stretch back through years of political deals, business deals, and family scandals covered up. Every family has dirty laundry, Mrs. Atchley, even fancy families: y'know, wrong love affairs, sleazy payoffs for even sleazier favors, maybe even a long-forgotten murder or two. The arrest and trial of your son could bring back those old scandals, ruin a lot of reputations and the careers of powerful people. And then there are those other people, the dangerous people. They're powerful, too, but deadlier. The Garraway case stirs up that other side of New York, Mrs. Atchley. The side with guns, the shadowy side where people don't like the Law looking into their business. People in that world can make James disappear, quietly, even while he's in police custody, and with him goes the investigation of the death of Eve Garraway. Just another unsolved murder in the big city. You look like you could use a drink, Mrs. Atchley."

I pour her two fingers of scotch, help her into one of my club chairs. She lifts her veil back over her hat, takes a good pull on the drink. The whiskey takes some of the gray out of her cheeks.

I refresh my own drink, sit down in the other club chair. "First of all, Mrs. Atchley, this is the first I've heard about your son's arrest, and I'm not any happier about it than you are." My Devil's bargain with Huber turns out to be all Devil and no bargain.

Mrs. Atchley says, "Have you changed your mind then about James's guilt?"

"I wouldn't go that far," I say, which evidently disappoints her, if the slump of her sealskin clad shoulders is anything to go by. "But Huber seems to be playing a fast game. Too fast. He doesn't know all the players."

"The dangerous ones," Mrs. Atchley says.

"Yeah, the dangerous ones."

"But you know them." She takes another pull on her drink. I take another pull on mine. We watch each other over the rims of our glasses. The formidable Mrs. Dierdre Atchley appears to be challenging me to do something about those dangerous people and their threat to her family. I'm trying to figure if she can handle what I have in mind.

There's only one way to find out, and the risk could kill us both. "Mrs. Atchley, if you want to save your son, it's time you met the most dangerous guy in town."

Mrs. Atchley's tense and quiet in the passenger seat of my Buick. Her gun's back in her handbag, an alligator number with a claw for a clasp. Between the alligator bag, the sealskin coat, and lambskin gloves, I'm tempted to think Mrs. Dierdre Atchley buys her clothes at a zoo.

My gun's in my shoulder rig. Sig's thugs will take it, and Mrs. Atchley's, too. I've already told her not to try to hide it from them. The boys will not be impressed. They'll search her in ways she's not used to. And they've probably never heard of the name Atchley.

I don't know what Mrs. Atchley's feeling, if she's scared or numb or maybe both. Her hat veil's down, and in the darkness inside my car, with only the light of street lamps and neon signs sliding through the windows as I drive down Broadway, her face moves from shadow to light and back again. Impossible to read her mood.

I know what I'm feeling, though. I'm damned scared. Bringing Dierdre Atchley to see Sig is a high-stakes play, maybe a deadly one if it annoys the lord of all crime. But Mrs. Atchley needs to come face to face with the threat to her son, and Sig has to come face to face with a woman who'll think he's dirt.

I'm also angry. I'm angry at Huber for double-crossing our little arrangement. If he really has a case against James, our Devil's bargain should've let me in on it. Instead, he's left me twisting in the wind, and he doesn't even know it. He doesn't know Sig's command that I bring Eve Garraway's killer to him. He doesn't know the penalties for failing Sig Loreale.

So yeah, I'm scared and I'm angry. But Dierdre Atchley won't see any of that. And neither will Sig. What they'll see is the Cantor Gold who's had enough of both of them, and enough of Lieutenant Norm Huber, too.

164

The street entrance to Sig's tower is closed for the night. The businessmen in their crisp fedoras, their secretaries in white gloves, and the stenographers with pencils behind their ears have all gone home. I ring the night bell. Mrs. Atchley's at my side. I hear her sharp intake of breath when she sees one of Sig's boys come to the door. I guess they don't grow them so bulky on Park Avenue.

I recognize the guy. It's Ham Face, the other member of the thug parade when I was here two nights ago. He says, "Mr. Loreale didn't say nothin' about expecting you, Gold."

"He's not expecting me, but he'll see me when you call upstairs and tell him I'm here with Mrs. Brooks Atchley."

He looks Mrs. Atchley up and down like he's trying to figure why his boss would want to meet with this snooty matron in a sealskin coat. He can't figure it, so he gives up, cocks his head for us to follow him to the elevator.

We walk through the lobby. Mrs. Atchley slides me a look that finally clues me in to her mood: annoyance, even disgust, but with a trace of curiosity. In her world, Ham Face is the kind of guy she'd have her butler phone up to fix the plumbing.

Ham Face calls up to the penthouse on the intercom next to Sig's private elevator, announces us to whoever picks up the line. After an, "Uh-huh," he says to me, "Gotta wait," then puts the receiver under his chin. He gives Mrs. Atchley another look-over. She raises her hat veil and gives him a stare that changes his mind about looking her over. He puts his attention back on the intercom instead, his flushed face practically begging for someone to come back on the line.

Someone finally does. Ham Face says, "Yeah, okay," hangs up, and says to me, "I gotta take your piece."

I open my coat, reach into my suit jacket, take out my .38 and hand it to him. "I know the drill," I say.

Ham Face puts my gun in his pocket, turns a smarmy eye to Mrs. Atchley. "You got a gun, lady?"

She doesn't answer, just continues to stare at him as if insulted by this challenge from a member of society's lower orders.

I say, "This isn't the time, Mrs. Atchley."

If her lips pursed any tighter, they'd crush her teeth, but she opens the claw latch of her handbag, slowly reaches inside.

Ham Face might be a dullard in the sophistication department, but he's wise to the ways of the streets. A slow hand could mean the wrong type of reach for a weapon, the type that ends up with a gun barrel aimed at your face. His street savvy brings his own gun out fast, aimed directly at the snooty lady in the expensive coat.

Only she doesn't look so snooty now. She's gone pale as paper, her body shrinking inside her coat.

I say to Ham Face, "Back off. She's not looking for trouble. She's just taking her gun from her bag."

Mrs. Atchley hands him her gun. Ham Face puts his away.

He unlocks the elevator. I follow Mrs. Atchley inside. When the door slides closed and we're alone, she finally breathes.

I hope I didn't make a mistake. I hope I didn't give Dierdre Atchley too much credit for guts. If cut-rate muscle like Ham Face can scare the air out of her, I wonder how she'll handle the first-rate murderer that's Sig Loreale.

The elevator opens at the penthouse floor. I take Mrs. Atchley's elbow and escort her to Sig's door. "If you want to save your son," I say, "you've got to stay steady."

The door's opened by Mike Mulroney, his weirdly pale blue eyes giving Mrs. Atchley an icy once-over.

Looking now at me, he skips any greeting, just says, "He's waiting for you on the terrace."

The terrace doors are across the living room. As we walk through, Mrs. Atchley appears surprised at the cozy décor, the fine art on the walls, and the sculptures around the room.

I say, "What did you expect? Tommy guns on racks?"

"Well, I certainly didn't expect such refined taste from an immigrant gangster," she says with an amusement that annoys me.

"Actually, Sig was born here, not long after his parents got off the boat," I say, matching her chilly amusement with some of my own. "By the way, Sig came by much of his refined taste courtesy of me, for a hefty price, of course. So I wouldn't underestimate immigrants, Mrs. Atchley. You'd hurt my Coney Island immigrant Mom and Pop's feelings. Of course, I'm sure you didn't mean to offend."

The look on Mrs. Atchley's face suggests she wishes she still had her gun.

I open the French doors, lead her out to the terrace. If she was surprised by the good taste in Sig's living room, she's right at home amid the gilt Gothic arches and the view that looks over the city and down on the people who live in it. The terrace is an expression of power and influence, two things Dierdre Atchley understands very well.

This may turn out okay after all.

The terrace wraps around the entire apartment. We have to turn two corners to find Sig. He's at the Fortieth Street side, overlooking Bryant Park and the big public library, the one with the famous lions out front. He's leaning against the terrace wall, smoking a cigar. The tip glows, giving a red tint to the smoke gathered beneath the brim of his homburg. In his black coat and hat, he's a silhouette against the light barely filtering up from the street and the lampposts in Bryant Park.

I'm holding Mrs. Atchley's arm. I feel her shiver. Sig has that effect on people.

He says, "Good evening, Mrs. Atchley." The chill of his slow, sharply articulated delivery makes Mrs. Atchley shiver again. "I understand your son was taken into custody by the police but has since been released." Sig takes a pull on his cigar. Its red glow illuminates his baggy eyes. He's not looking at Mrs. Atchley; he's looking at me, silently scolding me for letting the police get hold of James Atchley before he did. Taking the cigar from his mouth, he finally looks at Mrs. Atchley, and says through an exhale of smoke, "Why come to me, Mrs. Atchley? I had no hand in your son's arrest."

"Mr. Loreale," she says with more steel in her voice than I'd

167

expect after her earlier shiver, "we live on different sides of the street, you and I, but we both command considerable influence in this city. We both understand power. But your power moves in different circles than mine, darker ones. I am here to ask you to use that power to make sure that no harm comes to my son while I work to clear his name."

"And yours, Mrs. Atchley," Sig says.

"Indeed," she admits. "We understand each other then."

Sig answers with silence and another pull on his cigar.

Mrs. Atchley's confidence seems to have gone a little shaky under the force of Sig's brutal silence. She starts to say something, stops whatever she had in mind, then finally says, "Do you have an interest in the Garraway matter, Mr. Loreale?"

"I have an interest in many things, Mrs. Atchley," he says. He takes his time, as always, each word carrying the cadence of threat, as always. "And many people rely on me to keep those many things running smoothly, without interruption, and without drawing attention to those many things. Your son's murder of Miss Garraway, followed by a public trial—"

"My son did not murder anyone, Mr. Loreale."

"The police say he did, Mrs. Atchley."

"I would assume you are the kind of man who does not put his faith in the police."

Even in silhouette, I can see Sig's head tilt back. The glow from his cigar catches the lower half of his face. I see his mouth open in his silent laugh, his empty, cringe-inducing laugh.

Mrs. Atchley grabs my arm, an automatic gesture of shock. It's everyone's response the first time they're witness to Sig's bloodcurdling, soundless laughter.

When the laugh is finished and he's facing us again, he says, "You do not understand my relationship with the police, Mrs. Atchley. I have complete faith in them when I need to."

I say, "Which is why we're here, Sig. Look, there's no point in being dainty about it. The police—okay, Lieutenant Huber— screwed all of us: you, me, Mrs. Atchley, and certainly James. But maybe Huber screwed you most of all."

"And how is that, Cantor?"

"He was a very bad boy, didn't do what he was told—"

Mrs. Atchley cuts in, "What do you mean, didn't do what he was told? Told by whom?"

Sig says, "I suggest you do not ask too many questions, Mrs. Atchley." Sig's tone says it's not a suggestion.

"And why not?" she counters. "My son is in danger. I have a right to know why. Because he got in your way, Mr. Loreale?"

Another crushing silence from Sig. But this time it's backed up with a stare so steady and cold even the red glow from his cigar can't heat it up. It just makes it more terrifying.

I'd better calm this situation down before Mrs. Dierdre Atchley's name winds up on a Loreale death warrant. "Hold on a minute, everybody," I say. "Look, Sig, she's got a right to know what's going on. Her son's life is in the balance. But Mrs. Atchley," I say to the defiant woman at my side, the angry mother protecting her cub, "you may have the right to know, but it might not be a good idea for you to know. If you want to protect James, if you want to salvage your family's reputation, you should probably stay as clean as possible. The less dirt that sticks to you, the better. And there's plenty of dirt around Eve Garraway to grow a garden of poisoned tomatoes."

I turn back to Sig. "But about Huber, let's face it, he's busted the Garraway mess wide open. Maybe he arrested the killer of Eve Garraway, and maybe he made a mistake. But by jumping the gun he's forced you into taking care of the situation in less quiet ways than you usually like. And if he did arrest the wrong guy, you'll have to deal with the problem all over again. You'll have to deal with Huber all over again."

That got his attention. Sig looks at me like he's trying to drill into my brain, trying to read my thoughts, the thoughts he knows I didn't say, wouldn't say in front of a civilian like Mrs. Atchley.

After what feels like time crawling slowly through hell, Sig moves his gaze from me to her. "Your son is safe. For now. Good night, Mrs. Atchley."

She cringes at Sig's *for now*, his words a sharp slap in her face.

I take Mrs. Atchley's arm to escort her out. She looks back at Sig, starts to say something, but before she can get her words out Sig says, "Not you, Cantor. We still have business to discuss."

"It's all right," I tell Mrs. Atchley. "You got what you came for. You've saved your son's life. That's enough for tonight."

With a nod to me, her alligator bag firmly under her arm, Dierdre Atchley walks away with all the dignity she was bred to flaunt. Maybe she knows, maybe she doesn't, how lucky she is that her son's not dead and neither is she.

Sig watches her walk away. He's still as stone. When she's gone, he stays silent. Not quite the crushing silence of earlier, but heavy enough to make me stand around with my hands in my pockets like a kid waiting to have my ears boxed. Finally, he says, "That business about dealing with Lieutenant Huber. You are asking me to put a contract out on a cop."

"Hell no," I say. "You know that's a line I wouldn't cross. It brings more heat than it's worth. But I wouldn't mind if you found other ways to take care of Huber."

"I see. Maybe you'd like me to arrange his early retirement."

"Yeah, to a nice little cabin outside a town nobody's ever heard of in some backwater state far away," I say. *And you right along with him*, I don't say.

"But the lieutenant is not all that's troubling you, Cantor." He tosses the stub of his cigar over the ledge of the terrace wall, not giving a damn if the burning thing lands on a passerby.

I say, "I've got all sorts of troubles, Sig. Doesn't everybody?" evading a subject I can't bring up if I want to stay alive, the subject of the death of Alice Lamarr and my certainty he had her killed. I might end up following Sig's cigar over the terrace wall.

But Sig Loreale didn't get to be the biggest, deadliest big shot in town by being dull in the skull. It wouldn't surprise me if he knew about me and Alice. It wouldn't surprise me at all. The only surprise is that, so far, he doesn't seem to care about it.

He says, "Do you think James Atchley killed Eve Garraway?" He's leaning over the terrace wall, his arms on the ledge. Light

170

from the street brushes his face. I wish it didn't. I wish I didn't see the tension in his jowly jaw, the narrowing of his heavy-lidded eyes when he turns his head to look at me. Being under Sig Loreale's stare is like being mowed down by an oncoming train.

"I think it's possible he killed her," I say.

"But you are not convinced."

I light a cigarette, let the tobacco keep me steady, let the smoke keep some distance between me and Sig. "The guy had plenty of reason," I say, "but there's the little problem of how he got into the house and up to Eve's office with three other people in the place. That little detail is like grit in my eye."

"Then you must find out if that would have been possible. Now, is there anything else you want to tell me? Anything about the Tenzi matter?"

"You already know Tenzi's in the klink. He'll get the chair for the murder of Lorraine Quinn. That should end it." We're skating close to talking about Alice, and maybe talking about Lorraine's photos, too. I'm sure he knows about the first, but I'm not sure about the second. Both are making the hair on my neck twitch.

"Well then," he says, "we have nothing more to talk about until you bring me Eve Garraway's killer, am I right?"

"Can't think of a thing," I say.

The desk sergeant, a tired guy aptly named Withers who's counting the days until his pension, can't believe his eyes when he sees me walk into the precinct house. "Unless you're turning yourself in, Gold, you got a lotta nerve strolling in here."

"Turn myself in for what?"

"Pick something."

"Why, I'm just a concerned citizen come to share useful information with Lieutenant Huber."

"You? A concerned citizen? Don't pull my leg."

"I wouldn't," I deadpan. "And don't bother calling Huber. I know my way upstairs to his office."

Sergeant Withers doesn't pick up the phone, doesn't signal for help to any cops milling around. He just lets me go my way, figures he's better off letting me be Huber's problem.

Upstairs in the squad room, uniformed cops and detectives in boring suits are at their desks, some on phones, some taking statements from willing or unwilling witnesses or from people dragged in in handcuffs. The place is noisy with phones ringing, civilians complaining, other cops horsing around over coffee. The room is thick with smoke from cigars and cigarettes, but it doesn't blunt the stink eyes I get from the cops as I walk to Huber's office.

I raise my knuckles to knock on the door, then decide I don't owe Huber the courtesy. I just walk in.

He's at his desk in his shirtsleeves, his collar open and his tie loose, his fedora on his head. He's reading a police file when I come through the door. He closes it when he sees me. "Took you long enough," he says.

"If you figured I'd show up, then you know why I'm here." I sit down in the chair opposite his desk, the same chair I sat in four years ago when Huber thought a wallop across my face would loosen my tongue about a murder I didn't commit. It didn't.

He says, "You're sore I didn't let you in on the Atchley arrest."

"Y'know, Huber, you always did only get half the picture. This time, you've got even less than that."

He takes the stub of an unlit cigar from an ashtray that should have been emptied last week, lights the cigar, and blows the smoke in my direction. "And I suppose you're going to fill me in?"

"Actually, I was hoping you'd fill me in. That's why I'm here. Fill me in on what you've got on James Atchley."

"Sure, I'll fill you in, and then you can get the hell outta here. I don't need you anymore, Gold. I got Atchley dead on for the Garraway killing. Even the brass who wanted me off the case are playing ball with this one. And you know why?"

"I bet you're gonna tell me."

"Cut the smart-mouth, Gold, or you can get lost, leave here no wiser than when you walked in. Listen, the brass is playing ball because they don't like being pushed around either, and City Hall was pushing them around."

"And they pushed you around."

"Yeah. And then there was Atchley's fancy lawyer, a real slick operator dropping diamond-studded names. The names were good enough to get Atchley released on bail, but that's it. Mr. James Atchley is going to trial for murder. You and I both know he had motive, and his alibi is shaky for the time Eve Garraway caught it in the back. But here's the kicker." Huber's warming to his tale, leaning forward in his chair. "It turns out the knife that killed Garraway belonged to one Mr. James Atchley." He parks his cigar in the corner of his now triumphantly smiling mouth.

He's earned his triumph. That bit of evidence with the knife could sink James Atchley no matter how many high-priced lawyers his mother sics on the court.

I pull out my pack of smokes, light one up while I think things over. After a deep drag and a long exhale that helps blur my view of the filthy window behind Huber's desk, I say, "How do you know the knife is Atchley's? You said there were no prints on it."

Huber leans back in his chair, lord of his shabby office. "You should've seen his face when I had him in the sweatbox and I showed him the crime scene photos of Garraway dead on the floor with a knife in her back. He babbled that it was his knife with a look of panic on his face I'll take to my grave, smiling. And then he tried to sell me a cock-and-bull story that the knife was one of the antiques the family no longer wanted and put up for auction. Some coincidence, huh? The knife goes up for auction, and Eve Garraway just happens to buy the knife that will kill her?"

"Lieutenant, did you check with the auction house?"

"Don't play me for a fool, Gold. Of course I checked," he says, but his triumphant smile is gone, replaced by the pursed lips of annoyance. "They told me they had no record of a knife with a carved bone handle consigned to them by the Atchleys."

"That's because the handle isn't bone, lieutenant. It's ivory." Making a cop feel stupid is one of my great pleasures. Sometimes it's a risky pleasure, like that day Huber walloped my face. But I'm in no danger of another wallop tonight. The only danger I'm in is maybe being tossed out of his office and the precinct station.

But not yet. "Okay, I'll go along that the knife bit doesn't look good for James," I say, playing for time by waving an olive branch. "On the other hand, did you ask him how the hell he got into Eve's office without Desmond or me or Vivienne seeing him?"

"I never got the chance," he says with disgust. "His bail came through, and his lawyer had him out of there the minute Atchley babbled about the knife."

"Well, that's it then," I say and plunge my smoke into the overflowing ashtray. "I guess I'm really off the hook now for the Garraway killing."

Huber says, "I guess you are," as if he's swallowed sour milk. "But there's always a next time, Gold."

"You should live so long," I say and get up from the chair, ready to leave.

"And what's that supposed to mean?"

"Those higher-ups who were pushing you around? Who do you think was pushing them around? Those same people still want the Garraway case to go away, and if they have to sacrifice James to do it, they will. I would put extra guards on his cell, lieutenant. And while you're at it, maybe you should put some watchful eyes on Johnny Tenzi's cell, too. You wouldn't want him to imitate his wife and commit suicide, would you?"

Huber doesn't like my smart aleck suicide jab. His hollow cheeks turn dark, the skin stretched tight on his bones.

But I push ahead. "And maybe you should take on a partner. You know, to protect your own back."

I don't bother saying good-bye on my way out the door.

Chapter Eighteen

Desmond's not in. The windows of the Garraway house are dark, and there's no answer to the doorbell. I guess now that he's not at Eve's beck and call Desmond can trot around wherever and whenever he likes, at least until the will is read, the estate is resolved, and Desmond Mallory is either the new permanent caretaker of the Garraway house or out of a job and a roof.

I'll have to find the answer on my own about how James Atchley might've gotten into the house without being seen. Without Desmond to show me around unfamiliar parts of the house, I'll have to rely on what I've learned about architecture over the years. In my racket, understanding a building's architecture tells me how to get in, helps me figure the best route to where the goods are kept and the best route to get out again.

A quick glance of the area confirms that there are only two ways to get inside the houses around Gramercy Park: from the street or from a back garden if they have one. The Garraway house, being on the corner, has a third way, from the south side façade.

I go down the front stairs to the street, avoid the light of street lamps, and slide into the shadows along the house. I made friends with New York's shadows years ago, learned the difference between shadows of the day and shadows of the night. I've treated them with respect, and they've protected me ever since from nosy neighbors, passing pedestrians, and patrolling cops. A big house with lots of carved architectural details like the Garraway place casts a lot of shadows, especially at night. I have my pick.

The first thing I do is check the basement windows next to the front stairs and on the south side of the house. I have to push the thick shrubbery aside to get to the windows. They're all locked. Steel mesh screening embedded in the glass protects the windows from being smashed. Access into the basement through those windows would be impossible.

I look up to the first- and second-floor windows. Their sculpted sills, scrollwork, and cornices could provide good hand-holds, but there's no way to reach them from the ground without a ladder or something else to stand on. I suppose one could stand on a stack of garbage cans, but that would be noisy, disturb the neighbors, who'd no doubt call the cops.

I can scratch getting into the house unseen from the front or side.

That leaves the back garden, my next stop along the path of shadows.

The garden gate is locked. But I remember the paper clips from Otis Hollander's office that I'd fashioned into lockpicks. Luck is with me; they're still in my coat pocket. I put them back into service and unlock the gate.

The trees and plants in the garden are mostly in silhouette. Here and there they catch a bit of light from the rear windows of Third Avenue apartment buildings a block east of Gramercy Park. The Garraway garden is walled off from the street, and since the garden gate is probably always locked, entry would be difficult if you didn't know how to pick the lock. Difficult, but not impossible, especially for an athletic guy like James Atchley. He could scale the gate or the roughly eight-foot wall, but it would be tricky in daylight, which is when Eve was killed. Atchley may be an arrogant, self-important son of a bitch, but he's probably not stupid enough to climb the wall in broad daylight for everyone and their grandmother to see and who'd, yeah, call the cops.

But let's say he got away with it, got into the garden unseen. Maybe he found a shadowy spot along the wall. Maybe, like me, he's friends with shadows, though I doubt it. I don't think they'd go for him. He's not their type. But you never know.

In the thin glow from the windows in the apartment buildings behind the garden, I can just make out the back of the house. And I see a door.

It's locked, too, and my paper clip lockpicks aren't strong enough to open this more substantial lock. I can't get in.

It doesn't matter, though. It tells me what I need to know. If James Atchley was able to get into the garden and open this door, he could get into the house. If he was stealthy enough, he could slip through the basement and up through the house to the second floor without being seen. He could've been in the house for hours, waiting for the right moment to kill Eve Garraway and then escape the way he came.

He could do all that.

It's nearly ten o'clock when I get back to my place. I've got a headful of questions, but no solid answers. Just a lot of maybes. Maybe James Atchley killed Eve Garraway, or maybe he didn't. Maybe it was Dierdre Atchley who was behind the whole thing, or maybe she wasn't. Maybe Sig's connection to Sterling Auctions is somehow involved with the Garraway mess, or maybe it isn't. Maybe Sig knows what was in Lorraine Quinn's photographs or maybe he doesn't. Maybe Vivienne's moment of concern for me was real or maybe it wasn't. Maybe Alice . . .

The memory of Alice descends on me like a shroud. She'd asked me for a good-bye kiss and I ran out the door, afraid of her desire, afraid I'd be trapped by the need of her. Now I'm trapped by her memory.

I light a cigarette, pour myself a Chivas, and turn on the television. Maybe the box will take my mind off all the other maybes and the haunting memory of Alice. The Lux Video Theatre is starting a drama they stole from a movie, which stole it from a

Broadway show about a rich young woman who falls in love with a fortune hunter in New York's gaslight days. Nothing's changed. They could've written the script yesterday.

Two drinks later, the show's not improving my mood. I toss around the idea of going to the Green Door Club, let some pretty thing soothe my troubles, but the place carries reminders of Alice that are too recent, too fresh.

I pour another scotch. And then another.

Light comes at me, and some guy gabbing about . . . pie. Apple pie. I don't know where the light and the chatter are coming from. I don't know why there's light in my eyes since it occurs to me that my eyes are closed. I open them slowly; the light glares through my slitted lids. I figure out that it's sunlight through my living room window. The noisy blather about apple pie comes from the television, an announcer hawking Fluffo shortening. I see a woman's hand scoop out a spoonful of the waxy stuff, a gray glop in the black-and-white TV picture. My stomach turns over.

I'm still in my big red club chair. I remember sitting down in it, but don't remember falling asleep in it.

A hot shower fixes some of the kinks in my chair-bound muscles, clears my head of the alcohol haze. But my cleared head makes room for thoughts and memories to come rushing back in. Sig's threats loom large. Dierdre Atchley makes an appearance. So does Lorraine Quinn. And Eve Garraway. And Vivienne, Johnny Tenzi, and Alice.

Alice's funeral is this morning.

It wasn't all that long ago that the borough of Queens was mostly small towns, ash piles, factories, and potato farms. People in Manhattan never came out here, and people from the Long Island mansions just passed through on their way into town. But almost overnight after the Second World War the towns of

Queens burst with returning GIs and their new wives, new kids, new jobs, and new money. Tract housing grew faster than the trees that supplied the wood. The developments straddled town lines, so that where one town ended the next town now begins just across the street. Shops selling everything from televisions to dishwashers followed the new neighborhoods. These days, GI Johnny and his wife have wall-to-wall carpeting, a Chevy or a Dodge or a Plymouth in their two-car garage, a lawn in front of the house, a barbecue grill in the backyard, and a couple of kids. Queens is fat and happy, and the developers just keep building. The only things in their way are the dead. Queens is New York's borough of cemeteries.

I turn off Northern Boulevard onto 162nd Street and through the gates of Flushing Cemetery with a few minutes to spare before Alice's ten a.m. service. The gatehouse guy gives me directions to the Lamarr burial.

Her plot's at the edge of a treeless section. I guess it was the best Judson could get on such short notice. I pull up behind the only other car parked in the area, the hearse. There's no one at the graveside except a bored chaplain in a black coat and hat. He's checking his watch.

"In a hurry?" I say when I get out of the Buick and approach the graveside. Alice's coffin is on the platform ready to be lowered into the ground.

Surprised at either my question or my arrival, or maybe my black silk suit and tie under my unbuttoned coat, he stammers, "Oh, good morning. I was just wondering whether to start the service or wait for the mourners to arrive. You're the first." He might've bitten his own tongue if he'd seen my gun, but I'd left it home. I figured a funeral is no place for the violence of my life, and Alice's.

"What time is it?" I ask.

He looks at his watch again. "Just now ten o'clock."

I look along the road from the gatehouse. There are no other cars rolling toward Alice's burial.

179

The chaplain asks, "Did you know Miss Lamarr well?"

"Intimately," I say quietly. "Okay, let's start the service." I take my cap off.

He takes his place at one side of Alice's coffin. I take my place on the other. The coffin's a nicely polished cherrywood with brass fittings. Very classy. Alice would have liked it. Judson did well. There's no headstone yet, just a marker with "Alice Lamarr" written on it and the name of the funeral parlor Judson dealt with.

The chaplain does the ashes-to-ashes, dust-to-dust bit, commends Alice to heaven—if there is such a place, yeah, I hope she makes it—and then asks me if I wish to say a few words over the deceased. I'm sure I shock the guy through every organ of his body when I bend down to the coffin and give it a good-bye kiss.

I park the Buick at my place, but decide to walk up the street to Pete's for a bite of lunch, Doris's good coffee, and her good cheer. I need it. I'm just at the door when a cop car pulls up, and a hard-faced cop in a gray coat and fedora gets out of the car and follows me inside. He's accompanied by a young cop in uniform. The hard-faced guy grabs my arm, shows me his teeth, his detective's badge and identification. He says, "Cantor Gold, you're under arrest for the murder of Lieutenant Norman Huber."

Chapter Nineteen

I shout to Doris, "Call my lawyer, Winston Maximovic! He's in the book!" as Detective Sergeant Liam Adair and his uniformed sidekick lock the steel bracelets on me and hustle me out of the luncheonette. The uniformed kid pushes me into the backseat of the car, then gets into the driver's seat.

He turns the siren on to force our way through midtown traffic. The noise kills any chance of conversation. Just as well. I need to think, need to work through the mess that comes from a cop killing. I can't say I'm sad about Huber being gone from my life, but I'm not happy about the way he was taken out of the picture. Nothing stirs up the cops like the murder of one of their own. The whole department goes wild, like bees on a rampage, stingers out.

It's no use asking why they've stung me for the killing. I've been on their prize catch list for years. My testy relationship with Huber, and the Devil's bargain that threw us together, gives the cops a convenient hook on which to hang me. Whether they can make the charge stick is another story, something I leave Winnie to handle. It will be a lot easier for him if I can figure who's behind the Huber hit. My first thought is Sig. He was annoyed enough that Huber was disobeying Sig's behind-the-scenes orders. But I toss that scenario right away. Sig wants the cops complacent, not wild with fury. He knows better than to order a cop killing.

So who? Who would be stupid enough to kill a cop? Who would think they could get away with it?

By the time we pull up to the precinct house, an idea starts to take shape. An idea I don't like. But I like it better than getting wired up and fried for a murder I didn't do.

Sergeant Adair yanks me out of the car. The uniformed kid comes around my other side. The three of us walk into the station.

The desk sergeant, tired old Withers, enjoys his smug smile when he sees me bookended by Adair and the uniform. "You crossed the line, Gold," he says. "You crossed the line."

As Adair marches me through the building on our way to the holding cells, I get heavy stink eye, murderous looks, sour grins, even mocking catcalls from the precinct's cops. One guy even jokes, "Can I have your fancy suits after they fry you, Gold?"

I tell him, "The trousers would be too big in the crotch." This gets a laugh from the crowd.

Adair hauls me downstairs to the booking area. The green walls could induce nausea, and the scuffed and sticky linoleum floor is a color they haven't invented yet, though beige bears a distant resemblance. I don't know who the grimy room insults more, the unfortunate souls hauled in here in handcuffs or the booking cops forced to be here all day or all night. Today's booking officer, a lanky guy who looks like we just woke him up, adds his jeering smile to the ones already thrown my way. He takes too much pleasure in filling out my arrest paperwork, a task cops usually find tedious. I guess I should be flattered. I've made his day.

When he's done, he presses a buzzer and a police matron comes through a door. She wears one of those uniforms designed to turn a woman's curves into boxy boulders. Her billy club hangs from her belt.

The matron and I have three things in common: she's around my age, she's around my height, and both of us think that what the other is wearing is an insult to a woman's body. She takes my arm with a steel grip that mocks the idea of women as the weaker sex.

The matron takes me through the door to the women's holding area. She unlocks the cell, pushes me inside, locks the cell, and tells me to put my hands through the bars so she can unlock the cuffs. When she's done, she takes a seat at her desk nearby where she busies herself with a newspaper.

Three women are in the cell. Two of them are ladies of the night in tight skirts, tight sweaters, well-worn high-heeled shoes, and lipstick red enough to start a fire. One of the women is a bottle blonde with a once-upon-a-time pretty face, which could break my heart if I had the time. The other, a natural redhead, is tough and dull. The bottle blonde gives me a smile. The redhead doesn't bother. The third woman, though, the woman seated on a bench against the cell bars, her pale blue silk dress out of place in the sordid surroundings, the expression on her face like she'd jump off a bridge if given the chance, stops me in my tracks.

It's Vivienne.

Seeing me, she gets up from the bench, walks over to me, and slaps my face. Hard. Her expression has changed from despair to icy fury.

The bottle blonde who smiled at me says, "Looks like Miss Fancy Panties has some spine after all."

Vivienne says, "This is your fault, Cantor. I warned you not to drag me into this—this—whatever it is. My attorney should be here soon to arrange for my release, and when I'm gone, I don't ever want to see you again. You're too dangerous, Cantor. You're a threat to my reputation and my position at the museum."

"Slow down," I say. "First of all, what did they arrest you for?" I take her hand to calm her.

She yanks it away. "They said I was interfering with a police investigation."

"Which investigation? The Garraway murder? And just how the hell did you interfere?"

"I don't know. A Sergeant Adair showed up at my house this morning and arrested me. He didn't even give me a chance to get my coat. George was so shaken, I was afraid the poor man was going to have a heart attack. But why are you here? Oh god, maybe I don't want to know."

183

"I think you need to know, Vivienne. I don't think it's a coincidence that it was Adair who hauled both of us in on the same day. We might both be facing the fight of our lives. You want to fight this alone?"

The blonde says, "I'd listen to your friend, missy. Sounds like she wants to save your dainty little life."

"If you *please*," Vivienne snaps to my streetwise defender.

The woman gives Vivienne the once-over, looks her up and down like she's deciding if Vivienne's even worth talking to. "Suit yourself, honey. Hell, we're all sisters under the whack of the billy club. You just don't know it yet."

I take Vivienne's hand again, keep my voice gentle. She doesn't fight it this time. "Listen, Vivienne. Either somebody wants to tie a rope around the Garraway situation and drop it down deep where no one will find it, or someone is out for revenge. You with me?"

She gives me a reluctant nod, says, "So why are you here? Why did they arrest you?"

"Remember Lieutenant Huber? He's dead. They say I killed him."

I've never seen the color drain from someone's face as fast as it drains from Vivienne's. "Did you?" It comes out so soft, her voice so tight, it almost squeaks.

"This is the second time you've floated the idea that maybe I'm a murderer, Vivienne. Do I scare you that much?"

It's the bottle blonde who answers. "You don't scare me, sweetie. When we get out of here, look me up. Your money's good with me."

I give her a smile and a tip of my cap.

The sisterhood in our cell is interrupted by the ringing phone on the matron's desk. After her bored "Okay," she hangs up, comes to our cell jangling her keys, and unlocks our cell door. "Okay, Gold. Your lawyer's in Sergeant Adair's office. Get a move on."

I take Vivienne's arm as gently as if I'm escorting her to the opera. "Let's go," I say.

184

The matron blocks Vivienne with her billy club. "Not you. Just Gold."

I push the stick away, stare at the matron. "Step aside," I say.

The matron stares back, but she's no match for the steel-hard determination I'm throwing at her. I escort Vivienne past the matron and her billy club.

Sergeant Liam Adair's office could be a carbon copy of Huber's: cramped, dusty, with a battered desk and a greasy window that turns sunlight into an eggy ooze. Adair, though, is neater than Huber ever was. His gray suit, boring and cheaply cut, is nevertheless clean and pressed, and his tie, a black-and-green spiral print, is up to date. The ashtray on his desk has only a few cigarette butts, and the desk is less cluttered. But he has the same attitude as Huber. Behind his desk and his badge, he's all powerful and Vivienne and I are prey.

We're seated opposite Adair's desk. Winnie, elegant in a dark brown suit that gives his enormous bulk the dignity of a mountain, stands beside me. He says, "Sergeant Adair, on what evidence did you arrest my client, Cantor Gold?"

"Ask the prosecutor. He's obliged to share that information. My job was to haul her in."

"On whose instructions?"

Adair leans forward across his desk. The grin on his tough-as-nails face should be in a horror movie. "Ask the prosecutor that, too."

I say, "While we're all waiting breathlessly for the prosecutor to fork over, suppose you tell me just how Huber was killed."

"You shot him, Gold. In the back, like the cowardly scum you are."

I start to ask another question, but the door to Adair's office opens and a well-tailored gent walks in. "So sorry to be late. Friday traffic is wretched." He's one of those gray-at-the-temples types, with a thin, chiseled nose that always seems to sniff at the world. "Hello, Vivienne," he says. "They told me downstairs that you'd already been sent up here. Let's go."

Adair says, "And just who might you be?"

The guy whips a card out from his breast pocket, hands it to Adair. "I am Arthur Henley of the firm of Henley & Crown, Miss Parkhurst Trent's attorneys. The paperwork for her release is being signed as we speak. Hello, Winston," he says to Winnie in an offhand way that lets us all know he doesn't count Winnie among his more beloved courtroom comrades. "Vivienne, I have a cab waiting."

Vivienne stays in her chair. "Just a minute, Arthur. Cantor was about to ask the sergeant something, and I want to know what it is."

Henley says, "As your attorney, Vivienne, I advise you to have nothing to do with Mr. Maximovic's client or the charges against her."

Vivienne shoots me a look that carries tenderness and insolence at the same time, the eternal pairing of her aristocratic and savage bloodlines. "It's too late for that, Arthur."

Winnie says, "Yes, Arthur, it is rather late. I have an appointment at City Hall, which I should not miss. It would dearly disappoint the councilman." The hint of bite in Winnie's courtly delivery puts the hoity-toity attorney in his place, while Winnie's smile could charm a schoolmarm into stripping naked. To me, he says, "You were saying, Cantor?"

"Oh yeah," I say with a side-eye at Henley. "So tell me, Sergeant Adair, just where did Huber's killing take place?"

Adair gives me a frown and a disgusted *tsk*. "Keep pushing your luck, Gold, and I'll send you back downstairs so fast you won't even know you're outta that chair."

Winnie says, "Just a moment, sergeant. I am Cantor's attorney. You are obliged to inform me of the reason for her arrest and the nature of the resulting charges against her. So let's address that question again, shall we? I want to know where Lieutenant Huber was killed, the weapon used, and the hour of the crime. If you do not cooperate, I will be forced to file a complaint. Actually," he adds with his most winning smile, "I can do that while I'm at City Hall this afternoon. I'm sure the councilman can hurry the process."

That's why I have Winston Maximovic as my lawyer. High-priced, fancy attorneys like Henley might play the legal and courtroom games with panache, but Winnie Maximovic plays the game of power. It saves me every time.

It won this round with Sergeant Adair, who uncomfortably nods his cooperation. "Huber was coming out of the coffee joint down the block. He liked to get his mid-morning bagel and coffee over there. He said the walk helped clear his head. He was on his way back here when a bullet found him. Your bullet, Gold."

Winnie says, "How do you know the bullet came from my client's weapon? Was there a ballistics check on a gun you never recovered or that we never turned over to you? And did anyone at the scene identify my client?"

I jump on Winnie's bandwagon. "And while we're at it, what time did all this happen?"

Adair looks like his birthday cake's been rained on.

Winnie presses. "Answer the questions, please, sergeant. I do not want to keep the councilman waiting."

Adair leans back in his chair, loosens his tie, stares into space with the worried expression of someone watching his career shred in front of his eyes. "There are people," he says, looking quickly at Winnie, then at me, then at nothing again, "people who make decisions. I don't know who those people are. If the brass does, they're not telling. They just pass those decisions along, and guys like me are ordered to carry them out."

I say, "And I was one of those decisions."

Henley says, "And so was my client, Miss Parkhurst Trent. Tell me, sergeant, was any of this meant to stick? Or was it all just a warning." Henley's finally convinced me he's a savvy lawyer.

The question angers Adair. "When I make an arrest, counselor, it's meant to stick."

I say, "In that case, sergeant, let's see what you can do with the murder charge you've tacked onto me. What time was Huber gunned down?"

"Shortly before ten this morning."

"How shortly before?"

"Well, 9:56," he says. "If you've got an alibi, Gold, it better be solid."

"Solid as they come, sergeant. I'd just arrived at a funeral, burying Huber's previous case."

If Adair's sigh was any deeper, he'd be pulling air up from between his toes. "Lamarr," he says. "Alice Lamarr. I guess if I check, someone can confirm you were there?"

"Would you doubt the word of a chaplain?"

Adair shakes his head. "Huber said he didn't buy Lamarr's suicide. Do you?"

I answer with a shrug. That's all I'll give him. After my Devil's bargain with Huber, I learned my lesson about sharing anything with cops.

"Play it smart, Gold," he says. "Maybe we can clean this thing up together."

"Listen, Adair, the last time I made a deal with a cop, he wound up dead and I got arrested. Don't be nice to me, sergeant. We both might not survive it."

Chapter Twenty

Vivienne and I take Henley's waiting cab, leaving the flabbergasted attorney on the street.

I'd given Vivienne my coat when we walked out of the police station into the chilly September afternoon. Even in the cab, she keeps it wrapped close around her. By the time we arrive at her place, she's not shivering too much.

George looks like he's been given the go-ahead to breathe again when he opens the door. "Oh, Miss Vivienne, I'm so glad you've returned safely."

She says, "Thank you, George," with deep and genuine warmth, borne probably of being taken to the park by the faithful butler when Vivienne was a toddler and her parents were busy being New York swells. After George takes my coat from his mistress's shoulders and hangs the coat and my cap on the hall rack, Vivienne asks him to bring a pot of hot coffee and a tray of sandwiches to the living room.

George gives a dignified "Of course," and trots off to the kitchen. I follow Vivienne to the living room, enjoying the sway of her pale blue silk dress flowing around her with every step. Vivienne's curves know how to carry silk.

In the living room, Vivienne, exhausted from her jailhouse ordeal, floats down to the sofa with the delicacy of a shredding cloud. I head for the liquor table behind the sofa and pour us each a shot of scotch.

"Here, this'll stiffen your bones and warm your blood until the coffee gets here," I say and hand her the drink.

She nods her thanks, downs the scotch, puts the glass on the coffee table, then leans back against the sofa cushions and closes her eyes while the whiskey courses through her. The color comes back into her cheeks.

I watch all this from the chair opposite the sofa.

Vivienne opens her eyes, sees me watching her. She smiles a little. Just a little.

"Welcome back," I say.

"I didn't go far," she says. "Cantor, thanks for getting me past that dragon of a police matron."

"Then we're even," I say. "It evens us up for getting me past Huber the morning Eve was killed."

"Huber." Vivienne says the name as if she wished she'd never heard it or ever laid eyes on its owner. "Who would be crazy enough to gun down a policeman?"

"Someone who thinks they're safe enough to get away with it," I say. "They almost did."

The reality of what I just said works its way through Vivienne like a bitter pill dissolving slowly. She looks at me through widened eyes, sees me as one of the Law's condemned. "Cantor, how do you . . . I mean, when the police . . . Cantor, how do you survive?"

"I survive because I have to. I survive because I don't like getting pushed around just for living my life."

"And for who you take to your bed." She says it softly, almost sadly. I hope it's not regret for our one shared night.

I repeat, just as softly, "And for who I take to my bed," but there's no sadness when I say it at all.

"You're your own army," she says. "An army of one?"

"If I have to be," I say, shrugging it off. "Could be that army might get bigger. There's talk about organizing to get the Law off our necks, or so I've been told."

That prospect seems to please Vivienne. At least it kicked her sadness aside. She's the comfortably regal, elegantly alluring

190

Vivienne Parkhurst Trent again. "I think that's a marvelous idea," she says. "Maybe you wouldn't have to hide anymore."

"I don't hide now," I say.

"Which is one of the reasons you have those scars on your face. For heaven's sake, Cantor, wouldn't you want a life less chancy, less threatening? Maybe even a life where you could fit in with the world?"

"Fitting in might turn out to be a straitjacket."

George comes in with the tray of coffee and sandwiches, saving me from a discussion I'm not in the mood for. Right now, the hard realities of Sig's threats, the cops on my back, and the murder of three women loom larger than a hazy political future which might frown on the way I live as much as the straight-backs who frown on it now.

George asks if we require anything else, and when Vivienne gives him a pleasant, "No, thank you," he leaves us alone in the living room.

Vivienne takes up hosting duties and pours us each a cup of coffee.

The coffee's good and strong, the sandwich—I've picked up a roast beef on rye—takes care of the lunch abruptly postponed by Sergeant Adair and his uniformed sidekick.

"Okay, Cantor," Vivienne says after thoughtful bites of her ham sandwich and sips of coffee, "what are we going to do about the Garraway and Huber situations? They're really making a mess in both of our lives."

"We? Five minutes ago you were all knotted up about the danger in my life, and now you want to get involved in two murders?"

"Five minutes ago I was tired and hungry. Well, the coffee's perked me up, the food is comforting, and I don't like being pushed around anymore than you do. That sergeant and that police matron pushed me around, and I won't stand for it. And besides, you know I can handle myself in a tight spot. You've seen it."

Yeah, I have, when Vivienne made a crack shot across a room and saved my skin.

But this is different. This time there's at least one sharp killer out there, maybe two, and hovering over it all is Sig, who might not take kindly to interference by this scholarly curator. Sig has ways of taking care of people who interfere.

"Vivienne, I've got to handle this alone."

"Well, that's insulting," she says. "Your life isn't the only one that's on the line here, Cantor. I have a life and career to salvage, too. This scandal could sink me at the museum. And you can't cut me out of whatever you're planning to do because like it or not I'm already in the thick of it. So now tell me, who do you think killed Lieutenant Huber? Do you think it's the same person who killed Eve?"

She's sitting up straight, a woman with a hunter's heart and a marksman's eye, and the impatience to use both. In other words, it's Vivienne Parkhurst Trent at her most impressive. And her most beautiful.

She says, "What's so funny?" in response to the grin I can't control.

"I'm imagining you as a medieval warrior queen, galloping on your horse with your sword and your shield, determined to smite the invading barbarians."

"I'm certainly ready to smite the barbarians who've invaded my life. More coffee?" The Trent huntress and the Parkhurst hostess in the same magnificent skin.

I nod for the freshened coffee, watch the steady hand pouring from the silver pot, the same steady hand that can ease back a shotgun trigger with the delicacy of a tickle.

"I'm not sure who killed Eve or Huber," I say. "The police think James Atchley did the Garraway killing."

"Yes, I know. Dierdre phoned me after his arrest. She was furious."

"How furious?" I ask.

"As furious as a mother can be when her offspring is threatened, which is pretty furious. Oh! Cantor, you don't think—"

"I do think. But that's it, just lots of thoughts but no facts. Do I think Dierdre Atchley is capable of killing Huber in revenge for the arrest of her son? Sure. Do I think she's fool enough to do it on her own? And in broad daylight? Down the street from a police station? Maybe she hired someone to do it. I wouldn't put it past her. I don't know her well enough to answer those questions. But you do."

Vivienne relaxes back in the sofa again, at home in the familiar territory of discussing her social circle. "Let me ask you something, Cantor. If you lost everything that mattered to you, everything that shaped your life, made life worth living, how far would you go to get revenge on whoever caused your— well, heartbreak?"

There it is, the wound that won't heal, the pain I try to drown with women, whiskey, and the thrill of my criminal life. The wound won't heal because my vengeance failed. I couldn't save the woman who was everything, the woman who gave shape to my life, who made life worth living. The woman whose name I won't say because saying it crashes the scaffolding I've built to keep me standing.

"Cantor?" My name comes to me as if from far away. "Cantor?" Vivienne says again, luring me out of the wilderness.

"Yeah, Dierdre Atchley," I say, letting the feel of her name in my mouth be the final snap back into the here and now. "Furious mother taking revenge. Okay, maybe. But only maybe."

"Here's the part you're missing, Cantor. If Dierdre killed Huber out of revenge, it wasn't just vengeance for James's arrest. It was also revenge for what that arrest did to her life. If Eve's takeover of the Atchley banking empire had been successful, it would have embarrassed the Atchleys, taken them down a peg, but they would have adapted. They would have survived."

"Even while being snubbed?"

"Sure, the family would be snubbed in certain circles. It would hurt their pride. But the Atchleys would still have the power of their lineage, not to mention all that money. It could cushion the blow a bit. It's Eve, the pushy social climber, who'd be the villain in high society's eyes. But if the Atchleys have a family member arrested for murder? Maybe convicted? Condemned to a sordid death in the electric chair? A scandal of that magnitude would destroy the Atchleys. No amount of lineage or money could save them. They'd topple from the pinnacle of society to the gutter of the disgraced, well-upholstered as that gutter might be. Diedre Atchley would not tolerate being disgraced. She'd sooner die."

"Or kill."

Vivienne gives that a heavy nod, the sort of nod that accepts rotten news.

I say, "But let's not hang her yet. Just because she could do it doesn't mean she did. Like you said, who'd be crazy enough to kill a cop? Dierdre Atchley doesn't strike me as crazy."

Vivienne says, "Yes, you're right," with the relief of grabbing a lifeline. "She doesn't strike me as crazy, either. She's one of the most calculating women I've ever met."

Now, there's a new spin. Dierdre Atchley may not be crazy, but maybe she's calculating enough to figure her odds in getting away with taking revenge on a cop. The kicker of it is, the odds just might be in her favor, because the city's high and mighty string-pullers just want the whole Garraway business to go away, Huber included.

Funny, the only two people who might have plans for either revenge or deadly justice are Dierdre Atchley and Sig Loreale. I'd laugh if the idea didn't make my skin crawl.

"Listen, Vivienne, thanks for the lunch, but I've got to go."

"What are you planning to do, Cantor?"

"I have to talk to Dierdre Atchley again."

Vivienne waves the idea away. "You can't be serious. I doubt she'll see you."

She's right. I have to get around that. The question is how. I work through a number of possibilities, all of them dead ends. And then I realize that the answer I'd been avoiding, the answer that scares me with its risk, is sitting right in front of me. "You're a friend of Dierdre's, Vivienne. Any chance you could get me in to talk to her?"

"Are you asking me to come along?"

"It's against my better judgement, but I guess I am."

There are very few sights in life as pleasurable as seeing Vivienne Parkhurst Trent get her way.

I give the cabbie my address, explain to Vivienne's puzzled expression that I have to pick up a few things before going to the Atchleys' apartment.

When we reach my place, I help Vivienne from the cab, take her arm to escort her into the building.

She holds back. "How about if I wait here?" she says, her green gloved hands rubbing up and down the sleeves of her dark blue wool coat.

"On the street? You're already shivering."

"Well, in the lobby, then."

I want to ask her what she's afraid of, ask her if she's afraid of the memories she'd find in my apartment, memories of the night she showed up unexpectedly at my door and wound up in my bed. But I don't ask her, because to ask could embarrass her, and I know the answer anyway.

So I just nod, escort her into the lobby, and take the elevator up to my apartment alone.

I'm back down to the lobby a few minutes later, equipped to take on Mrs. Dierdre Atchley.

I escort Vivienne to my car.

One likes to think of residential architecture as welcoming. Even an apartment building like mine promises a little bit of "Home Sweet Home" to the residents, and a note of "Nice to See You" if you're a visitor. But the ritzy apartment towers lining Park Avenue don't even try. Their facades were designed to ignore you if you're not a resident, to be sentinels against the undeserving Everybody Else. Erected mostly during the late teens and 1920s, these la-di-dah buildings changed the definition of residential luxury from an ornate townhouse with a bunch of rooms stuffed with gewgaws and an army of servants to dust them, to spacious apartments with fewer rooms, fewer gewgaws, so requiring fewer servants. The rich love to save labor costs.

The building housing the Atchleys boasts of being the most exclusive on Park Avenue, the occupants among the wealthiest and most prominent people in town, people whose tentacles of influence reach across oceans. Perched atop this stately stone pile is the Atchley family.

Guarding the entrance to the tower is a beefy doorman in full livery of chocolate brown with brass buttons and gold braiding. His "Good afternoon," is friendly enough, but the way he looks me over isn't. But that's okay. I'm used to it. "Are you expected?" he says to Vivienne.

In her bluest blueblood tone, she says, "Miss Vivienne Parkhurst Trent to see Mrs. Dierdre Atchley."

With another disapproving glance at me, the doorman dials the intercom mounted beside the imposing entry door of etched glass accented with pointy-ended curlicues of iron. He announces Vivienne, adds "and guest," then waits for the reply. After a wait of a few moments, presumably while the maid or butler checks with the family, the doorman hangs up. He says, "Sorry, folks, I can't let you go up."

Vivienne says, "Is the family not home?"

The doorman puts up his hands as if ready to shoo away the riffraff. "I've been instructed not to let you up. Now, just move along."

I sense Vivienne stiffen beside me. Not only doesn't she like being pushed around, she's not used to it, and this is the second time today she's gotten pushed around. Her annoyance, and her frustration that there's nothing she can do about it, tightens every muscle in her face.

But there's something I can do about it. I give the doorman a nod, give Vivienne a smile, and gently take her arm. "Let's go," I say.

She reluctantly lets me lead her away.

We're a few steps along Park Avenue, walking toward the corner, when Vivienne turns her head to look back in the opposite direction. "Your car's the other way," she says.

"We're not going to my car."

"Then where are we going?"

"To talk to the Atchleys." We turn the corner.

The Atchleys' apartment building extends about a third of the way along the expensive street of elegant brownstones and the few remaining robber baron mansions. The service entrance is toward the back of the building, where tradesmen bring in the residents' grocery deliveries or wrestle a new sofa inside.

Vivienne, realizing where we're going, says, "This is a waste of time, Cantor. The building staff won't let us in here, either. Don't even bother to ring the bell."

"I'm not planning on ringing the bell."

"You mean you're breaking in? You're going to get us arrested. Again."

I half expect her to stamp her foot.

When we arrive at the door, I tell Vivienne, "Stand behind me."

I reach into the inside pocket of my coat, take out the leather case of lockpicks I took from my apartment. I took my gun and shoulder rig from my apartment, too. I'm still not sure if the Atchleys are killers, but I'm not going to be caught naked, especially with Vivienne along for the ride. I'm already feeling rotten about the deaths of Lorraine and Eve, and my guts were shredded with the murder of Alice. If anything happens to Vivienne, I don't know if my soul could stand it.

I examine the lock on the service door, pull out the correct hook and pick, and with a little probing the lock clicks open.

I say to Vivienne, "Stay here; don't come in until I tell you it's safe."

"Safe? Cantor, this is Park Avenue, not a Mob joint."

"Tell that to Lucky Luciano. He lived down the street at the Waldorf. Now, stay behind me and don't come in until I tell you."

I turn the knob, open the door.

A guy in green work clothes and surprise on his boiled potato face is quick to the door. "Who're you? And how'd you get in here?" he says, eyeing me like he's never seen a coat and cap before, or at least never seen them on the likes of me.

Telling him who I am and why I'm here won't get me past him. And it's pretty clear I'm not delivering anything.

There are two ways that might get me through, get me and Vivienne to the service elevator and up to the Atchley penthouse. The first way is usually reliable in these situations. If it fails, the second way often does the trick, though leaving blood drops could jam me up later if the guy squawks to the cops or other wrong people.

I reach into the back pocket of my trousers, take my wallet, slip out a twenty-dollar bill. I say to the potato-faced guy, "You never saw us, understand? If there's any trouble, I'll know it was you who squealed." I take out my .38 to make the point.

The guy's gone gray as dust. He takes the twenty.

I motion for Vivienne to come in.

She says, "Good afternoon," to the guy, gives him a smile.

He says, "Yeah sure, you too, lady."

We walk into a large dingy room lit by glaring overhead bulbs with no shades. Hard shadows rake across shelves crammed with tools, electrical supplies, cleaning supplies, and other equipment to keep the building shipshape. There's a battered desk with a cheap tin ashtray half filled with butts, coffee-stained paperwork held down by a telephone, and a desk chair with a torn seat.

I say to our potato-faced host, "How about you just sit down and pay no attention to us." I indicate the chair with a wave of my .38. He sits down. I smile.

Vivienne and I walk across the room to a wide hallway and the service elevator. I lift the grating, and we walk in. After I close the grate and press the button on the brass panel for the penthouse floor, I notice Vivienne staring at me. If looks could kill, well, maybe I wouldn't be dead but I'd be good and bloody, and there'd be wet red drops among all the dried paint drips on the elevator's wooden floor.

She says, "Did you have to scare that poor guy by waving your gun around?"

"Yes," I say.

"Would you really have shot him?"

"Waving my gun around made sure I wouldn't have to shoot him."

I guess that satisfies her since she gives it a nod and a hint of a smile.

We don't speak again until after I lift the elevator grate at the penthouse floor. Vivienne says, "Are you going to wave your gun in the servants' faces, too?"

"Depends on the faces," I say.

That gets a *tsk* and an eye roll from Vivienne and a smile from me.

We step off the elevator into the concrete gray-walled service hallway, then go through a door into the thickly carpeted main hall. Here, the walls are papered in silk and decorated with hand-painted scenes of colonial era New York. It probably cost more than most people's yearly rent. Besides the service door, there's a door at each end of the hallway; one is a double door of carved dark wood and big brass handles, the other's a standard door with a standard doorknob.

Vivienne starts toward the fancy double door. I hold her back, say, "This way," and lead her to the standard door.

She says, "But that's the kitchen entrance."

"Where we have a better chance of not having the door slammed in our faces."

"Ah, I see your point," she says. I start to press the button for the bell, but Vivienne stays my hand. "Try the doorknob." In answer to my lifted brows, she says, "It's often left unlocked during the day so if a servant arrives carrying things for the kitchen or the family, they won't have to fumble for keys or wait for someone to answer the doorbell. And now I'm sorry I told you."

My eyebrows go up again, but then I get it. I give her a wink and a smile. "Good thing I do my best break-in work at night after they've locked the kitchen door. You're off the hook, Vivienne."

"Very funny," she says, not laughing.

I turn the doorknob slowly, quietly, and open the door. It takes a minute for the cook, a slender woman in whites, to look up from stirring something on the stove, its pungent aroma of lemon and garlic tempting me to try a spoonful. Seeing me and Vivienne, the cook stops stirring and opens her mouth to say something, her eyes wide. But a finger to my lips and the no-nonsense set of my face—helped by my scars, no doubt—quiets her before she can get even a single word out.

I follow Vivienne through the kitchen, which leads into the dining room. Tall windows along a wall covered in peach damask send streaks of sunlight across the rosewood table. There's enough art on the walls to fill the Early American galleries of Vivienne's museum, and what I'm pretty sure is an original Paul Revere silver coffee and tea service is on the sideboard.

My appreciation of the Atchleys' taste and their ability to pay for it is interrupted by a woman's scream coming through the dining room's closed double doors. I pull out my .38 and tell Vivienne to wait here, which she answers with, "Like hell I will."

We make a dash to the doors. I slide them open. We're in the living room, a palatial gold-and-white cavern where Dierdre Atchley, in a green taffeta dress more suited to a cocktail party than a brawl, is screaming, "Brooks, no!" over and over as she runs out to the terrace. A tall guy in a navy blue suit has James Atchley pinned on the ledge of the terrace wall. One wrong move on either man's part and James could go over, fall twenty-eight floors to the street.

Dierdre tries to pull her husband off her son, but she can't shake his violent grip.

I shout to Dierdre and Vivienne, "Grab James's arms!" and when they do I slam Brooks Atchley's head with the butt of my

200

.38. Stunned, he lets go of James while Vivienne and Dierdre pull him safely off the terrace ledge.

Dierdre, crying, hugs James. She wipes blood from his cheek and fingers the blood on his white shirt in a way that's somewhat more than motherly.

I notice Vivienne wince.

Brooks Atchley, silver-haired, ramrod straight but unsteady and a bit wild-eyed from the smash to his head, mutters, "Vivienne?" as if surprised she's here.

Vivienne says, "I thought you were in Geneva, Brooks. Maybe you should have stayed there."

He puts a hand to his head where I walloped him. "I—I returned late last night." He has a boardroom voice, smooth as polished wood-paneled walls.

We've been joined on the terrace by the Atchley butler, a guy with a round face tight with horror. "I heard a commotion," he says with the understatement of the butler's trade while trying not to trip all over his terrified tongue. "Do you need assist—"

Brooks Atchley cuts him off. "It's all right, Evans. You may return to your duties."

The butler answers with his obligatory, "Yes, sir," and makes a quick exit from the terrace and out through the living room, disappearing in that way that butlers do.

Dierdre Atchley, slowly uncurling from her embrace of James, says, "Vivienne, I instructed the doorman not to let you up. I have nothing more to say to you. You are as much to blame as Cantor for the catastrophe facing my family."

I say, "And you're welcome, Mrs. Atchley, for Vivienne and me saving your son's life. You might be the only one who thinks it's a life worth saving. The police certainly don't, and it looks like your husband doesn't either."

Brooks says, "Vivienne, who is this person?"

His wife answers, "It's Cantor Gold. The thief I told you about, Brooks."

"I see," he says. He gives me the Park Avenue version of the look I've gotten ever since I put on my first set of lapels as a teenage Romeo. Instead of a sneer, Brooks Atchley regards me with a raised eyebrow and the pinched nostrils of a sniff. "Well, you may have successfully bullied your way into our home, but you are not welcome here. You will kindly leave." He turns his attention to Vivienne. "I'm disappointed in you, Vivienne. I would not expect you to keep such low company."

"And I would not have expected you to try to kill your own son," she says. Her tone of voice, her confident posture, challenges him, blueblood to blueblood. But Vivienne has that trace of Trent ferocity to give it heat. Atchley's outmatched.

He retreats into proud sniveling. "I did not try to kill him, merely beat some sense into his bumbling brain. And in any event, he is not my son. No son of mine would be such a blunderer. I'm sorry I ever allowed him to take the Atchley name."

James's lips are so tightly curled it twists his patrician face into the grimace of a gutter punk. He says, "And I'm sorry my mother ever married you," practically hissing it. "It was your philandering that got us into the mess with Eve Garraway. She hated you for abandoning her, and you know something? I don't blame her."

I say, "Speaking of Eve Garraway, her murder case has gotten a lot messier. Maybe you've heard that Lieutenant Huber is dead? Yeah, he was shot in the back a little before ten this morning."

The silence on the terrace is so complete, the whoosh of traffic filtering up from twenty-eight stories below seems loud.

All three members of the Atchley family look like they've stopped breathing until James says, "Good riddance."

His mother snaps, "Be quiet, James."

Brooks says, "Vivienne, you and your friend will leave here now, or I will—"

"You'll what?" I say. "Call the police? The Atchley family is in enough trouble with the cops already, what with James looking at the electric chair for the murder of Eve Garraway. They have a good case, too. I'm inclined to go along with it, but I can't figure one thing. How did you get into the house, James, without being seen?"

All three of them are quiet again, but this time they're smiling. It gives me the creeps. It gives Vivienne the creeps, too, judging by the tight grip she suddenly has on my arm.

"On the advice of our attorney," Dierdre Atchley says, "we will not answer any questions, Cantor. You are wasting your time here. In other words, go to hell." I'm not surprised it's Dierdre Atchley who speaks up. She seems to be the only one of the Atchleys with backbone.

It's my turn to smile. "My time with you is never wasted, Mrs. Atchley."

Chapter Twenty-One

The doorman's surprised to see us when Vivienne and I come out through the building's Park Avenue entrance. I tip my cap to him, just for the fun of seeing the confused expression on his face. After the ugly drama of the Atchley household, I'll take a little fun wherever I can get it.

I say to Vivienne, "I could use a drink. Care to join me?"

She looks like the air's been kicked out of her. "I think I'll just go home, Cantor. I need to be alone for a while."

"Sure," I say. "Come on, I'll drive you." I take her arm to escort her to my car.

She holds back. "No please, don't trouble," she says. "I'll just take a cab."

"It's no trouble, Vivienne. I don't mind." I start us along the avenue again.

Again she holds back.

I say, "Vivienne, what's wrong?"

"I just . . . I just really need to be alone, that's all. I feel like I'm turned inside out by what happened up there. I thought I knew those people, but it seems I don't know them at all." She shakes her head as if shaking it will reassemble an ugly tableau into a prettier one.

I lift her chin, say, "For what it's worth, you were magnificent. You stood up to the Atchleys and called them out for the pompous asses they are."

Those fabulous eyes of hers, those eyes of a pampered palace cat, glisten in the fading late afternoon sunlight, hinting at the seductive contradictions that live in Vivienne Parkhurst Trent: darkness and daring, passion and aloofness, elegance and ferocity. Right now, most of all there's sadness.

She says, "Do what you have to, Cantor, to find out who killed Eve Garraway and Lieutenant Huber. And if it was any of the Atchleys, feed them to the lions."

Turns out Vivienne was right; it's time to be alone, time to quiet the noise surrounding the Garraway killing, the Huber murder, and the Atchley circus of horrors. So I'm home now, slowly sipping a Chivas in the comfort of my favorite chair while I watch the evening float down on New York through my living room window. The city's lights are coming on as the neon colors of my neighborhood's theater marquees, nightclub billboards, and neighborhood joints tint the air.

Feed them to the lions, Vivienne said. Best idea I've heard all day. Trouble is, the Atchleys might tear themselves apart and gnaw each other to the bone before the lions get their share.

There's one lion who has the biggest bite in town. And after what I saw of the Atchleys, I might not feel too guilty about feeding them to him after all.

I finish my drink, get my coat and cap. It's time to go back into the lion's den.

After the usual routine of handing my gun to the thug at the door—it's my old pal Mike Mulroney—and traipsing behind him across the lobby to Sig's private elevator, Mulroney calls up to the penthouse and tells the upstairs thug that Cantor Gold is here to see the boss.

We wait the usual minute until the upstairs thug gets back on the line; then Mulroney says, "Okay," hangs up, and unlocks the elevator.

Five minutes later I'm in Sig's living room, where a big surprise is seated on a sofa: Mom Sheinbaum, a hefty empress in a sensible brown dress. She's drinking a cup of tea.

Sig's standing in the middle of the living room. His white shirt is crisp as frozen snow; his red and brown tie is neatly knotted. The libation in his glass is a lot stronger than tea.

I feel like I've walked into Nostalgia Night at the home for criminal old folks. Handling these two separately is tough enough. Being in the same room with both of them is like an endless scolding by a family who never thought much of you in the first place.

Sig says, "Come in, Cantor." His words emerge slowly, as his words always do, giving the greeting the rhythm of a dirge. "I was about to send the boys out to find you."

"Well, I guess I saved them the trouble," I say. "Hello, Mom. I didn't expect to see you here."

Her tiny eyes are hard and flat as buttons. "I came here, Cantor, because you have been causing trouble again, and I've come to see if maybe Sig can fix things. Maybe Sig can control you. Somebody's got to." Her Lower East Side lilt does nothing to soften her ever present disappointment with me.

"What's the trouble this time," I say.

"Policemen came to my house," she says as if the idea is as unbelievable as pastrami on white bread. "Policemen! With their questions about you and the killing of that *mamzer*, Lieutenant Huber. Not that I'm sorry he's dead. But I don't allow those Cossacks to cross my doorstep—okay, so maybe the police commissioner. He sometimes stops by for a glass of wine and a *bissel* honey cake. But no other policemen would dare enter my house, not since the night—" she grabs her chest, the memory of that painful night choking her—"the night my precious daughter died. And you, Cantor, you were also there that night. And so was that Huber. What do you do, bring those *mamzerim* police with you?"

Sig says, "I warned you, Cantor, about Lieutenant Huber. You wanted him out of the way, and now he's been shot in the back."

206

"And you think I did it?"

"I think you caused it."

I can't argue with that, at least not entirely.

Sig's not through with me. "You have fumbled the simple task I gave you, to bring Miss Garraway's killer to me so that the police would not be involved, City Hall would not be disturbed, and the business could be taken care of quietly. Instead, you've gotten a policeman killed. The police do not look the other way when one of their own is murdered, Cantor. They are like rabid dogs let out of their cage."

I've had about as much of their scolding as I can stand. "I didn't send the cops to your door, Mom, and I didn't fumble the Garraway business, Sig. I've been trying to get out from under the murders of three women: Lorraine Quinn, Eve Garraway, and Alice Lamarr." I give Alice's name a little zing, and look straight at Sig.

The cold son of a bitch doesn't even blink, just says, "You are mistaken, Cantor. The police have determined Miss Lamarr's death was not murder, but a suicide. You should not pursue it any further." He sips his whiskey. The look he gives me over the rim of his glass hovers somewhere between advice and warning.

"Yeah, sure, suicide," I snarl almost under my breath. "Meantime, while you were busy doing favors for the city's higher-ups, arranging to keep the cops quiet and keep Huber off the Garraway case, those higher-ups were busy trying to stick the murders on me. If I didn't have a good lawyer, I'd still be in the slammer. Now, listen you two," I say, sliding a look from Sig to Mom, "don't you even want to know why I came over here?"

I take off my coat and cap, toss them on the sofa opposite Mom, light a smoke with a silver lighter on a side table, and sit down. I look at Sig, then at Mom, then at Sig again. Neither of them have softened toward me, but both of them look curious.

"All right," I say. "Here it is: I was at the Atchleys' Park Avenue place this afternoon, and what I saw turned my stomach. Underneath their shiny veneer they're as vicious as rats fighting over garbage. I think any one of the Atchleys is good for the Garraway and Huber killings. They had motive by the bucketload, and enough vengeance in their greedy souls to push them over the edge."

Sig says, "You have proof of this?"

"Well, there's the wrinkle," I say. "There's two things I still can't tie up: which of them actually did the killings, and how did Eve's killer get into her house without being seen. But there's no doubt in my mind that any one of them could commit murder. Hell, I saw Brooks Atchley nearly kill James today."

Mom gives that a disgusted *tsk* and wave of her hand. "What kind of parent is that? To kill their own child. A monster, that's what."

I say, "James is Dierdre Atchley's son from her first marriage. He's only Brooks's stepson. Brooks allows him to use the Atchley name to keep the dynasty going. He blames James for failing to protect the family from Eve's plan to force them out of their own bank. If Vivienne and I hadn't gotten there when we did and stopped Brooks, James Atchley would be a pile of pulp and broken bones on the sidewalk."

Sig says, "I don't think Miss Parkhurst Trent's involvement is wise, Cantor." It's not a statement. It's another warning.

"She held her own," I say, swatting his warning away. "Now, here's the rest of it. Remember that chat you had with Dierdre Atchley last night, Sig? She was the loyal mother, right? The loving matron protecting her family? Well, from what I saw today, Dierdre Atchley's attachment to her son goes somewhere beyond motherly. And she's so full of revenge over his arrest, and so convinced her high social position enables her to get away with anything, I wouldn't put it past her to take revenge on Huber with a bullet in his back. Did you know she almost killed me? Yeah, arrived at my door last night with a gun in my face because she blames me for James's arrest."

Mom slides a fast look at Sig, then looks away before he notices. "Sure," she says, "it's a mother's job to protect her child." She's not talking about Dierdre protecting James from the cops. She's talking about her failure to protect her daughter from Sig.

208

I'll feel bad for Mom's loss until the day I die, but tonight's not a good time to hold Mom's hand. Not that she'd let me.

I keep to business. "But then there's Brooks Atchley. The guy almost committed murder today, so he's got it in him to kill. He was out of town for the Garraway killing, but came back late last night, so it could've been Brooks who decided to avenge the family's name by killing Huber. Look, what I'm saying, Sig, is go ahead and take them all down. They deserve it, the whole bunch. But be smart about it. Feed them to the cops. Let the cops have the glory. It will settle them down, get them back in their cages. You own the cages, anyway."

My speech is met with silence. Sig's silence is hard and cold. Mom's is more thoughtful, as if she's considering what to do about the unruly upstart who just lectured the city's royalty of crime.

But then Sig says, "I have misjudged you, Cantor. You have done well."

I never thought I'd live to see the day. I pick up my coat and cap, get up from the sofa. I can't get out of here fast enough, away from these two suitcases full of our shared pasts. "If you don't mind, I'd like to get back to my life now."

Sig says, "That is a good idea, Cantor. Live your life. Keep your eye on your business. And by the way, it was very thoughtful of you to arrange Miss Lamarr's funeral and to attend this morning. I understand you were close at one time."

If there's anything in this town, in this world, that Sig Loreale doesn't know about, then it simply doesn't exist.

Mom says, "Cantor, you came here in your car, yes? Good, you can drive me home."

Even in the safety of the passenger seat of my Buick, Mom clutches her mink coat around her and keeps her handbag tight to her lap as if someone might reach in and rip them from her. A hard life will do that, and back in the gaslight days Mom's immigrant life was as tough as they come. Cramped and crowded tenement hovels freezing in winter, stifling in summer.

Rats in the hallways. Sweatshop work that paid pennies by the piece, and never enough to eat. So now, even after she's made millions, Mom's fist remains tight. Her fist is her way to hold fast to her gains, and a weapon to smash anyone who tries to cheat her out of so much as a dime.

She looks out the window as I drive through midtown. "I don't get above Fourteenth Street much anymore," she says. "So many new buildings now they have in this neighborhood. So what was wrong with the old ones?"

"Progress," I say. "There's a lot of money in the city's real estate since the end of the war. Even Sig's put money in."

"I don't like that kind of money," Mom says. "You can't look a building in the eye and see if it's going to cheat you. So listen, Cantor, when are we going to do business? You haven't brought me any goods in a while."

"If I get anything that needs to move outside of my own clients, I'll let you know. Haven't I always?"

She answers that with a shrug, then goes quiet again, looks out the window, watching the city change from midtown's skyscrapers to downtown's walk-ups. She seems to relax a little. I guess the older neighborhood suits her better than midtown's modern buildings. Unlike Sig, who mastered the modern methods of power even back in Coney Island, Mom holds onto the gutter power of the old ways. Maybe that's another reason why she disapproves of me. The old ways nearly smothered me, so I said the hell with them and put on a suit.

After another silence, she says, "So tell me, what's the story with all those Garraway *tchotchkes* now that she's dead? Any chance you can get your hands on them and move them through me? We could make a bundle, Cantor."

"Eve's only been dead a few days," I say. "The estate hasn't been settled yet. And I'm sure she made plans for her collection in the event of her death. In the meantime, Desmond Mallory's still at the house serving as caretaker until the lawyers and the courts get things settled."

"Maybe he's hoping the Garraway woman threw some things his way."

"Maybe," I say. "He was certainly loyal all those years."

Mom's "Hah!" is sharp and cunning. "Loyal shmoyal. Where else was the broken-down grifter gonna go? Okay, we're here."

I pull up in front of Mom's brownstone, get out of the car to open the passenger door for her. She takes my hand to help pull her bulk out of the seat. Before going up the front stairs of her house, she says, "You were smart tonight, *mommeleh*. You gave Sig what he wants. You'll live a little longer."

Chapter Twenty-Two

There's a lot in my life I want to get back to. My business is one; good times are another. I wouldn't mind a drink and a twirl around the dance floor at the Green Door Club with a sweet somebody to ease me away from all the death and vengeance of these last few days.

It's a little past eight, according to the Buick's dashboard clock. The crowd at the Green Door Club will be just starting to get comfortably juiced. I put the Buick in gear.

But there's an itch that I haven't been able to scratch ever since this whole Garraway business started, an itch that just keeps crawling along my skin.

That drink and dance will have to wait. I drive to Gramercy Park.

I'm in luck. Lights are on in the Garraway house. Desmond's in.

He answers the door, says, "Hiya, Cantor," with as much enthusiasm as his thin, feathery voice can handle. "C'mon in. Have a drink with me."

I follow him into the living room. In the glow of shaded lamps, the overstuffed room has even more of the feel of a bygone lair of power than it did when Vivienne and I were here yesterday.

I toss my cap and coat over a chair while Desmond pours a Chivas for me and a Jameson's Irish for himself. His yellow shirt and dark red cardigan spiff up his skinny frame, throw a little color on his hollow cheeks and hard gray hair.

He hands me my drink, says, "So what brings you around, Cantor?" and sits down in the same spot on the sofa he sat in yesterday.

I take a seat in the big chair across from him. "It looks like the cops might make their case against James Atchley for Eve's murder after all."

"I'll drink to that," he says and takes a swig.

I join his toast, take a pull on the Chivas. "And now that one of their own took a bullet in the back, the cops are really on the warpath."

"Sure, I saw the story in the paper. The television people made a big deal about it, too. It was that Huber fella," Desmond says as if Huber's name is acid on his tongue. "He was the cop who was here when Miss Garraway was killed. Any idea who did the deed? Tell you the truth, I'd like to shake their hand. Never did like cops. Bet you have no love for 'em either, Cantor."

"Can't say that I do. But getting it in the back, that's not the work of an honorable killer."

Desmond nods, says, "True. People like you and me, we respect the code," warming to a subject that puts him back in his outlaw glory days. "How much you wanna bet the shooter was civilian. My money says it was an amateur with a grudge."

"Very likely," I say, and just leave it there. I don't want the conversation to get sidetracked with my latest suspicions about the Atchleys. I'm here to try to scratch the damned itch that's driving me crazy. "Listen, Desmond, have the cops been around anymore since yesterday? Maybe have a look around the house, figure how James got inside without being seen?"

"As a matter of fact they did. Left about an hour ago. A guy named Adair."

That sits me up. I guess I ought to give Adair a little credit. He sure didn't let grass grow under his feet after he turned me loose this afternoon. "And?"

"And I showed him the tunnel."

What's that they say about a light appearing in the darkness? This one glares so damn bright it zaps my brain, and I can only blurt out, "There's a tunnel?"

Desmond says, "Sure. Miss Garraway never mentioned it? Well, maybe she wouldn't. The Garraways loved their secrets, y'know."

A grin spreads across my face, the kind of satisfied grin that comes from finally soothing an itch you couldn't reach no matter how far you stretched. *Gotcha, James Atchley. You've just hit the cops' trifecta. Your motive: revenge. Means: a knife you admitted was yours. And opportunity: a secret tunnel into the house.* My life's my own again. I just might get that dance at the Green Door Club tonight.

Desmond, caught up in reminiscing, says, "Oh, Miss Garraway loved the tunnel when she was a tot. She'd giggle and tease her Dad to find her, then swear me to secrecy with her sweet smile." Desmond's face almost glows with the memory. You'd think he's witnessing a beatification. Tears even well up in his eyes.

"Why did John Garraway put a tunnel in the house?" I ask.

Desmond wipes his eyes with the back of his hand, then takes a swallow of whiskey. "It wasn't Mr. Garraway who dug the tunnel," he says. "He told me it was Mr. Aloysius Sloan, the first owner of the house, who'd put it in. Mr. Garraway told me all about it. Quite a lusty tale, too. It seems Mr. Sloan liked certain types of ladies, the kind you pay, if you get my meanin'. He liked 'em even more than he liked his wife. But he didn't want to patronize the bawdy houses. A gentleman could have his pockets emptied by the house's thieves while he was, y'know, attending to business. So the tunnel was how the ladies came in to see Mr. Sloan. They'd come at night, after the missus had gone to bed."

"Does the tunnel go up to Eve's office?"

"Sure. It wasn't an office in Mr. Sloan's day," he says with a wink. "It was where the fella would have his trysts with the ladies. C'mon, I'll show you. Take your coat. We have to go outside for a bit."

Desmond takes his overcoat and hat from a rack by the front door. Outside, he leads me down the front stairs.

At the side of the stairs, left of the below-stairs windows I couldn't get into last night, he wrestles with the tall, heavy shrubbery. "Give me a hand with this," he says. "These shrubs have gotten real thick over the years, and I'm not as hefty as I used to be."

I help Desmond press the shrubbery aside. It's sturdy stuff, but not much of a struggle for me, probably not for Sergeant Adair, either, and certainly not for the athletic James Atchley.

With the shrubbery cleared, all I see is a wall of brownstone blocks with carvings of vines and flowers, topped by the edges of the front stairs to the house.

Desmond, chuckling at the puzzled look on my face, says, "That Sergeant Adair didn't see nothin' either until I showed him. That's because it wasn't supposed to be seen, especially not by Mr. Sloan's wife. But look here." He's pointing to a large carved flower just below my eye level. "See that petal on the flower? Give it a push."

"I suppose you're going to tell me to say 'Open Sesame,'" I say, and press the flower petal. Yeah, it gives, and a section of brownstone blocks swings slowly back. I don't know whether to applaud Aloysius Sloan's ingenuity or be annoyed at the guy for cheating on his wife right under her nose, or under her bed, it turns out.

I follow Desmond through the opening. Inside, he turns on a light switch at the side of the entrance. "Old Man Garraway had the tunnel electrified. He used the tunnel, too, for what you might call sensitive meetings with political people or people he didn't want to be seen with. But there's still a few of the old gaslights." He points out a couple of small curlicued bronze sconces on the walls, their glass shades, etched with flowery designs, dusty but still intact. One of the sconces has fallen to the floor, its shade shattered. Desmond picks it up, puts it in his coat pocket. "I should probably get this repaired," he says, "in case the lawyers want an inventory of everything. Sooner or later they'll find out about the tunnel, and it won't do for them to think I didn't take care of the place. Could make me look bad."

215

The tunnel is a length of rough concrete walls and ceiling, and a floor that's a little smoother. Desmond leads the way until we come to an old-fashioned spiral staircase made of iron, its steps covered in fraying red carpet. Aloysius Sloan thought of everything, including carpeting the stairs to muffle the sound of feminine footsteps as the ladies made their secret climb to a rendezvous with the master of the house.

There's a door at the top of the stairs. Desmond takes a set of house keys from his pocket, selects one, unlocks the door and switches a light on in the vestibule ahead. I follow him through. I realize I'd seen this door before. I'd thought it was a closet door, but it's a door from the tunnel into the vestibule fronting Eve's vault of treasures.

There's another door to my left. A door I'd also been through before. I open it and walk into Eve's office. It's dark except for the luminous dial of the clock on the desk, and quiet except for the clock's tick. Both give me a chill.

The clock reads 9:20.

Desmond turns on the torchiere in the corner near Eve's desk. The lamp throws a soft light around the room and onto the floor. The sprawling red-brown stain of Eve's dried blood and the cops' chalk outline of her corpse uglies the carpet.

I wander around, get a feel for the scene, imagine James Atchley coming through the door from the tunnel and then through the vestibule door into the office. I imagine the knife in his hand, imagine him stabbing Eve Garraway in the back. I try to see his face, but can't get a lock on it, can't see his expression of revenge or hate or desperation or whatever it was that could drive him to murder.

Desmond's at Eve's desk. He leans against it, almost limp, like he's using the desk to prop himself up. He looks like he'd rather be anywhere but here. He wipes his eyes with the back of his hand again. "Sorry, Cantor. It's just hard for me to be here, you understand, seein' that blood and that outline of Miss Garraway's body on the rug."

"Sure," I say. "It's not a pretty sight."

Desmond says, "Let's go back downstairs and have another drink. Maybe it'll wash away the memory of Miss Garraway lyin' there."

"In a minute," I say. I'm back at the vestibule door. The vault's in front of me, its fortune of treasures locked away, out of my grasp. If I could get into that vault, I could get the stuff out through the tunnel. It's a perfect setup. I think of Mom Sheinbaum's idea of getting my hands on the stuff and fencing it through her. We'd be rich beyond our wildest dreams, and our dreams are pretty wild. Mine are, at any rate.

Too bad I didn't catch the combination when Eve turned the tumblers. I give a thought to coming back sometime with a stethoscope, give a shot to listening to the lock's tumblers while I turn the dial. I haven't cracked a safe in a long time, and Eve's vault door looks like one of the latest modern jobs, a lot tougher to crack, even with sharp ears and delicate fingers. But the fortune inside that vault door could set me up for life.

The scenario of that tempting opportunity slips out of mind because another, more immediately relevant thought replaces it. "Desmond," I say, "how would James Atchley know about the tunnel?"

"Oh, he'd been to the house before, came around to try to pressure Miss Garraway out of her designs on the Atchleys' banking stuff."

"So he was here. So what? It hardly seems likely she'd show him the tunnel. Why would she?"

"Well, maybe he heard about it from his dad. That's probably it. Y'know, Dad had been pretty chummy with Miss Garraway. Maybe they had some spicy playtime in there." He gives that a laugh, a breathy rasp with a vulgar edge that might've gotten him fired if he was still a butler.

But he has a point. Eve might've showed Brooks the tunnel. You share all sorts of things when you're in love, things that come back later to haunt you, or kill you.

217

Desmond says, "That Sergeant Adair grinned from ear to ear when we came in here from the tunnel. He was one very happy cop. First time in my life I ever made one of those devils happy."

"Yeah, well," I say, "cops like things neat and tidy and all wrapped up in a bow. Even if the bow isn't tied right."

"What do you mean, not tied right?" Desmond says with a snap of impatience. "Adair says he has it all wrapped up. James Atchley has a date with the electric chair. Good riddance, too. What more do you want?"

"Nothing, I guess. All right, let's get that drink."

"Now you're talking." He starts for the office door.

"Mind if we go back through the tunnel, Desmond? I'd like to have another look." There's no sense wasting the chance to give it a good going-over. Who knows? Maybe I'll come back with that stethoscope.

"Suit yourself," he says. He turns off the torchiere.

The room goes dark except for the light from the vestibule and that eerie green glow from the desk clock. I follow the silhouette of Desmond out of the office, close the door behind me. Desmond opens the tunnel door, locks it behind us after we step through.

We make our way down the spiral staircase, then walk along the tunnel. I try to get a picture of James Atchley making his way through here, knife in hand, vengeance in his soul.

I remember that knife. Remember it sticking out of Eve Garraway's back. I remember that fancy carved ivory handle. It's the sort of weapon that was good for murder in, say, medieval Baghdad. It was an antique.

Thoughts suddenly tumble through my head, snatches of things said since Eve's death, things said by Desmond, by James, by cops, even by Judson. The tumble of thoughts congeal into just one. "Desmond, I guess you made your peace with Eve and John Garraway after what happened to your daughter."

The guy stops walking. He goes as ashy gray as the rough concrete walls of the tunnel. He has that "caught naked" look, as if his pants fell down in a crowded room and everyone sees

218

his festering sores. After a moment of licking his lips, he says, "She didn't mean it. Miss Garraway . . . didn't mean it. It was an accident." He stumbles through every word.

"That's mighty big of you, Desmond. If someone killed my kid, and then their powerful daddy got it hushed up, I'd be mad as hell. I sure wouldn't want to work for them. Have you been mad for twelve years, Desmond?"

He raises his arm, wags his finger at me, fast and sharp, like he wants to slice me. "You got it all wrong, Cantor. I was mad at first, sure, but I'd been working for old John since Miss Garraway was a baby. She was as much a daughter to me as my own Fiona." He's not wagging his finger now. He's rubbing his eyes again. "I saw how upset Miss Garraway was. She was . . . she was—"

"She was what? Guilt-ridden? Tearing her hair? Rending her garments? Seems to me she went right on living as daddy's little girl."

"Why are you asking me about all this, Cantor? That's water under the bridge."

"Because that water might drown James Atchley. Maybe it's drowning the wrong guy."

"No, they got the right guy. That arrogant son of a so-and-so hated Miss Garraway."

"Funny, just today he told his father he even felt sorry for her for the way Brooks Atchley treated her."

"Is that so?" Desmond thrusts his hands in his pockets, ambles around, shakes his head. "He didn't sound so sorry for her when he tried to get her to stop acting against the Atchley banking business. The guy was seething with vengeance. Vengeance is a very powerful thing."

"Yeah, it can fester for years, can't it, Desmond."

"Well, it sure festered in James Atchley. You should've heard him, Cantor. He wasn't exactly making polite conversation with Miss Garraway. He'd even grabbed her. I told you yesterday, remember? Left a bruise on her arm. Now, if you're finished with this nonsense, let's get that drink." He claps me on the back like we're drinking buddies again.

"Not so fast," I say. "Something else is bothering me, Desmond. The knife that killed Eve."

"What about it? That Adair fella said James recognized it. It was Atchley's knife."

"Yeah, *was*," I say. "The knife was an antique. Not the first weapon you'd pick out of the drawer to commit murder. It was an antique that the Atchley family auctioned off along with a number of other things. And you know who bought those things?"

"Wait a minute, Cantor. What the hell are you saying?"

"I'm saying Eve bought that knife when she bought the Atchley auction lot. Sounds to me like she was digging into the Atchleys every which way she could, even buying up their hand-me-down antiques. The knife came along with the other stuff. It wasn't a high-priced item. Maybe Eve left it lying around in the office. Maybe she kept it as a symbol of what she had in store for the Atchleys. Maybe she even gave the knife to you. You said she was generous to you. What I'm saying, Desmond, is I'm starting to think it wasn't James Atchley's revenge that killed Eve Garraway. It was yours."

After an accusation like that, you'd think the guy would be angry, or even scared. But Desmond's smiling. The smile gets wider, wilder, until it becomes a giggling laugh scraping through his old man's wispy voice. "You really have got it all wrong, Cantor. I didn't feel any revenge. I knew my Fiona could be a handful. She had her mother's quick temper, and nasty sometimes, too. I'd seen her nearly scratch her friends' eyes out. There were times I wanted to—well, never mind. That don't matter." His laugh grows darker. There's no humor in it, just bleak whimpers. "What matters is I loved Miss Garraway like she was my own."

"So why did you kill her, Desmond?"

He digs his hands deeper into his coat pockets. His whole body shrivels around his bones. His eyes get teary again, only this time he doesn't bother to wipe the tears away. He opens his mouth to speak, but no words come out, just a gag trying to block a deep pain. It takes him a minute to swallow it and finally speak. "Because she told me I was fired. That's right, after you left the other day, she told me I was getting too old, that I'd dropped too many things lately, that I was forgetting things. She told me I had to clear out by the end of the month. Then she turned her back on me. Me, who'd been loyal to her dad, who'd supported her, stood by her even after she murdered my Fiona. She was throwing me out into the street. And that knife, that knife—" He's talking faster now, his body tensing, his tears faster. "You're right about that knife, Cantor. Miss Garraway used it as a letter opener. It was on the desk. And after she told me I was fired, I grabbed it and I—" His hand is out of his pocket. He's holding the bronze sconce, making a stabbing motion with it, his face scrunched up in a horror movie grimace, but with tears in his eyes.

And then his eyes find mine as he swings the sconce against the side of my head.

I hear his breathy, "Good-bye, Cantor." I see his face fade behind white sparks in front of my eyes. The sparks flame out. There's nothing.

Chapter Twenty-Three

I think my eyes are opening, my lids lifting slowly. At least that's what it feels like. But I don't see anything, just darkness, a thick, black, smothering darkness. There's a pain on the left side of my head. It slices like razors through my skull. Something warm and wet slides down my cheek. The floor's hard and cold. The air's gritty.

All these sensations swirl like a windstorm inside my brain and finally fuse together into awareness. I'm in the tunnel of the Garraway house. The warm, wet stuff on my cheek and oozing into the corner of my mouth is blood dripping from the wound made by the sconce Desmond smashed against the side of my head.

Standing up is no easy business. My legs can't make up their mind if they're made of soft rubber that won't straighten or brittle sticks that might snap. Somehow or other, using my hands to push against the wall at my back, I manage to stand up. My legs aren't happy about it. My head's not thrilled about it, either.

I know what I have to do. I know because it's not the first time I've been knocked around. It comes with the life I lead, the dangerous way I make my dough. It comes with the fists of bully-boy cops or society's snarling straight-backs. I know that I have to take long, deep, slow breaths to stop the dizziness. I know that I have to ignore the pain in my head, push it out of consciousness. And I know that I have to get out of here.

I fish around in my pockets for a book of matches. No luck. I'll have to make my way in the dark. I remember Desmond turning on a light switch at the street entrance to the tunnel. I remember there's a door at the top of the spiral stairs. But I'm in no condition to climb a spiral staircase in the dark. I'll have to make my way to the front of the tunnel.

But which way is the front? There's no left or right, front or back in pitch dark.

Only one way to find out. I start walking, keep one hand along the wall to help me stay on my feet.

Wrong way. I've just bumped into the stairs.

I turn around slowly to keep the dizziness from coming back. Little by little I traipse through the darkness, one hand against the wall, my other hand stretched out in front of me to tell me when I've reached the front of the tunnel.

My hand bumps against the stone door. I've made it.

I reach over to the side, find the light switch and flip it on. The world rights itself.

I check to see if Desmond might've made off with my wallet, my lockpicks, or my gun. They're all there. The old thief must be slipping, or maybe he thought I'd never be found until I was a desiccated corpse some future resident of the house stumbled across. Or maybe his long-ago outlaw instincts to make a fast getaway got the better of him, and nothing else mattered.

There's no visible lock on the door, no flower petal to push. There's got to be a way to open the brownstone blocks; otherwise, there'd be well-dressed skeletons of Mr. Sloan's ladies of pleasure lying around. But after pushing and pressing several spots on the stone and getting nowhere, I forget about it. I stand a better chance upstairs at the vestibule door.

The spiral staircase isn't helping to keep the dizziness away, so when I reach the top I stand still and take a few deep breaths to keep the world from spinning.

When the world settles back into place, I take out my lockpicks, make quick work of the lock on the vestibule door, open it, and turn on the light. A moment later I'm through the door to Eve's office. I make my way across the room by the light from the vestibule, don't bother to turn on any lights in the office. I'm not interested in the office. There's nothing to see here but Eve's blood and the chalk outline of her corpse. I don't feel like lingering with either.

Outside the office I open the other doors surrounding the mezzanine, look around in bedrooms and storage rooms. I figure Desmond is long gone, but I check anyway. The guy's old. Maybe he tripped and fell. Maybe he's out cold on the floor. But I don't find him anywhere.

It's the same story downstairs. Desmond is nowhere in the house.

A mantel clock in the living room surprises me with the news that it's a few minutes past ten o'clock.

I look around for a phone. There isn't one in the living room, but I find one across the hall in the library. It's on the massive walnut desk, the kind of desk where big plans are made. I bet Boss John Garraway hatched more than a few political deals and dirty tricks in this room.

I make my first call. The officer tells me Sergeant Adair's gone home for the night. I tell the guy it's important, tell him it's life and death on one of Adair's cases, and to have him call me back at this number, pronto.

There's a liquor cabinet behind the desk with a selection of libations. I pull out a bottle of Chivas, don't bother with a glass. I need a long draw, fast, to keep the world steady. It does the trick.

I make myself comfortable in the desk chair, a cushy oxblood leather number where I imagine little Eve sitting on her daddy's knee while he instructs her in the ways of power. I imagine daddy's daughter listening and learning. This charming fantasy is interrupted by the ringing phone. "Adair?"

"Who's this?"

"It's Cantor Gold. Listen, you've got the wrong guy. James Atchley didn't kill Eve Garraway. Desmond Mallory did. It was Mallory who knifed her in the back." So much for Desmond's

224

story about respecting the underworld's code of an honorable murder.

There's silence on his end, just the sound of his uneasy breathing. I can almost see his nostrils flare and his lips tighten. "And you know this how?" he finally says.

"He told me." I give him the story.

He says, "I'll bring him in."

"First you'll have to find him."

"He's an old guy. He can't get far."

"I wouldn't bet on that," I say. "Check your department records. You'll see the guy was a pro in the old days. Did time, but got away with a lot of stuff before they nailed him. They say he killed someone years ago, too. He knows the ropes and the roads. Good luck finding him, sergeant." I hang up.

I take another pull on the Chivas while I think about making another call.

Of course I make it. It's the deal we made.

When I get Sig on the line, I give him the same story I gave Adair. All Sig says is, "Thank you, Cantor." The phone feels like ice in my hand.

By the time I get back to my apartment, I let go of the idea of a night at the Green Door Club. Twirling around the dance floor would kick the dizziness back into play, and the bloody wound at the side of my head would probably put off the lovelies. It might also cause a snicker or even a lecture from Peg. She might even push one of those magazines in my hand, like the one she gave Rosie, and tell me to read all about how I don't have to fight my battles alone.

Well, maybe she has a point. I suppose I should give it some thought. Battles aren't won by an individual soldier; it takes a whole army. If nothing else, the sisters and brothers of my romantic persuasion would certainly make a colorful army. Sharp suits and sequined gowns clashing with cops. I have to admit it has its appeal.

225

But that's an idea for another day. Tonight, after all the death and ugly vengeance of the last week, plus the guilt I feel about Lorraine Quinn and the grief I carry for Alice, all I want is that rarest of things in my life, peace and quiet. And anyway, whatever politics Peg tries on me, she knows I have my own ways of fighting my battles. The face looking back at me in the bathroom mirror has the scars to prove it. They tell the story of my survival, the times I stood up after being knocked around, the times I managed not to get killed by cops or thugs or Sig Loreale. There'll be two more scars to add to the story, the one at the corner of my mouth courtesy of Tap Tenzi's flashy pinkie ring, and the one caused by Desmond's wallop to the side of my head. I survived those attacks, too.

I wash the blood off my face, go into the kitchen, make a chicken sandwich on rye with plenty of mustard, fill a glass with water, and take my little supper to the kitchen table. The sandwich is good, but the water's a bore. I toss it, take the glass and my sandwich to the living room, and pour myself a hefty dollop of Chivas.

I turn on the radio, hum along to Tony Bennett singing "Rags to Riches"—a sentiment I think is swell—and take the glass of Chivas and my sandwich over to the window. Lights are on all over the city now. Rooftop electric advertising signs glow in bright colors against the night. Down below, people are on the streets, hailing cabs or walking home from nearby theaters, or heading into the neighborhood's nightspots for the late show. New York's streets are never empty. Makes it easy to get lost in a crowd if that's what you need to do.

It's what Desmond is probably doing until he makes it out of town. The chances of Adair finding him are slim. The chances of Sig finding him are good. The chances of Desmond surviving Sig's dragnet are zero.

I should feel guilty. I probably condemned the guy to death when I made the call to Sig. But Desmond left me for dead in a tunnel. I don't owe him any favors. Besides, even if Adair is lucky enough to find Desmond before Sig does, the state will fry him anyway.

Tony Bennett is followed by a singing commercial for Wildroot Cream Oil hair tonic. I make it fast to the radio to turn it off. I don't want to hear that commercial. I used to use that hair tonic brand. The woman who mattered more to me, the woman whose name I can't say without falling to pieces, liked what it did to my unruly hair. I can't use the stuff anymore. I can't listen to that tune anymore.

I turn the dial to turn it off, but a news bulletin cuts in, stops my hand: *We interrupt this program for a bulletin from the New York City Police Department. Mrs. Dierdre Atchley, socialite wife of prominent banker Brooks Atchley, has been arrested for the murder of police detective Lieutenant Norman Huber. Brooks Atchley is being held for further questioning in the matter. Their son, banker James Atchley, previously arrested for the murder of Eve Garraway, daughter of the late political leader John Garraway, is also being questioned in relation to the Huber murder. Stay tuned to this station for further developments as they become available. We now return to our regularly scheduled programming.*

Well, that didn't take Sig long. I guess he took my advice and gave the glory to the cops.

So it's all coming out right in the end. Johnny Tenzi will fry for Lorraine's murder; one way or another Desmond will get what's coming to him for killing Eve Garraway; and the Atchleys, that terrifying excuse for a family, will disappear from the elegance of the *Social Register* and into the disfiguring clutches of the Law. And I'll go right on taking pleasure in pretty women and poking my finger in the Law's eye.

The radio is playing Jo Stafford's latest hit, "Make Love to Me." Her smooth-as-smoke voice is backed up by a hot instrumental arrangement, giving the song a sexy kick.

I guess I'll go twirl around with a pretty little thing at the Green Door Club after all.

Acknowledgments

A lot of this book was written in Paris during what was supposed to be a three-month adventure of writing, exploring, and socializing. It was a trip I'd scrimped and saved and given up a lot for. Then came the Covid-19 pandemic. After my first two weeks in Paris, my social and exploring plans were squashed as the entire nation of France, indeed all of Europe, went into pandemic lockdown for the next two months.

So instead of my original idea of writing for four hours each morning and then spending the afternoon and evening galivanting around town, with side trips to the south of France, maybe quick weekends in Venice and Florence, I would now be shut in with nothing to do but write from morning till night. The writing part of my Paris adventure became the *raison d'être* for each day.

The pandemic, of course, was awful. France, like everywhere else, suffered terribly. But if a writer finds herself locked away in a city, what better city to be locked away in than Paris? And in a genuine garret with the iconic view of the Paris rooftops above a courtyard?

So first and foremost I must thank the City of Paris for its nourishing spirit, even during the worst of times. I felt the Parisians' lust for life, their storied *joie de vie,* while in my garret and when I went out for the permitted errands of shopping for necessities. Paris has fed the creativity of writers and artists for centuries. No plague was going to stop it.

There are people in that glorious city who made sure this American in Paris never felt stranded or alone. They called or emailed me regularly, checking in to share a laugh or just a shared moment of the day, and keeping me informed of the French government's evolving Covid regulations. My deepest gratitude goes to Claudine Dumoulin, Claude Pollack, Stephanie Olen Kleindorfer, and to my hosts Richard and his son Sacha, who made sure I knew where to go and who to see for supplies and services in a difficult situation.

Stateside, I'm grateful to Richard Eagan, Liz Ostrow, AE Cavalieri, Carol Seibert, Stan Coplan and Jan Schleiger for their encouragement and support of my vagabond adventure. Special thanks to my buddy Allan Neuwirth for taking care of two of life's most important tasks: collecting my stateside mail and generally being a pal.

A special shout-out goes to Debbie Fahlman, who came up with the terrific name "Liam Adair" for one of the characters in this book.

And finally, loving thanks to Bywater Books for adopting Cantor Gold when she was orphaned.

About the Author

Native New Yorker Ann Aptaker's Cantor Gold crime/mystery series has won both Lambda Literary and Goldie Awards. Her short stories have appeared in two editions of the *Fedora* crime anthology, *Switchblade Magazine*'s *Stiletto Heeled* issue, the *Mickey Finn: Twenty-First Century Noir* anthology and in *Black Cat Mystery Magazine*. Her novella, *A Taco, A T-Bird, A Beretta and One Furious Night,* was published by Down & Out Books for their *Guns and Tacos* crime series. Her flash fiction, *A Night in Town*, appeared in the online zine *Punk Soul Poet,* and another flash fiction, *Rock 'N Dyke Roll,* is featured in the Goldie Award-winning anthology *Happy Hours: Our Lives in Gay Bars.* Ann has been an art curator, exhibition design specialist, art writer, and professor of Art History at the New York Institute of Technology. She now writes full time.

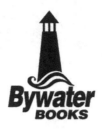

At Bywater Books, we love good books just like you do, and we're committed to bringing the best of contemporary lesbian writing to our avid readers. Our editorial team is dedicated to finding and developing outstanding writers who create books you won't want to put down.

For more information about Bywater Books our authors and our titles, please visit our website.

www.bywaterbooks.com

CPSIA information can be obtained
at www.ICGtesting.com
Printed in the USA
JSHW021118120721
16662JS00004B/12